ABC's *20/20 Friday*, January 14, 2000

Concluding comments by Barbara Walters and John Stossel, after John's poignant *Give Me a Break!* segment revealing the hypocrisy of politicians over pot:

Barbara: "John, it is *very* confusing...on the one hand, as you know, the politicians make light of their own drug use; on the other hand, the severe laws continue."

John: "It feels very wrong. In a free society we lock up *so* many people. A million people are in jail, many of them non-violent people doing what these politicians did. We arrest more people for marijuana than for rape, robbery, murder and aggravated assault *combined*. It doesn't feel right."

Barbara: "Yet, as a campaign issue—how severe the laws should be, or what should be our point of view—it has barely emerged as a campaign issue."

John: "Everybody just says 'we're tough on drugs,' and that's it."

Barbara: "Hmm...so give us a break. Thanks, John."

Come along with some homegrown terrorists as they band together and move from innocence to angst, then on to freedom again in their struggle for legal and social fairness in 2000 America. The problem: politicians *still* have not separated soft drugs from hard drugs, resulting in asinine mandatory minimum sentencing laws that are corrupting greedy local police and prosecutors. Good people are being jailed, and assets belonging to otherwise upstanding citizens are being wrongfully seized.

Victor Stamate is a highly-decorated Vietnam veteran and muscle car collector. He suffers from PTS, but he's also into illegal extreme fighting. He's picked up by the Feds for growing weed on his Minnesota River bluff property, but *two years* after he'd already been fined and put on probation by Bunyan County, Minnesota. A case of double jeopardy? Not in this drug case. Victor's beautiful wife, Jade—and two close friends—Buck Foster and Charlie Pierce—must work to free him. Buck is a wannabe stand-up comedian. Charlie (Charleen) is the adventurous narrator of this story. They have a hard time figuring out just whom they can and cannot trust, a task made more or less difficult—depending on how you look at it—by consuming way too much schnapps and smoking a ton of hash (discovered in the trunk of the Sheriff's car). Bunyan County Chief Prosecutor Joe Schruder commits suicide not long after Victor is taken into custody. But is it really suicide?

When a bomb threat doesn't work to get Victor released, his friends hatch a bolder plan—a *ransom for justice*. Young, bitchy Kimberly Patch is chosen because her father is U. S. Senator Warren Patch, a strong proponent of mandatory minimum sentencing. But the team of helpers must avoid Luther Sullivan. He's a former State Police bodyguard, now the owner of a string of *gentlemen clubs*. He wants the Stamates' property for yet another strip-joint. Fat, greedy Sheriff Rudy Tipton is on the take too. He's a problem until Buck is forced to back him down with his hunting bow. Then cub investigative reporter Tucker Westmoreland has to be "detained" after being caught snooping too near the rescuers' wooded hideaway. Victor's wife, Jade, begins to show signs of suffering a nervous breakdown.

Punctuated with humor both light and dark, *Ransom for Justice* is a unique and compelling story—a journey, really—of steadfast friendship and loyalty in the face of outrageous injustice coming from corrupt officials and bad law. It's *exactly* right on time!

Ransom for Justice

R. L. Voyles

Hallmark Emporium
Bloomington — Minnesota
2000

Ransom For Justice
by R.L. Voyles

Published by: Hallmark Emporium Publishing
9201 Russell Ave. S
Bloomington, MN 55431

Cover design and artwork by Trebor E. Selyov

ISBN: 0-9665055-2-2
Library of Congress Catalog Card Number: 00-90524

Printed in the United States by
Morris Publishing
3212 East Highway 30
Kearney, NE 68847
1-800-650-7888

For Pat

Introduction

This novel was written with the hope of better things to come for America in this election year, 2000. To that end, there wouldn't be much point in me writing a book like *Ransom for Justice* if I couldn't piss at least a few people off. (Uh, no, not at me.) I hope I've succeeded in turning my own moral outrage against some of our politicians into something positive and good, because in America right now certain prosecutors have the power of accuser, judge and jury, and some of them are using their power to seek higher political office. How good can *that be?*

Many Americans are becoming frustrated by the lack of justice in America today, not just me. Murderous Mafia hitmen—who've snitched for the government—and brutal killers such as O. J. Simpson are free to cruise our neighborhoods. And our President can lie to *we, the people* under oath and somehow still remain in office. Yet the same morally corrupt White House can spend millions of our tax dollars to plant sneaky anti-pot messages into the TV shows we watch. And the same White House would like to have a heavier hand in monitoring the internet for us, too. (For our *safety*, you understand.) Certain politicians would also like to censor communications on the internet, but how much should our civil liberties be curtailed in pursuit of drug enforcement, say, or violence? Maybe we're not that far removed from having *bad* books and *bad* movies destroyed, too. Easy Rider is definitely a threat to America! Powerful media conglomerates aren't satisfied with merely helping the government in controlling our thinking with subliminal programming. No, they'd also like to rewrite the meaning of our Bill of Rights. Ha! Without knowing it, they are stupidly preparing for their own free-speech problems down the road.

Police departments across America are coming up with all kinds of amazing new ideas to fight crime. If a check-point for drunk drivers is such a good idea, then—hey, why not throw up a few *drug* road-blocks too? And why not just go right on ahead and establish some *exclusionary zones* where certain undesirable people aren't allowed to go? The accepted practice of "profiling" Afro-Americans driving down some our highways has now expanded to profiling weird-looking students walking down school hallways. They'd better not start running or they might get arrest-ed—or even maced or shot in the ass with rubber bullets! Students are now being routinely drug-tested by schools and parents alike. America's workforce is being drug-tested more and more too, and not just in jobs where public *safe-ty* is the big concern. (How about those welfare people!) Testing companies are advertising their services and getting filthy-rich at the expense of our personal liberties. Forget your piss, now it's your *hair* they want. But why aren't politicians routinely drug-tested themselves if they think it's so great for the rest of us to be insulted this way?

Jane Smith is irresponsible enough to kill someone while driving drunk, and she's still allowed to possess a gun for self-protection or to go hunting, while John Smith is convicted of having too much marijuana, and he's denied the *right* to bear arms for the rest of his life? A whole class of people. Why can't Second Amendment *rights* be restored, anyway? Who says no? I believe it's up to people like Buck Foster in this story—and people like you and me, to get the pro-freedom message out. We have to make others understand what's at stake here. Together, we can hopefully make a difference in stopping some of the bullshit. I'd like nothing more then to see *young people* with a lot of energy rise up again with some passion! Nothing will change—except at a snail's pace—unless *we, the people* keep pushing for our natural-born freedoms.

R. L. Voyles
January 1, 2000
Bloomington, Minnesota

"The prestige of government has undoubtedly been lowered considerably by the prohibition law. For nothing is more destructive of respect for the government and the law of the land than passing laws which cannot be enforced."
—Albert Einstein

"Latent in every man is a venom of amazing bitterness, a black resentment; something that curses and loathes life, a feeling of being trapped, of having trusted and been fooled, of being the helpless prey of impotent rage, blind surrender, the victim of a savage, ruthless power that gives and takes away, enlists a man, drops him, promises and betrays, and—crowning injury—inflicts on him the humiliation of feeling sorry for himself."
—Paul Valery

Chapter 1

Just who I didn't want to see, Buck Foster. I was in a hurry to meet my best friend, Jade Stamate, and I didn't feel like chatting with a screw-up with a lot of bad habits.

Don't get me wrong—Buck's all right most of the time, and loyal to a fault. He's usually good for a few laughs, too, as long as he hasn't been drinking too much. A good sense of humor. It's not that I don't like him at all...he's just such a *pain in the ass* most of the time.

Buck Foster tried stand-up comedy a few times, but he never had much success at it. He'd always end up drinking too much on account of the pressure and then start cutting into the audience—especially fat people in the audience. For instance, there was the time he was fired on the spot for telling a fat woman she looked about the same whether she was standing up or sitting down. And there was the time he got smacked right off the stage by a big mama who didn't appreciate being asked to diaper her kid's face. He'd made the mistake of goading her further: "Why'd you bring your stupid kid here in the first place anyway? Do you see any other kids here? Loud-ass *brat,* making all that noise...breaking my concentration." "I'll break your concentration, you bastard!" the woman had yelled back at him just before hurling herself up over the edge of the stage. She smacked the hell out of him with her purse, knocking him off the stage and giving him a bloody nose. It was unpleasant, very bloody.

Along with fat women, Buck doesn't like rich people—rich people like my friend, Jade. I guess her husband, Victor, is okay because he didn't originate from money, he only married into it.

I waved at Buck Foster half-heartedly and sped up, hoping he wouldn't turn around, but when I looked in the rearview mirror of my yellow Mercedes CLK 320 convertible, I saw that he was already behind me, flashing his headlights like a mad European. *Shit, what does he want to talk about so bad? Pain in the ass!*

It was always something with him—there was always something to bitch about, always something wrong with society that he knew exactly how to fix. His quirky world seems to be defined by bottom lines and the big picture. He's got far too many opinions—*that's* a bottom line. Thirty-four, stocky and single, he runs two businesses, one as a tree doctor and one as a creator of rustic furniture. The two jobs go hand-in-hand quite well. He's unusually competent with a chainsaw, even a hundred feet up and surrounded by thick leaves and branches. He's also extremely sexist, so whenever I feel the need to get even with him about something, I call him a *tree jumper,* which I've heard is prison jargon for a sexual predator.

He's not bad looking. He's got humorous, twinkling hazel eyes and he wears his sandy hair close to the bone. Served as a marine during Desert Storm. I guess he was one of the few jarheads to actually get shot. His unfaithful girlfriend, Beth Ann, works as a flight attendant for Northwest

Airlines and claims to have "movie star or else model potential." Not exactly my kind of people. You could say that Buck's part privacy nut, part anti-gun-control freak, and part conspiracy theorist all wrapped too tightly into one. He seems to be prematurely disappointed in the future. But he *is* very loyal to his few friends. Actually, his real name isn't even Buck, but he's an avid deer hunter and so the name somehow stuck. He attracts deer by rattling and smashing antlers together to imitate the sounds of bucks fighting, then he kills them with a bow and arrow.

Why Victor Stamate likes Buck so much, I'm not sure. Probably finds him entertaining. Or maybe it's enough that they're both veterans and into late '60's muscle cars. They do have one other thing in common too, though: they both grow and smoke a considerable amount of marijuana.

What a royal pain in the ass!

I turned off Bunyan County 42 onto Big Pine Road and punched the convertible's accelerator to the floor, heading south toward Crystal Lake. I pretended not to see the flashing headlights behind me. Buck quickly shot up alongside me in his old red and black Torino. I smiled and waved. He looked angry, and he impatiently motioned for me to pull over.

After we'd both stopped on the shoulder of the road, he hollered through the open window of the Torino, "What the hell's the matter with you? Why'd you make me push this piece of shit so hard?"

The '69 Ford Torino with the big 428 Cobra Jet engine was a beautiful machine, probably the last of its kind still terrorizing Twin Cities area roads, but right now its tired engine was smoking and heaving, in desperate need of an overhaul.

I noticed that one of Buck's front teeth was broken off at an angle and nearly half gone.

"Hey—relax man," I said calmly. "I didn't see you turn around. And you shouldn't talk about your car that way. What happened to the tooth?"

"Forget the tooth for now," he grumbled. "That's pure bullshit, Charlie. You thought you could outrun me with your *fancy-rich-girl* Mercedes—a favorite among gentrifying scum, I might add. Listen, are you headed over to Victor and Jade's house?"

"No," I answered. "Why?"

"Come on, let's cut through it," he said. "I'm in a hurry. Are you going to see Jade or not?"

"Maybe. What's it to you?"

"What's it to me? I'll tell you, Charlie—the shit's getting ready to hit the fan, *that's what it is to me!*" he yelled. "And I'm not just talking bullshit, either—Sheriff Tipton and some mean-looking bastard just left my place about a half-hour ago, looking for Victor."

"Wonderful."

I thought Victor's little problem with the law was pretty much over with, except for the probation part. He'd gotten busted for growing weed two years ago and had gotten off fairly light under Minnesota law, probably because of being a Vietnam vet suffering not only from Post-traumatic Stress Disorder, but also from Tourette Syndrome and Obsessive Compulsive Disorder. The recent push for medical marijuana undoubtedly helped him, because he ended up only getting lengthy probation and a stiff fine. The Feds had initially shown some interest in the case. From what I've heard, they can jump in and prosecute any drug case they want to—and not always in a timely manner, either. But Victor's case was already settled. Besides, that'd be like double-jeopardy, wouldn't it? Maybe he'd broken his probation.

"Did you just hear me?" Buck shouted. "They were looking for Victor! Have you seen him? Damn it, Charlie, where are you going? We've got to find Victor before they do!"

"I'm on the way to see Jade right now," I said. "She's not at home, though...she's at her folks' house."

"Over by the West Park boat launch?"

"Yeah, not far from the launch."

"I'll follow you there—wait!" He studied the vapors seeping out from under the Torino's hood. "Can I ride with you?"

"I prefer if you don't," I said. "Is the seat of your pants clean?"

"You can be a real bitch at times, Charleen, can't you?" he said. "Come on, we don't have time to waste."

"Don't call me Charleen," I said. "I warned you about that before, *asshole*. Come on and get in. And keep your hands to yourself."

He looked surprised and smirked. "Hey, I was drunk and that was two weeks ago. You're not going to let me forget it, are you?"

I decided to give him a break. It's true that he'd been

drinking, but with him that's always too much and most of the time. Maybe it has to do with the four bullets he'd caught in Kuwait. I decided to go easy on him. He hadn't really been that hard to deal with anyway, partly because I grew up with five brothers. Also, I make my living operating a large construction crane; it's not glamorous work, but the money's good.

Buck locked the old Torino—including the hood locks—and walked over and stood in front of my car with outstretched arms and raised eyebrows, a silly, questioning look on his face. He made several faces and obscene gestures at me, then came up very close to the windshield and stuck his tongue out. "Okay, that's enough about *that* little incident," he said. "How many times do I have to tell you 'I'm sorry?' Actually, I've never been that interested in you anyway...I was just drunk. Come on, let's hurry up and find Victor."

He looked so vulnerable, I couldn't resist needling him. "Sure thing, Mr. Macho. Got your gun with you?"

A city of Burnsville police car slowly passed by. In my peripheral vision, I saw Buck wetting his lips. He looked at his Torino, then at the mostly-white patrol car again. "Very funny, Charlie," he muttered.

I said, "What'll you bet some Minnesota-nice person called in about an old, weird-looking car tearing up the roads right around here."

"I wouldn't doubt it," he answered. "Again, very funny. Hey, you know how Victor's always half-kidding about the boogie-man coming? Well, I just met the boogie-man a little while ago, and he looks like a real prick to me. Victor's in for some trouble—I can feel it coming."

"I hope not," I said, trying to sound optimistic. "Maybe they're just squeezing him on the probation thing...something like that."

"Uh-uh," he answered seriously. "It's more than that...it's something worse, much worse. I could tell from Sheriff Tipton's face, the fat bastard. They wouldn't tell me anything. Just kept asking me about Victor—when I'd seen him last, stuff like that. Like they were in a big hurry to find him."

"I think he's with Jade right now," I said.

Buck frowned and jerked his head back. "Why in the hell didn't you say so in the first place? Call ahead and find out, will you? Wait, no...well, go ahead, but don't mention any names."

"Settle down, will you?" I said, "you're making me nervous, and probably over nothing."

"I hope so," he said mournfully.

The weight of his premonition made my body feel heavy, like I'd suddenly put on about twenty pounds. I didn't like the feeling, so I punched the Mercedes' accelerator down sharply as though to carry the extra weight.

Jade's parents were away for the entire month of July vacationing in Spain, so she and Victor were taking care of their large estate for them. It wasn't an easy task either, because the estate was really a well-stocked hobby farm. Besides eighteen lovable llamas to take care of, there were also a half-dozen miniature horses and many other smaller birds and animals to feed and water as well.

The Mastersons' log home is perched on the second-highest hill overlooking Crystal Lake in Bunyan County, about three miles Southeast of Burnsville. The estate is fairly isolated considering its closeness to the Twin Cities. The valuation of the thirty-seven-acre estate was most recently put at around two million dollars, plus. Seven lighted ski runs a half-mile away on Buck Hill can be seen from the west-side windows of the massive log home. The views of star-shaped Crystal Lake are breathtaking year around—like living postcards. A wooden deck goes all the way around each of the three stories, and a smaller fourth floor comprises a small greenhouse and an open garden. The many decks and walkways are lined with shrubs and vines and colorful flowers, and some of the walkways continue down over the grounds, ending up at the bottoms of ravines. Some of the ravines have tiny, spring-fed creeks running through them. One of the little streams has native brook trout in it.

As far as I can tell, Victor never tries to take advantage of Jade's wealth. He doesn't seem to be that interested in money. He's very handsome and intelligent and several years older than she is. He served in the Army as an Airborne Ranger and he still keeps his black hair short, though not as short as Buck's. He earned a ton of medals, but he doesn't talk about them. He's tough and masculine, but also quiet and mellow, and he has a high degree in something he calls *The power of Ki*, which has to do with blocking pain. He's also into illegal extreme fighting, so I imagine *The power of Ki* can be quite helpful to him.

Victor's a high achiever despite his medical problems.

He often seems uncomfortable. He once told me that people are usually more interesting and pleasant to be around when they're stoned—they seem to be more accepting and mellow. He claims that smoking pot helps to take the edge off the reality of having to constantly deal with his brain chemicals being out of whack. That's along with dealing with post-traumatic stress from his days in Vietnam. Pot helps him not care as much, he says, the same way having a few drinks helps certain people feel more sociable. He strongly resents being treated like a criminal for doing something that helps him cope with an oft-times difficult life.

A few years older than me, Jade's *about* forty and still very beautiful, with thick black hair, brown eyes that are dark yet soft, and a full mouth. That's the Spanish blood she got from her mother. She seems fragile, but she exercises regularly, and she's very conscientious about what she eats. Her occasional outbursts of passion are usually directed at crooked politicians and injustice wherever it's found. She especially despises hypocritical politicians, including a distant neighbor of her parents, U. S. Senator Warren Patch, who looks like an evil puppet when he talks.

Patch is a strong proponent of mandatory minimum sentencing, a concept that Jade finds particularly troubling. He's on some kind of Justice Department committee that recommends judicial nonsense to Congress. He's got a daughter named Kimberly. I've seen her around a few times. Blond-haired and in her early twenties, she's just the kind of person Buck loves to hate—a snobbish rich bitch. She's too young for him anyway.

We breezed through the open gate of the Mastersons' estate. A sleek, dark green '99 Jaguar was parked next to a new thirty-two-foot travel home. The car was Jade's.

Buck and I found her feeding the llamas hay a hundred yards or so down one of the wider, paved trails. She was in a sunny opening with a little red and white barn in the middle of it. She was happy to see us, though surprised to see us together.

She soon saw something in Buck's face that made her frown. I suddenly wished he hadn't come, even though he was only being loyal to his friend.

"Where's Victor?" he asked Jade, breathing hard. Though powerfully built, he was out of shape from too much partying and not enough exercise.

Jade tried a weak smile and brushed a few strands of long black hair out of her pretty face. "Hi Charlie. Hi Buck...you didn't even say hello, Buck."

Before he could answer, I jerked my thumb his way and said, "Sorry about...*this*."

Jade chuckled, but her brown eyes looked worried. "Is something wrong?"

"Buck thinks there may be," I said. "He says someone is looking for Victor...go ahead and tell her all about it, Buck."

"That's right—I'm sure as hell not making it up," he said. He looked at me coldly, waiting for a response.

"What?" I said.

"Ah, never mind...it isn't worth it right now." He looked back at Jade. "Victor's in trouble," he said. "They're looking for him—Sheriff Tipton and some real mean look-ing prick in civilian clothes. Whoops, excuse me. The guy made me nervous right away. Mean eyes...probably a fed."

"They didn't say what they wanted?"

"Nope, just that they were looking for Victor. I imagine they were already at your place. Where is Victor, anyway? I don't mean to be rude or anything, Jade, but may I simply ask you, *where in the hell is Victor?*"

Chapter 2

Victor hurled the pitchfork he'd been using in the hayloft into the ground about a foot and a half from one of Buck's feet and yelled, "Hey, you down there! What do mean talking to my wife that way!"

He must've ridden over with Jade, because his favorite classic car—a lime-colored '68 Plymouth GTX with a dark green vinyl top—wasn't anywhere around.

In addition to collecting late-60's muscle cars, Victor also sold one now and then. But unlike Buck, he always kept to the letter of the law. He never sold more than five vehicles per year—which could be increased to ten with Jade's help. He didn't need the money. It was mostly just a thoroughly enjoyable hobby.

The handle of the pitchfork was still quivering when Buck whirled around and looked past it up at Victor, who was chuckling with amusement.

"Sorry," Victor said, "I didn't mean to get it quite that close—I was off a few inches. Hey, what happened to your tooth?"

"Damn it, Victor!" Buck sputtered, "if that was any-body else but you up there I'd be even more pissed than I am right now!" He was angry for only a moment. He glanced sheepishly at Jade, then scowled at me before explaining to his friend, "Oh, I got sucker-punched by a cop with a big ring on. I learned something out of that fight too...never to raise both of my fists to a cop at the same time. I left myself wide open. If you think the tooth looks bad, you should see the big bruise on my gut." He looked at me and scowled again, adding the expression of, *Okay, you can leave now, Bitch.*

I said, "Hey, what'd I do? I'm the one who just brought you here, remember?"

"Yeah. Thanks. You were making light of my mission, being a smart-ass as usual. Well, I don't need you any more. Good-bye."

"*Good-bye?* Fuck you, Buck," I said. "I'm here to see Jade. Why don't you go shovel some llama shit or something...make yourself useful as long as you're here."

He retorted, "I'm too fucking busy, that's why—and vice versa! It's a good thing you're a woman, or I'd probably smack the hell out of you right now." He turned to Jade. "I'm sorry for getting a little up-tight there a second ago. It's just that—and sorry about bringing the bad news, if that's what it is. It probably is."

Smiling, Jade said, "That's okay, Buck, we appreciate your concern. "Don't we Victor?"

"I don't know yet," Victor answered from the hayloft. He jerked his shoulder three or four times in rapid succession. "Who likes bad news, anyway?" He slowly twisted his neck, then nodded his head sharply once."

Buck was agitated and turned to walk away. "Come on Victor," he said. "We need to talk—in *private*."

"I'm wondering whether you guys should be talking in private about this," I said, wincing. "I mean, maybe four heads would be better than two."

Buck had already taken a few steps back up the paved trail. He stopped abruptly, but didn't turn around. I didn't have any trouble imagining the expression on his face.

Victor jumped down out of the hayloft, ending up in a crouch. The llamas scattered and regrouped at the farthest corner of the sunny clearing.

They were normally very relaxed animals, soft to the touch and not at all unfriendly to visitors. Jade's parents showed them often, and they'd won several awards. The Mastersons had stopped at a llama farm in Wisconsin one day and they'd become fascinated by the gentle creatures. Now the expansive walls of their log home were decorated with more than a dozen valuable wall hangings made from llama wool. The llamas and the little horses didn't cost much more to raise than dogs, because they mostly ate hay and grass.

"The best thing about these llamas," said Jade, looking directly at Buck, "is that they make you feel so mellow when you're around them, because of their relaxed nature. They help me to slow down and relax whenever I'm here." She paused and smiled sweetly. "Let's hear Charlie's idea, Buck. How about if we all put our heads together over as much cold German beer as we can drink in—oh, say about an hour? How about it?"

Seeing a distant helicopter passing high over Crystal Lake made me remember one of Buck's trigger-points. He scores pretty low on the emotional stability scale when paranoia creeps in, so I thought maybe I could jar him into forgetting he was angry with me long enough for everyone to start pulling together as a team.

I touched Jade's arm lightly and said, "Buck, We need to talk a second."

Taking their cue, the Stamates began walking back up the hill. Victor turned around and jerked his shoulder once, then winked at me. "Take it easy on her, Buck," he said, grinning. "And let's not make these llamas any more nervous than they already are, okay¿"

I waited a minute and said, "Buck, how long do you think it's going to take for the cops to show up¿"

He did a double double-take, trying to discover any hidden agenda on my face and asked, "What are you talking about...*here¿*" He looked up to the top of the hill, beyond where Jade and Victor were walking arm-in-arm. The dense forest of giant oaks and maples and white pines effectively blocked his view of the gate and any police cars that might be slowly cruising up to it.

Then the expression on his face quickly changed. He looked back at me and grinned. "Now you're the one full of shit, huh¿"

"Buck," I said, managing to keep a straight face, "we need to be serious here a minute." I nodded my head toward the Stamates. "For them. I don't want them to worry unnecessarily, but I'm beginning to think you may be right about Victor being in extreme danger. Remember that police car we saw right after you got into my car¿"

Buck suddenly stopped grinning and nodded seriously. He glanced back up the trail and began peering into the dense woods as though expecting to see brown-uniformed

Sheriff's deputies emerging with shotguns and dogs at any moment.

"You probably didn't even notice that helicopter going overhead a few minutes ago, did you?" I asked him.

"Huh?" He immediately looked up. "I didn't see no damned chopper. "Wait—I might've *heard* one a minute ago now that you mention it...."

"So neither one of us is full of shit now, right?" I said, confident once more. His paranoia was back on the upswing. Pretty soon he'd be a nervous wreak, no longer mad at me.

"I see the problem," I went on, "the big picture. They're messing with people like you and Victor—and me and Jade—because the small guy has lost his voice. That's not to say I necessarily agree with you on your whole pot-conspiracy theory, but I *am* beginning to see your point about the political prisoner part of it."

Buck looked astonished. "You are?"

I nodded and gave him a weak smile, trying to look more uneasy than I actually was. "Sure—they probably want to make Victor one. A political prisoner. Probably the Feds."

"Yeah." He shook his head vigorously. "That's it—you bottom-lined it. Thank you very much!"

"So don't worry, I don't think you're not crazy."

Seeing the sudden sparks in his eyes, I laughed and said, "Just kidding. Lighten up, will you? Seriously though, I'm beginning to see it now. It's the redneck group representing your generation that's to blame, beginning with Clinton—the one who didn't want to serve when he was supposed to. You know, Buck, the cowards and the pro-testers who wanted to wait and join the government later on. They've basically infiltrated the government, and now they're not representing people like us."

All the sparks were gone. He was warm putty in my hands once again.

"The way I'm seeing it, Buck," I continued, "—adding to your own views, I mean—it's the damned mandatory minimum sentencing laws that's to blame. Ever since the politicians tied the hands of judges by taking their discretion away, why, prosecutors and law enforcement working hand-in-hand have had a field day. Have you noticed how many prosecutors move right up the ladder into politics? I have. A whole slew of them, all across America. That's the purse and the sword coming together, Buck.

"Look at the Governor of Iowa. Another big advocate of the mandatory minimum laws. Used to be a prosecutor, now he's moved up. Remember him? He's the one who slapped that kid in the joint for twenty years for hitting his girlfriend. Mandatory minimums. Zero tolerance, even with soft drugs like pot."

Buck looked puzzled.

"The purse and the sword," I repeated. "Don't you get it?"

"I guess so," he said. He studied the dark forest. "Come on, let's get going."

"Buck, what I'm trying to say is, a local purse-and-sword team may be trying to take *Victor's* purse away—his land, or more money. Get it? If so, we may need to help him. Think about it, will you?"

He didn't think about it at all, but laughed loudly instead and said, "Now I know just how fucked-up in the head you really are, Charlie. I don't want to get anything going again, but now I know. You just tipped your hand. You're out of your fucking mind even worse than I thought...even worse than I am. We need a smoke break."

He sat down on a decayed log by the side of the trail and, grinning, lit up a joint. He slowly shook his head back and forth. "You think I don't see right through you, huh? You're just trying to buzz me up. And there wasn't any damned chopper, either."

"Yeah—why'd you look up, then? And why do you keep looking in the woods. You afraid of the boogie-man or something?"

"Boogie-man...that's pretty good, Charlie. Victor would appreciate that."

"He might not have much of anything left to appreciate pretty soon," I said. "Think about it. He got off pretty light for growing a couple of hundred plants. The Feds were interested in the case at first, remember? We thought they were interested in the track of land he got caught growing it on—a wedding gift from Jade's parents. But there was that sticky point, something about a short-term clause Jade's father had put into the land deed. I remember Jade telling me about it. In other words, maybe they weren't satisfied with the outcome...plus he had a bad attitude."

Buck frowned and passed me the joint. "What's that got to do with it?"

"Hey, attitude's everything," I said, pausing to take a small hit. "They were pissed because he wouldn't tell them anything, like even where he got the seeds. He didn't give them jack-shit." I blew out the tiny bit of leftover smoke, then continued. "I've heard the feds can jump in on any drug case they want to, and you pretty much have to snitch on somebody to get them off your back."

"Victor would never do that."

"I know. But the bottom-line is, they're probably coming back for more, even though he already paid that outrageous fine. It's the purse and the sword coming together, Buck. The judges' hands are tied."

"I know," he said. "It's not that complicated...it's called double-jeopardy. It sounds like a game, doesn't it? But it's not a game. That sinister-looking bastard...he's probably a stinking, no-good Fed. Come on Charlie—let's get going."

I felt like saying, *Don't do anything stupid, Buck*, now that I was guilty of turning his aggression over to the Feds to handle.

"You should leave your guns at home," I advised him.

Quite naturally, he took offence. "What do you think I am, *stupid?*"

"No—I just don't want you to get carried away trying to help your friend out."

"Oh, you mean like how I was overdoing it on the way here, being overly concerned, right? Listen to you...the one who's trying to buzz me up. Don't make me laugh, Charlie."

I was glad things were back to normal between us. Unfortunately though, what I'd just told him made pretty good sense to me too. That's what had me worried.

Jade was close to tears. Her hands shook noticeably as she got us all mugs of ice-cold German beer from one of the fancy taps in the basement den.

"I can't believe this is happening...again."

"It isn't," said Victor. He was stone-faced.

"I'm not much for social tinkering," Buck began, "but—"

I rolled my eyes.

"What? Don't start in again, Charlie, *please*, because I'm trying to be serious here now, okay? I might have some strange ideas about some things, but as far as social tinkering—actually doing anything—no, I don't get too involved. That's true. I leave the street stuff to tough people like you—and Jade here. I just kind of help the process along with a lot of bitching and complaining."

He was good for something. Jade couldn't help smiling. "I just hope you're complaining to the right people, Buck," she said.

"Can a prosecutor be sued?" Victor asked of no one in particular.

"I've never heard of it before," I said.

"I don't think they can be, Honey," Jade said. "They have immunity. Look at those cases where people are wrongfully imprisoned for years. They can't sue their prosecutors for compensation, can they? You hear about police departments being sued, but not judges or prosecutors."

Buck said, "I know a soldier can't sue the government. There were a couple of drill sergeants I wanted to sue. Dirty bastards. They were just doing their jobs though. Hey Victor, wasn't that Schruder guy a federal prosecutor?"

"No."

"He's the one who showed so much interest in your land, though, right?"

Jade answered, "Yes, he was one of them. But he dropped out of the picture—and coincidentally, not so long after the $75,000.00 fine was paid."

Buck was amazed. "Whew! Was it that much?"

"It was worth it at the time," Victor said. "I'm not so sure about it now."

Buck drank thirstily from the large ceramic beer mug, then remarked almost offhandedly, "Well, maybe someone will just have to be punished." He tipped the mug again.

I remembered the joint we'd just smoked. *This might get good*, I thought.

Jade said, "Oh, please don't say that Buck."

"I was just speaking figuratively," he said, belching loudly. "Wow, this is strong stuff—and good!"

Victor stood by the largest den window and looked down at Crystal Lake a half-mile away. A small window-tunnel had been carved through the rocks and roots for a distance of four or five feet to make the view possible; the Mastersons had wanted to keep all natural landscaping up close to the home in that spot. The edges of a half dozen large, moss-covered rocks were in view up close to the window, along with a clump of white birches, then open-ness until the lake. Victor seemed to be counting the boats on the lake. He *was* counting the boats on the lake. It was part of his obsessive-compulsive disorder to count them.

I watched him, being mindful of Jade. Victor was a hunk, and I didn't want her to think I was interested in him. I was always careful of that.

Without turning around, he angrily put his hands up to his hips and said, "It's probably just more money there're after."

Jade said, "Honey, maybe we shouldn't jump to conclusions."

Buck interjected, "You'd jump to conclusions if you saw that prick that was with Tipton this morning...whoops, sorry. I'm almost positive he was a damned fed."

Victor sadly turned away from the lake view. He had a light tan and was very handsome, in superb physical condition. He certainly didn't look forty-seven.

"You know what really gets me," he said, pausing to jerk his right shoulder a couple of times, "is just how much manipulation there is in politics. It's like I heard somewhere, 'Politics isn't about the truth, it's about what people believe.' Propaganda. I mean, it's all getting to be so fake...so obvious and measured. Now they take polls to find out want the people want to hear."

Jade said, "Well, I guess one has to be a salesman to be in politics. I imagine it's difficult to pose as a servant while actually wanting to be a master."

Victor was obviously getting upset and stressed-out. He arched his neck and moved his head back and forth slowly, as though to loosen stiff muscles. He jerked his shoulder. "It's all manipulation," he said. "I'm still madder than hell about getting busted in the first place. Do I sell pot? No. I only grow it for myself—and to share with a few friends. It shouldn't be anybody else's business. It's the damned politicians you're always complaining about, Jade. They can't seem to separate soft drugs from hard drugs.

They should've done that during the last thirty years, but instead it's only gotten worse."

"Yeah," said Buck, "just like the Kennedy thing."

I rolled my eyes. Buck didn't see me, but Jade did and smiled. "Buck, I think you're *really* missing the point," I said.

Buck's eyes were very glassy in the subdued light of the den. He slowly turned his head my way and pretended to see me for the first time by jerking his head back in mock surprise. He roared, "Ha! Ha! When did you get here!" He grinned mischievously. "Don't make me lose my train of thought...damn it, now where was I at? Oh. That whole Kennedy thing, it's getting worse, too...what they're finding out, I mean. And I'm not talking about that asshole Ted, even though they should be taking another look at him too. I'm talking about the Old Man's ties to the mob, and those Dr. Feelgood shots ole Jack was getting, and all the women—the whores—he was banging. Not to mention that he almost caused the destruction of planet Earth by fucking up with Castro. Ha! He came out of that mess looking like a big-shot hero...so then he gets us started in Vietnam. I'm actually thinking about maybe getting a petition drive started to re-name some public places carrying the name 'Kennedy.' A High School or two to start...maybe that one in East Bloomington. See, history is just now re-writing that whole fucking *Camelot* crock of shit. It's starting to fester and come to light—and it's about fucking time, too, I might add. And here Clinton wants to emulate him...you can see what an asshole *he* is, too."

"Okay, good point," I said. "Do you mind if we move

on now?"

"All I'm doing is agreeing with Victor...from a historical point of view, it's all getting worse. And you know why? Mostly because of that butthead Clinton. Look at all the dumb-asses he appointed, starting with Reno. Why, I wouldn't piss on that big, raw-boned Texas bitch's *panty-hose* if it was on fire! You ever notice how many big, raw-boned people come out of Texas? Like Janis Joplin and Lyndon Johnson. Now Reno. Stupid names, too.

"Who do you think was behind that Waco fiasco? Shining those bright lights on everybody? Kids too. Playing that loud, crappy music...even playing rabbits being slaughtered. Monks chanting, too, if you can believe that. Gee's, no wonder they thought the world was coming to an end! They could've picked that asshole Koresh up quietly, but, oh no, they had to be big shots. I guess that's why they set the place on fire with those pyrotechnic things, to show them who the boss was—or who the anti-Christ was, or whatever. And Ruby Ridge. Deliberately plugging that poor woman while she was holding her kid. I'm not forgetting *that* shit, either.

"And how about that Madeline woman...what's her name? Fucking up royally. See, Clinton's big mistake was hiring a bunch of women to do a man's job. But then I guess he owed a bunch of them for getting him elected, along with another group or two I won't mention at this time...like all his homosexual supporters out in Hollywood. I heard most faggots are democrats—you could've knocked me over with a pink feather when I heard that!"

The monologue ended with him staring at me with a stupid, open-mouthed, broke-toothed grin on his face. "Well, don't you want to add anything?" he asked.

"I guess not," I said sarcastically, "you've about covered everything."

"Not everything," he said, smiling at me drunkenly. Dark beer foam covered his upper lip and one side of his mouth. "I haven't gone full-circle yet. About what Victor was saying, I mean."

"And what was that?" I joked. "It's been so long ago now, you probably don't even remember."

"Sure I do," he said. "About how the rednecks are still in power after all these years...after they didn't want to serve when they were supposed to. Now they've infiltrated the government—stealing and shit, grabbing all the power they can. Grabbing ass, too...I know a little bit about politics. It's all smoke and mirrors and polls. Have you ever been polled? I have never once been polled in my entire life. Never, not once. Not even *one* time."

Victor looked tired and sat down. "It's pretty weird alright," he said, slumping back and putting his hands behind his head. "It's like certain prosecutors—working with local police—have taken the place of the British back in the 1700's. History is repeating itself. We don't deserve what's happening to us any more than the colonists did back then. America just can't get around to separating marijuana from hard drugs, because of all the politicking. So as a consequence, we have to worry about our rights being violated."

"It's a conspiracy," said Buck. "Maybe a loose—"

"—History is repeating itself," Jade interrupted, "like Victor said. What were the reasons we fought against the British? I'll tell you—I used to teach it to my eighth graders when I taught years ago. It was mainly because laws were being applied unfairly. Sound familiar? It wasn't just over taxes. Corrupt British officials were selectively seizing property. And sometimes they used fabricated evidence. I bet there were plenty of snitches back then, too. The similarities are scary...this is what mandatory sentencing is causing right now."

"Yeah," Buck agreed, "we're basically being picked on because of suck-butt laws, just one part of the overall conspiracy...a loose theory I've got."

Victor said, "I heard someone say once that politics are based on the indifference of the majority. They won't separate soft drugs from hard drugs," he repeated. "It's the way they classify drugs, and it's all political. Nobody cares about your rights if drugs are involved—even if it's only pot. It's the way it's hyped, especially in the media. They always put a big, bright-green pot leaf right there with all the white powder. It's ridiculous. But never mind about alcohol and tobacco, even though those drugs are destroying peoples' lives every day."

Jade was becoming angry and indignant. "There's the hypocrisy!" she exclaimed. Just like you can kill a whole busload of children while driving drunk and still have the right to bear arms, but what about someone busted for growing pot? The Federal Government can take away *her* right to bear arms for the rest of her life. A whole group of citizens are being denied their second amendment rights.

Politics have invaded the judicial system...maybe that's what happens when too many prosecutors move into politics."

Buck managed to bottom-line the situation without giving me any credit at all—not even so much as a glance my way. "It's the purse and the sword, man," he said. "They're coming together again, just like back during the Revolution."

It was a profound statement coming from Buck Foster. I looked at him—my *student*—and smiled broadly.

The Stamates looked at one another, puzzled. They smiled along with us, though they couldn't understand Buck's newfound intelligence.

"Maybe it was an accident," I mumbled.

Chapter 3

Buck had been looking down and away—slightly embarrassed, I think—when he suddenly sprang to his feet. He took two or three steps, then quickly dropped down to one knee, frozen in place. He stared down intently at a pile of rolled-up newspapers collecting for the Mastersons' return. From where I was sitting, I could barely make out the black and white image of a man's face on one of the newspapers, the one Buck quickly snatched up.

"That's him! That's the son-of-a-bitch right there!" he yelled. The veins on his neck stuck out and his entire head was red from bending over so long. He viciously stabbed his finger into the man's face four or five times, then brought the newspaper up for a closer look.

"That is him! I can't believe it. This is the guy who was with Tipton, the fat fuck!" He looked at Jade. "Sorry." He threw the newspaper across the den to Victor.

Victor jumped up and caught it easily, then quickly sat back down and leaned forward and smoothed the newspaper's front page down on a smoked-glass coffee table so we could all get a good look at the enemy. The Sunday edition of the *Star Tribune* was dated July 3rd, which made it a week old.

The man Buck so despised was named Luther Sullivan, and he wasn't a fed. I knew Buck would be disappointed.

Below Sullivan's picture, in large bold type: *Wisconsin's problem, soon to be Minnesota's.*

And obviously, Victor's now too, I thought after taking one look at the guy. Buck was right. He looked like a prick—enough like Stephen Segal to be his brother. Darkly handsome, strong, dangerous-looking. Almost a description of Victor, I suddenly realized, but without his gentle side.

Buck was now almost out of control. He shouted, "He looks like a real prick! That's what I said to myself the first time I saw him, walking up to my door with Sheriff Tipton, the fat...never mind. I said to myself, 'You look like a real prick.' See his eyes? Something about his eyes makes you feel nervous. Deep and penetrating—that kind of nervous."

Jade and I glanced up from the newspaper together. He hadn't met anything by it. We looked back down together.

"What's it say about him?" Buck demanded to know. "Anybody...look for the keyword 'federal.'"

It was fun breaking the bad news to him. "Buck, he's not a fed."

"Huh—you sure?"

I saw his disappointment and smiled. "Not the work 'federal' anywhere. Just a bunch of stuff about strip joints."

"Strip joints?" He was suddenly very interested again. "What's it say? Just the highlights, please."

"Read it yourself," I said.

"Come on, I just smoked that jay, plus it's a little dim in here, anyway."

"Okay," I answered, "back off though, will you?"

I read for awhile, occasionally stopping to glance up at Luther Sullivan's picture. Buck was right—the man's dangerous-looking eyes were deep and penetrating. *"'Luther Sullivan: errant former state boy and big shot body guard to a previous Governor of Minnesota. Now the proud owner of a string of strip joints plastered all along the East side of the Mighty Mississippi.'"*

It made very little sense. Why would this guy, Sullivan, be in the company of the Sheriff of Bunyan County, and why would they be looking for Victor Stamate together? I read on, giving Buck the highlights: *"'Favorable Wisconsin Supreme Court ruling. Nude dancers. Protest signs. Six border county locations. Communities scrambling to stop him. Liquor licenses. Stillwater. Near recreation, antique shops, trendy coffeehouses. St. Croix River, tubing on Apple River, concerts. Somerset. First Amendment lawyer. Secondary adverse effects. Opposition to planned expansion.'* Then girls-girls-girls," I told Buck, "just stuff about bending over to pick up tips and how far nude dancers should legally have to be from their customers—details you wouldn't be interested in."

"I'm interested," he said, "keep reading."

"Most drooling, sexist pigs would be—forget it, read it yourself."

"Hey, I have a lot of respect for women," he said, pretending offence. "I always pay my girlfriends for everything they do."

Jade said, "Are you guys going to stop that any time soon? You're going to end up hating one another."

"We already do," Buck said, grinning. "We love to hate each other—don't we, Charlie? Do you mind if I get another mug of beer, Jade?" he asked. "It sure is good on a hot summer day."

"Help yourself."

I answered Buck's other question, "Yeah, except that—for some reason—we mostly hate one another more after we're been drinking. We need to stop drinking together, Buck...only not today. This German beer is good."

The doorbell rang. It was Tipton and Sullivan.

When Victor answered the door, possibly worried about trumped-up charges leading to life in prison, Buck went with him and stood slightly back, wobbling loosely at the waist. Jade walked over to a small side-window and peered out. I quickly joined her.

There were two police cars parked in the shade near the house. One was a mostly white Burnsville squad car, the other one was dark blue and new-looking, unmarked. A cop dressed in a brown uniform stood leaning against the squad car, basically covering the front of the house. Tipton wasn't in uniform. He was wearing a loud, mostly-yellow, loose-fitting Hawaiian shirt.

"Hi Victor," he said casually.

Victor didn't return the pleasantry. "I heard you're looking for me."

The fat Sheriff hoisted his trousers and shifted his gaze over to Buck. "News travels fast, doesn't it?" he said. "Matter of fact, too fast." He asked Buck, "Is that your old red Ford sitting by 35W and County Road 42?"

"Old red Ford? You're talking about a *classic!*" Buck exclaimed, disdain written all over his face. "It might be mine. What's it to you, anyway?"

"How long you had it?"

"That might just possibly not be any of your business," Buck answered. "Why do you want to know?"

"Never mind for now," Tipton said. "That's not why I'm here...we're here to see you, Victor. Do you mind if we talk in private somewhere?"

"That won't be necessary," Victor said. He leaned forward just far enough to see the two police cars parked outside. "Just tell me what you want and then leave, okay?"

Luther Sullivan cleared his throat. "Um, actually, that's *not* okay, Victor. I went to considerable trouble to find you, and I'd really like to talk with you...right now."

"I don't have anything to say to you, Mister," I heard Victor tell Sullivan. "Our interests are neither mutual nor compatible."

"Oh? What do you know about my interests?" asked Sullivan.

"Just this," said Victor, thrusting out the newspaper with Sullivan's picture on it.

The strip-club owner remained cool. He didn't even bother to look down.

Buck began prancing up and down on his toes. "So if you've got anything else to ask me about my car," he said haughtily to Tipton, "you can do it through my lawyer. We don't have to tell you *jack-shit!*"

Tipton swiveled his porky head around to look at the deputy outside for effect, then swiveled it back around to look at Buck again.

"And another thing," Buck said, growing more obnoxious, "I've never sold a car to anyone who didn't deserve it!" He was obviously feeling the strong German beer now. "Yeah, so why don't you and your friend here—*Mr. Girly-flesh-man*—go fuck off!"

Having made himself abundantly clear, he retreated past me with a broad smile on his face, back toward the fancy beer taps. He was apparently satisfied for the time being, except for some final muttering. "And you'd better leave my fucking car alone too or I'll sue your fat ass...they should have better standards, weight limits would be good for starters...."

Sullivan looked at Victor coldly.

"You sure we can't talk?"

Victor easily met Luther Sullivan's stare. "We don't have anything in common. Go away now and leave me alone."

"Um, Victor," Tipton began, "you don't even know—"

"—Good bye, gentlemen." Victor started to close the door.

Sullivan said, "We can make some very good money together, Victor. I'd like to build a nice place on your land overlooking the Minnesota River, and—well, from what I understand—you've got a lot of bartending and bouncer experience. Maybe you could manage the place for me. No problem with re-zoning that particular piece of land...I've got connections. What would you like to name it?"

"I'm not interested," Victor said. "It's out in the middle of nowhere, anyway."

"That's just it, Victor," Sullivan said. "Actually, it's *not* out in the middle of nowhere. It's just a few minutes away from 169, and close to Bloomington, Eden Prairie—a lot of expendable income. There'd be plenty of room for parking, too."

"I'm not interested. Goodbye."

"Victor," Sheriff Tipton said, "I think you should listen to Luther here, because, well—I hate to put it like this—but that bad luck you had a few years ago is still up in the air a little bit, if you know what I mean."

I sensed Victor getting pissed. I saw him arch and twist his neck back and forth slowly a few times, then he jerked his right shoulder three times very hard.

Sullivan was surprised. "Are you all right?"

"Just fine," Victor said. "Goodbye, gentlemen."

"I just want you to know that I seldom take no for an answer," Sullivan said. "The same goes for second chances. That's just my nature—as well as it being a matter of principle." He waited for his words to sink in.

"You know what part your problem is Victor?" he continued, "The good citizens out there don't care what happens to drug fiends. They just don't give a shit about people like you—or for people like me either, for that matter."

"I'd rather smoke a little pot than be a crooked bastard like you," I heard Victor respond coolly. "I'm warning you both just this once to stay away from me and mine."

Then I saw him kick the heavy wooden door shut in their faces.

During his first run for Sheriff, Rudy Tipton had boldly claimed to be descended from General Armstrong Custer. The golden-haired fool was his great-great-great-grandfather, if you were willing to believe Tipton, though he himself probably couldn't even get on a horse, yet alone dash about smartly. It's much more believable that he inherited his love of the limelight from the General, because Tipton loves publicity.

He was the first Sheriff in Minnesota to have a public gun sale after lawmakers gave their nod to the idea of reselling confiscated guns. Why destroy valuable guns if some of the proceeds from selling them can go toward buying another squad car? Better yet, why not keep a few of the special ones for yourself? Tipton's personal gun collection supposedly includes fully automatic machine guns and antiques dating back to the Revolutionary War.

His antics sometimes attract unwanted attention, like the time folks started complaining when he loaned ordinary citizens radar guns after they kept pestering him about speeders in their neighborhood. It's a good thing the Governor stepped in before that one went national. No tickets were given out, only warnings. Then there was the embarrassment on TV just last month when he made a fool of himself complaining about the poor quality of convenience store videotape used to crack a murder case. Not an iota of gratitude for the storeowner, who he completely trashed—and she wasn't even required to have a camera on her property in the first place.

I'd only had one run-in with Tipton myself, and that was a long time ago. My brother Edwin and I had bought a car together to fix up and re-sell. Edwin sometimes sold more cars than he was supposed to—like Buck. The state would always get their cut in taxes, so it shouldn't have been a big deal. The car was in my name, so nothing ever became of it.

The voting public took Tipton for his word when he promised he'd make speedy improvements in the Sheriff's Department. He said there'd be no more coddling of the prisoners. No more idleness, either. There'd be no more tobacco or coffee—they were better off without it anyway. No more fancy, hot meals. Sandwiches would be good enough. And there'd be no more silly recreational programs—everyone could work for the county to stay in shape. That one went over real well. Punishment would come in, rehabilitation would go out. There'd be no more "perversion of tax dollars."

On *This Week with Sam Donaldson and Cokie Roberts*, Sam asked Sheriff Tipton if maybe he hadn't gone a bit too far. Tipton's response, as nearly as I recall, went something like this:

"Sam, I haven't gone far enough yet. I haven't had time what with implementing all my other new changes." Sam then asked him, "Well, aren't you concerned about prisoner complaints reaching your Governor's ear? I can't imagine Jesse Ventura letting you treat Minnesota prisoners the way you do!" Tipton's answer: "Me worried about him? Hell no! Have you seen him lately, Sam? He's the very least of my concerns. He doesn't even have time to work out anymore—just like me. Why, it'd be music to my ears to hear that Potato-head complain. That's just the kind of publicity I need, because it'd bring attention to how much tax money I'm saving folks back home. There's no way in hell my prisoners are going to live better in jail than folks do on the outside—not as long as I'm the Sheriff of Bunyan County! Ha!"

Why'd he have to mention Bunyan County—or even Minnesota, anyway? Then he finished the segment with an insult to Sam, right after agreeing with him that, yes, life was too short to deal with dull people. He told Sam that he'd be a good one for a future Star Trek episode, because of his eyebrows.

We rejoined Buck by the beer taps, where he happily greeted us by lifting his ceramic mug up higher and higher to each of us, respectively, as we came over to him.

Jade was angry and spoke bitterly. "Most of the locals around here know all about the special help Tipton's been getting in his *courageous* fight against crime," she said. "The Sheriff's Department has really grown, too."

"Yeah, with considerable help," I agreed.

Jade said, "Warren Patch is a former Bunyan County prosecutor himself, you know."

"I didn't know that," I said. "That could help to explain the rumors I've been hearing, I mean, about him being on the take...nasty rumors about seized assets, that kind of thing."

"Joe Schruder has to be involved," said Victor. "As the Chief Prosecutor, he'd have to share information with the Feds. He's probably getting a nice piece of whatever action Tipton drums up too. I've heard that Joe Schruder has a serious gambling problem."

"What an asshole," said Buck.

Jade picked up where Victor left off. "It's also rumored

that Schruder was a draft dodger during the Vietnam days. Shot himself in the foot."

Buck's interest suddenly picked up. "What an asshole! No wonder everyone hates him."

"He's a former cop too," she continued. "Staunchly in favor of gun control...very anti-NRA. The story goes that he...well...he may have tried to commit suicide two or three times. Of course we don't know whether that's true or not."

"I heard he's mean to his kids," said Victor with a chuckle, "and to the family dog, too."

"It's probably all true and even worse," I said, chuckling along with him before getting serious again. "Schruder's the one who prosecuted Steve and Mary Goode. Remember them...the storeowners? Mid-thirties. Had a couple of small kids. Steve was a decorated Desert Storm vet."

I glanced at Buck. He was listening intently.

"Yeah, they ran *Northern Lights Garden & Hydroponics* for about ten years," I continued. "They sold typical hardware, but the place had become popular with pot growers. The story goes that when Schruder approached Steve about setting set up a sting operation, he refused to help bust his own customers. Schruder told him he'd take away his store and put him in prison if he didn't cooperate. Well, he got federal agents to set up surveillance despite Steve's lack of cooperation. I heard it was Schruder's idea to watch the store and follow certain customers home."

"The dirty son-of-a-bitch," Buck said sourly.

I went on. "Yeah, I remember from the newspaper. And

Tipton carried it even further by having his deputies go through all the suspects' garbage. They finally got one of the growers to say that Steve had given him some seeds and advice."

"Right," Jade said, nodding her head. "I remember now, too. That's all they needed for a conspiracy charge. The Goodes ended up losing even more than Schruder had threatened. Besides the business, they also lost their house, vehicles, money—even their kids. The last I heard, the Department of Justice still has them locked up in a Federal Corrections Institution...somewhere down South, I think."

Victor said, "Yeah, I followed that case closely myself. Minnesota got a lot of negative publicity over it nationally. The Governor wouldn't do anything about it, either...that was before Ventura came to power."

"The bastards," Buck said. "And Tipton went through their *garbage*, you say?"

Now he's really going to become a conspiracy-freak, I thought to myself. To Buck it was simple: them against us. And now some of them included Tipton and Sullivan, and probably Schruder—maybe even Senator Patch. A potentially dangerous team working together against us, no doubt.

I said, "Well, I guess it's obvious they're looking for some more assets to take over."

Buck handed Victor a froth-topped mug of cold German beer. "I don't think they like us anymore, Victor," he said.

"They never did."

"What're we going to do?"

"Nothing," said Victor. "Unless they start messing with

me."

"Messing with *us*," Buck corrected him. "Then what?"

Jade walked over and put an arm around Victor's waist. "Let's not talk about it any more. For awhile anyway, okay? Do you mind?"

I quickly cut in, "Come on, Buck, I didn't plan on staying very long, anyway. I've got a sky-diving lesson to go to, then it's off to the race-track."

He looked surprised. "Whew—you've got more extra money to spend than I do," he said. "Okay, sure. How long are we going to be gone, Baby?"

"Forget it, I'm dropping you off at your car. If it's still there, that is."

He suddenly looked worried.

"What's wrong?" I asked.

"Oh, nothing," he muttered, "just that I left a half-ounce of good weed in it. It's a good thing I stashed it up under the dash." He looked at Victor and Jade and suddenly brightened up. "Hey, are you guys going to be all right? Maybe I should stay here for awhile. If you want, I can go hide down by the road and let you know if any trouble's coming. To be honest with you, I'm expecting some trouble." Turning to Jade, he said, "I don't mean to alarm you unduly, but does your father happen to have any guns around...hunting rifles, shotguns, pistols, anything like that?"

"Buck, what the hell's the matter with you?" I scolded him. I was beginning to feel the strong beer now too. I slapped his arm.

He drunkenly stumbled back a few steps. "Well damn!

Shit! What'd I say to piss you off this time, *Girlfriend?* Let me rephrase that, then. Jade, would your father happen to have anything like a crossbow or one of those heavy-duty slingshots lying around? Anything. Even a throwing knife is better than nothing at all. Boy, I'd like to stick a dagger right in Tubby Tipton's fat gut right now...the nerve of that fat bastard, hinting about my car like that, like maybe he—"

I took a step toward him and raised my arm menacingly. He backed up laughing and said, "Then I'd like to twist it and watch him dance!"

"Okay, let's go," I said. "See you guys later. I've got to *try* to get this asshole home in one piece. I'll call you later, Jade."

Chapter 4

I dropped Buck off at his car and decided to go past the Stamate's property on my way to the Flying Cloud Airport for my skydiving lesson. I crossed over to 169 and went north until I came to Riverview Road, then went west a mile or so until I came to Homeward Hills Road. The property was located just southwest of the intersection, near Walnut Ridge. I parked my convertible under a very large oak tree near the road, thinking, *At least I'll fit into the neighborhood.*

The property was heavily wooded with mostly oaks except for a clearing of about two acres, which was serving as pasture for two pinto horses and a foal. A watering trough was positioned in the center of the clearing near a single large oak tree. Behind the horses to the south was a spectacular view of the Minnesota River Valley, including the far distant cities of Burnsville and Savage.

Also just over the ridge behind the horses is where Victor had been growing his marijuana plants when he was busted. It'd been in late September, and the two hundred or so female plants were about eight feet high and thick and heavy with buds. He was pleased with how well they were doing in the naturally fertile, loose soil. The area was surrounded and protected by patches of wild black-raspberry bushes and thick brush. Deer and rabbits didn't pose a problem, Victor had said, but bugs were a hazard to the plants for a time in late June and early July. The mosquitoes were a pain in the ass all the time, but especially after heavy rains.

I briefly imagined how spectacular the view would be at nighttime, with no bugs, looking out an enormous window—not the window of a gaudy, lit-up, nude-dance club. No, it'd be a *private* window, perhaps the window of *my* darkened bedroom. It was just a fleeting thought, and I tried to leave Victor out of it.

I was worried for the Stamates—and for Buck too, though not as much, and I couldn't help wondering if Tipton or Sullivan had gotten my license plate number. It seemed likely, which possibly meant that I was already involved in the Stamate's problem—whatever it was. The idea of helping my friends didn't bother me. Quite the opposite, I looked forward to helping them.

I filled my little cream-colored ceramic pocket bowl with some good Minnesota homegrown and walked over to center of the clearing and took a couple of hits, facing the valley. The horses stopped grazing and studied me for a minute, then they went back to nibbling at the grass. The wind was blowing in gently from the south. When I exhaled, looking up, my face and hair were washed-over with some of the sweet-smelling but pungent smoke. The ancient oak trees presented me with an unbroken ceiling of branches and leaves. As I drifted forward, the green and brown ceiling magically switched over and became a downward-flowing green carpet stretching a half-mile or so to the wide, mud-colored ribbon of water below.

I thought about the possibility of kidnapping Senator Patch's daughter, Kimberly. It wouldn't be for money, it would be for justice—a ransom for justice. Buck would love the idea of kidnapping a *rich bitch* to help out his best friend. Release Victor and we'll release the girl. Simple. Buck would get it right away. And it was a plan he and I could pull off without anyone else's help. But the plan somehow sounded too simple. Something didn't sound right. I laughed to myself after finally realizing why the word *idea* sounded better.

I decided to blow off the skydiving lesson and instead do a drive-by of the Senator's home. As I headed back toward 169, I continually reminded myself that kidnapping Kimberly was just an idea, not a plan. Certainly not a *simple* plan. It would take disguises. Maybe a rented car or two. I had a bit of extra money available, which was a good thing because Buck wouldn't have a spare dime. Jade had plenty, but I didn't want her to be involved unless it became necessary.

The hard part would be penetrating any tight security surrounding a senator's daughter. But then, maybe the spoiled brat didn't like tight security. Maybe she liked to venture off by herself. That'd make it easier.

I imagined different scenarios. Buck would drag her, screaming, out of her car while I waited nearby in another car. We always wore disguises. He pushed her into the back seat and got in beside her—no, he tied her up and put her in the trunk of the car. The car was a plain color. Kimberly would scream, so Buck would have to gag her the next time before putting her in the trunk. I didn't know where we were taking her yet.

Then my mind jumped to Victor thanking me—and hugging me. Then my thoughts zinged so far out-of-place that I decided to turn around and go to my skydiving lesson after all, for punishment. I figured I could still make it in time if I pushed it real hard. Saving Victor could wait until later.

To escape my earlier bad thoughts, I cranked the volume of the radar detector to maximum and put on The Best of the Animals.

Buck called me after I got home from my skydiving lesson, wanting to meet with me again right away, but he sounded like he'd carried his earlier drinking home with him, so I told him it could wait until the next day. After some confused thinking, he said he'd be home by 2:00 o'clock, after working out with Victor. I agreed to stop by his home about that time.

Victor was punishing himself for his upcoming fight. The night of underground fighting was being billed as *The Suicide Man Extreme Dueling Show*. It would be a night of pure violence, though there wasn't any mention of the word *violence* in the billing—or the word *fight*. Those words could stir up too much unwanted attention, especially after all the anti-violence crap coming from the media in the wake of the recent shootings.

The thin cardboard tickets were printed plainly and numbered by hand in fine calligraphy. An *unspoken* name went out with each and every ticket card, which meant that they were somewhat protected by folks who wanted to keep their reputations for secrecy intact for future ticket-selling. That's how it worked. A couple of hours before the show was to begin, the calls would go out. Hopefully, the place wouldn't be raided. If it got raided, all the money would simply vanish—it was better that way. Even the fans understood. No show, no refunds. Token payments to the fighters. House bets *might* be returned, later, if all the cash wasn't confiscated. It was part of the chance everyone took, and it could end up messy, very messy. There were quite a few variations in how the illegal fighting matches were handled, and Victor was familiar with all of them because he'd been part of the secrecy for several years.

The winner of this Friday night's *show* would get a so-called guaranteed purse of $10,000, plus five percent of profits on house bets, which could double or even triple the purse itself, depending on how honest the particular sponsor was. Victor knew most of the big-time sponsors. One of them had suggested that Victor was getting too old to fight and asked him to be his partner. Victor told Jade he didn't know whether to take it as a genuine offer, or as a slam on his age.

Victor's philosophy about extreme fighting isn't complicated at all: if sane adults want to batter themselves for money, it's basically nobody's business but theirs. What good is freedom of choice if there isn't anything to choose from? The rest of society can butt out. If an adult wants to kill himself riding a motorcycle without a helmet, that's his prerogative. Same with seatbelts. Leave people alone—especially in their homes. It's nobody's business if you drink or smoke...whatever. The same goes for growing marijuana for your own use.

On the way to Buck's house I came to realize that the Feds were beating us up with another bureaucratic catch-22. *About like a loose conspiracy,* as Buck would say. Studies proving pot's good benefits aren't being recognized by the FDA, but the FDA isn't approving further research, so pot is still classified as a schedule-1 drug along with cocaine and heroin and meth, which means that it's still considered as having no therapeutic value. The bottom line, of course, is that pot can't be legally prescribed for people like Victor. To make matters worse, Minnesota's would-be medical marijuana program is relying on—and waiting for—federal changes. We're essentially on hold by the feds. We're waiting in vain to implement a workable state system. Hopefully, Ventura would help change all that.

I arrived at Buck's little cabin on the west shore of Bloomington's Normandale Lake at 2:00 o'clock and waited and waited for him, but he didn't show up, which was typical.

Then, just as I started to leave, his red and black Torino came peeling up the driveway. I wondered whether the reckless driving was just part of an elaborate excuse for being late, or if there was actually some kind of emergency. It was unusual for him to be cutting up so close to his home, because of his Minnesota-nosy neighbors; they were always quick to call the police on him.

He burned another good layer of rubber off the Torino's tires by sliding in sideways within a few feet of my Mercedes. He didn't care about the tires. It was part of the price of having fun. He didn't care much about having to replace universal joints and an occasional rear-end either. But he was careful with the transmission and the Cobra Jet engine. He always kept a close eye on the tachometer.

"Shit, I forgot all about Rosie!" he yelled, slamming the car door shut. Thick white smoke from the Torino's tires drifted northward away from the driveway, into the birch and pine woods, like the aftermath of a Revolutionary War skirmish. He ran past me and bounded up the wooden steps leading into his run-down house. A few seconds later I heard the back door slam.

Buck's home was just a summer cabin when it was built during the Great Depression, and that's what it still is, a run-down summer cabin, the last home left on the banks of the small lake. The city of Bloomington, prompted by the wealthy homeowners on the hill overlooking Normandale Lake, had tried unsuccessfully to buy the little cabin from Buck, but he wasn't selling. Not even for twice its value. The other homes had all been torn down after the city banned further improvements on them. The idea was to quickly rid the lakeshore of its few unworthy inhabitants.

Buck, being the last holdout, now enjoys making a nuisance of himself. He makes a lot of noise and keeps Rosie O on his property, for starters. Because of a grandfather clause, a few of Bloomington's ordinances can't be applied to the old homestead which he inherited from his parents when they died in a car accident. He can still have farm animals, for example, like Rosie O. Buck re-named the huge Hampshire sow-due to deliver any time now—back during all the gun-control commotion caused by the school shootings. In fact, I happened to stop by his house the very afternoon Tom Selleck appeared on Rosie O'Donnel's talk show. Buck'd been drinking and was all fired up, and he'd gone into one of his long tirades.

"She's so damned shallow, Charlie...I don't like her at all anymore. Look, you can watch her for thirty seconds and see what an asshole she is. I hardly ever watch her stupid program. She acts like a fool most of the time. Here she invites a fellow actor on her dumb show and then she ambushes him. Look! About like that Jenny Jones woman, or that stupid woman with red glasses—you know, the one who likes to send kids to boot camp all the time. No class. Knee-jerking all around her podium there. Listen to her! It wasn't that long ago she was attacking Charleston Heston. I won't forget this!"

I'd known better than to say anything.

"What the hell does she know about gun control? Or freedom? Just takes it for granted. She was just born into it, never had to protect it. What a dumb ass! Why, the very foundation of our freedom is the right to bear arms! It's not about crime—it's about keeping our ability to revolt! To keep the feds in check. Okay, that's it, I've had just about enough of this shit...the first thing I'm doing is changing the damned channel, and the next thing I'm doing is changing Janet's name to Rosie, Rosie O, in honor of that *stupid cunt* right there! Okay—*shazzam*, it's done!"

He came back through the house and let the front door slam shut. "Sorry I took so long," he said. "Come on—take a look. Rosie's had her pups."

"There not called pups, Buck," I said. "They're called piglets. Where in the hell have you been? I've been waiting around here forever for you."

"I said I was sorry, Charlie," he whined. "Gees, Victor wanted an extra-hard workout, and I—"

"Damn it!" I yelled at him. "I've got better things to do than to wait around for you to finish working out with Victor—waiting around at this *dump*, and for what? To see your stupid pet pig? I don't think so. I don't care about your stupid pig—or your stupid pig's piglets, either. I don't care how many there are, or what color they are or anything. And I *sure* don't want to smell them, or their mama! Come on now, let's get away from here so we can talk."

"Okay," he quickly agreed, probably relieved to be out of trouble with me so soon. "Mind if we take my car? Me and a friend just did a valve job on it—we stayed up practically all night. Matter of fact, I was testing it out and kind of forgot the time...if you can believe that."

"Sure I believe it," I said. "It makes perfect sense. It even has a ring of truth to it."

"You don't have to be such a smart-ass about everything I say, Charlie," he said.

I didn't mind that much riding with Buck. He's a good driver—though too daring at *times*—and he keeps the Torino nice and clean, unlike his home. The old muscle car has an immaculate black interior, with bucket seats and a Hurst four-speed transmission.

Though he didn't know it yet, we were on the way to Chief Prosecutor Joe Schruder's house in Burnsville.

We headed south on Normandale Lake Road, then took Old Shakapee west to 169 and headed south again. Buck punched it going over the new four-lane bridge crossing the Minnesota River. The Torino's exhaust pipes resonated low and mellow as he shifted gears. We seemed to fly through the branches of the huge cottonwoods growing up from the swamp below off to the right. I felt like I was in a fast-moving ultralight plane, and I marveled at the engineering of the high new bridge anchored to solid rock many feet below the surface of the swamp.

I was leaning back, glancing out of the corner of my eye, watching the Torino's speedometer needle floating somewhere between 115 and 120, when Buck finally braked hard for the next exit. Valley Fair was nearby, to the west. Schruder's house would be in a cul-de-sac just about a mile to the south, off Savage Street.

"You mind telling me where we're going now?" Buck asked. "And why?"

I said, "Listen, I'm not interested in doing anything radical, okay? Only what's required to make them back off."

"Uh, okay," he answered. He still had a lot of adrenaline pumping from the mad dash to Burnsville. "You're talking about Victor...and the current pot laws, right? Yeah, I'm following you. Good, because I'm getting tired of all this good-humor bullshit anyway. What did you have in mind?"

"Buck," I said, "first of all, I'm only talking about helping Victor. Nothing else. Please listen carefully...I'm not getting involved in some kind of bizarre campaign with you to fight anti-pot forces at the national level, okay? Let's be real now for a minute."

"Hey, I didn't know," he said defensively. "I thought maybe you were talking about mandatory sentencing laws, you know, because of how they relate to Victor's situation."

"Well, I am, but not directly—okay, I see what you mean. I guess we're close to being on the same page, but what I mean is...just don't go wild on me, okay?"

Buck pretended mild offence. "What do you think I am, some kind of nut ready to just march off and martyr myself for the first hopeless cause that comes along? I told you before that I'm just one of the guys who stirs things up for other people to take action on, remember? Unless it involves one of my friends."

"Well, this definitely involves one of your friends," I said. "And that's where we need to keep the struggle— right there helping Victor, okay? Limited warfare...turn to the right up there and slow down a little. Joe Schruder lives somewhere right up ahead there. I want to see what the layout of his house is, just in case."

"You really believe they're serious about fucking Victor over, huh?" Buck said. "It's not just me. Well, I'm glad you're thinking the way you are, Charlie, because one of the first things they teach you in the Corp is, *know thine enemy!* Yeah, let's see what we can find out, starting right here, right now. Good thinking, Charlie. Seriously. And you know what? I was starting to feel more like *doing* something lately, anyway, instead of just talking all the time. You know what I mean? Like, ninety-five percent of everybody you meet out there are assholes, and sooner or later you'll probably end up having to *do* something, you know? To be honest with you, Charlie, I kind of feel maybe even a little bit like hurting somebody. I hope that doesn't bother you...it doesn't bother me."

"Just do me a favor and keep it in check," I said, "at least while we're working together. Save it for—"

"—I know," he said, putting his hand up. "I only meant to help Victor."

I suddenly remembered something I wanted to ask him about. "Do you know anything about miniature tape recorders? I was just thinking, it could be extremely useful to get something on tape that Schruder shouldn't be saying, like something we could use to turn the tables on them."

Then I remembered something else I wanted to talk with him about too. "Wait—never mind the tape recorder thing for a minute, Buck," I said, "did you hear about what happened to Paul and Joan Steward on the news this morning?"

"No. Who?"

"That old couple who were living in that weird-colored shack down by the Minnesota River...you know, that purplish one close to where the old Bloomington ferry bridge used to be."

"Yeah, I remember them. The old man—Paul—used to grow pot to help the old lady with her pain. He caught me and a friend ripping off a few top-buds one time when I was a kid. Didn't even say much to us—just *get your own*, something like that. He was actually pretty cool about it. Why'd you say they *were* living there? What happened? I remember the old man used to give us nickels on Halloween. Drove that old pale-blue Chevy truck...a real menace on the road, I recall. He wiped out a whole slew of young turkeys once. White ones. Man, that was a long time ago. Why, what happened? One of them die?"

"Yeah," I answered, "the old lady went around behind the shed in their back garden and blew herself away."

"Yeah? No kidding?"

"Yep," I said, "with a shotgun. I heard Schruder was trying to get her to testify against Paul."

Buck suddenly became very pissed. He slammed a fist into his hand, making me wonder whether I'd be able to trust his emotions and judgement. There was his drinking to consider, too. I figured he'd probably have to be kept on some sort of leash, I just wasn't sure how long it'd have to be.

He whined, "I thought they weren't allowed to do that?"

"They weren't legally married," I said, "they'd been living together all these years. I heard the acreage the old house sits on is worth a small fortune. Apparently, a task force made up of DEA agents and Tipton and I don't know who else grabbed a couple hundred thousand dollars of their stock last week, along with the property. It was on the news this morning. I figured you'd want to hear about it, especially with this shit going on with Victor. Supposedly, the Sheriff's department had already budgeted some of the money for new bomb-squad equipment. That's how it came to light...some clerk at a bank. I still can't believe it. Here she killed herself, basically over a few dozen plants, just so she wouldn't have to testify against Paul. They weren't selling anything. And here Paul's a veteran, too—not to get you going or anything. It said on the news that the old fart had never even had a traffic ticket. Just one ticket from the DNR when he was in his early twenties, for poaching a muskie."

Buck's eyes were glassed over. "Yeah...they used to always fed the deer down by the river in the wintertime...they had a salt lick down there too. The last time I saw the old geezer, he talked to me about maybe getting a travel home."

"You got a doobie on you, Buck?"

"Always," he said. "What size you want?"

"Size?" I asked, chuckling. "I didn't ask you for a damned dildo. I asked about a *doobie*."

Buck laughed. "I heard what you said. You've got some pretty nasty thoughts cruising around up there in your brain. I wonder if I trust you while you're high."

"I was just joking, Buck," I said. "Don't get any false ideas over it. And don't forget about Beth Ann—you've still got a star to answer to, remember?"

"Forget her—she'll more than likely be heading to Hollywood pretty soon anyway."

"Serious?"

"Just kidding," he said. "Gee's, I didn't know he was a veteran."

He lit a large joint and passed it to me, then slowly swung his head back and forth. He couldn't wait to talk and some of the smoke escaped his mouth while he said, "Now that's the part...that really pisses me off. Like I

said...I feel like doing something. I'm getting tired of the—
whew! Bullshit. That was a good hit."

I tried to think about who we could possibly hit besides
Schruder. Sullivan, maybe, though I didn't think he was the
top thinker in the apparent grab for the Stamate's land.
Tipton? He would more than likely have good security—
and at taxpayers expense, of course. I sensed that Tipton
knew better than to cross Victor. Sullivan would be tough
to squeeze. Schruder seemed to be the most vulnerable,
and probably the easiest to monitor because he obviously
spent a lot of time away from home, gambling.

"Let's go," I said, "I don't want anyone to get suspicious
of your car. Do you know anything about those little tape
players?" I asked him again.

"Why, you thinking about breaking in or something?"

"Only if they continue to mess with Victor. Maybe
Schruder's got some personal files it'd be helpful to take a
look at. I'm certainly not opposed to blackmail. It'd probably be a lot easier to pull off than a kidnapping."

"Ha! You'd get less time—that's for sure," Buck said.
"We can probably break in, all right, Charlie, but that'd be
a stiff charge, too. I'm willing to take a chance to help
Victor, though. One good thing, I've got a clean record.
Another good thing is that I'm a vet."

"They don't give a shit about that, Buck," I assured him,
pointing. "There it is over there... 4200 Cumberland."

"Huh! You get the right judge, it matters plenty. Like a
judge that's been in the Service himself."

"Shit, Buck, he'd probably hit you even harder thinking
you should be setting a better example."

"See, now there's the primary difference between you and me, Charlie," Buck said. "You think negatively, while I think positively—most of the time, anyway. That's why I don't think breaking into that place right there will be much of a problem. The dumb-ass has big bushes up close to the house, for one thing. I've got one of those little recorders you're talking about, too, by the way."

"You do? I'm not even going to ask you why you have one."

"Don't worry, I never used it on you," he said laughing. "I used it for a couple of classes I went to."

"That's a relief," I said. "But getting back to business now, Schruder'll be our first target then—our first victim if need be, okay?"

"Sounds good to me," he agreed, reaching for my outstretched hand.

We shook on whatever it would mean.

Chapter 5

As a new radical of sorts, I was beginning to see that our fight wasn't necessarily going to be against a judicial system gone mad. Nor was I going up against *The Government*. That was Timothy McVeigh's big mistake, according to Buck...body counting with innocent people when he should've been going after the *individuals* actually responsible for the clumsy Waco disaster. "Same with Ruby Ridge." I was relieved when he added, "Go right to the source," because then I had some hope that the scope of our fight would at least be somewhat limited.

Four of Tipton's deputies in two squad cars showed up to hustle Victor away in handcuffs and belly-chains. Then they transferred him to a Federal Detention Center in Green Bay, of all places. Apparently, they were confident of being able to meet the burden of proof for a speedy re-prosecution on the old charge of cultivating marijuana.

Victor had been doing a final light workout for his upcoming fight. His opponent had already been selected—a loudmouthed but impressive weirdo with a scarlet mohawk and deeply pierced eyebrows. *Bloody Hugo* also sported about a dozen mostly-red tattoos, and both of his front teeth were missing. Bloody Hugo had been known for his fancy footwork as a boxer in his early days, which is precisely why he was permanently disqualified from professional rings: too much kicking.

Right after they picked Victor up, Buck went to the library to do some research on Senator Warren Patch. He wanted to come over to my apartment in Bloomington to show me what he'd found. He ended up showing me how Patch was a major part of the overall problem, just as we'd suspected all along. Even if he wasn't directly involved with Victor's case, he was still guilty of *fostering the climate*, as Buck put it. We figured the Senator was probably being rewarded beyond mere back-patting for his tough stand against drugs.

According to one news account, the Senator had but one child, from his first marriage. Nothing else about Kimberly, just that she attends a private college out East. But I already knew much more about her—what she looks like, where she lives, the kind of car she drives. Even the fact that she's home on summer break.

Buck practically screamed, "It says right here he's in favor of increased forfeitures of assets in drug-related cases!" He slammed the handful of remaining news articles down on my dining-room table. "This is where it's coming from...right here from Minnesota...in our own back yard!"

"Get a grip," I said. "Have you been drinking? Look at yourself. Do you think I want to be hooked up with some-body who might be emotionally disturbed while trying to help Victor? Yeah, I agree, it sucks...it's not only hitting too close to home, it's coming from home."

"You make it sound like you're the main one trying to help Victor," Buck said.

I retorted, "No, I'm just the one trying to stay calm and

collected here...one of us has to."

"Fuck you, Charlie."

"What else did you dig up...anything worthwhile?"

"Yeah—this one here. It's about a bunch of small-town newspapers disappearing during the last election for Bunyan County Sheriff. Nothing was proven, though. The papers carried a story about Tipton's gun collection, and it wasn't flattering. There was also mention of a long-ago suspicious land deal, but there aren't any details about it in this article. Too bad. Boy, I'd like to find one of those old rags Tipton had his supporters pick up."

"Anything else on Patch? Like how he might be affecting local politics?"

"Yeah, but just a minute—look at this one. Right from the Office of National Drug Policy, which reports directly to the President. Here's direct proof right here. Says the White House is opposed to efforts to reduce wrongful searches and seizures. Against medical marijuana too. Can you believe it! Here: *opposes* marijuana initiatives on state ballots, saying they would prejudge clinical research to determine the drug's safety. Straight from Clinton, that fucking asshole. Supposed to be representing the boomers. Lying bastard! Got away with cheapening the oath—with the Democratic media's help, of course. Why don't they do a follow-up poll to see how the American people feel now? I'd give them an earful...."

"Buck."

"No wonder he's always hitting on other women, hooked-up with that barracuda wife of his. Doesn't it just make you sick every time you see that asshole and his bitch wife getting off a plane? Ha! Like they're some kind of royalty. She'd like to be a senator. What pure, fucking, unadulterated nerve. She's as crooked as he is. The same as that Jim and Tammy Bakker deal, and look how she got off. What nerve! All that pomp and ceremony at taxpayers' expense—*my expense!* We're paying for that stupid dog, too. A dumb breed, just like its master...what's that they say about dogs and their masters?"

"Buck, you're going to have to give me a break."

"Everything's quieted down. Nobody—even Congress—gives a shit about the oath...."

"Buck, I wish *you'd* quiet down. In fact, I wish you'd shut the hell up."

He added, "Nobody gives a shit anymore...that's what pisses me off." He looked away like it was hopeless.

"Except us, Buck," I said. "We give a shit. And we're going to do something about it...a couple of local yokels are going to do something. Hey over there! Are you still with me, or did you let Clinton bust your spirit?"

"Yeah, I'm still with you," he said hoarsely. "That ass-hole."

"Now that you let off most of your steam, how about a beer?"

His eyebrows lifted just a bit little slower than usual. "You might've saved your ears some of that if you'd offered me one right away, you know."

"That's debatable," I answered.

"Here's the last article...about Patch again," Buck said. It's from a speech he gave last year from Washington while he was the big-shot Chairman of some Law Enforcement Judiciary Committee. See, politicians get too involved with the judicial system, Charlie. Listen to these outrageous highlights. '*We need to empower prosecutors and local law enforcement in this war against drugs...we can't allow soft-on-crime judges to mess up the system...we all know that drugs cause our young people to lack discipline...they're unhealthy, dangerous, and just plain wrong...these so-called soft drugs—like marijuana-are gate-way drugs, which is why I'm pushing for an increase in drug-related seizures and mandatory federal sentences.*'

"Charlie, there it is right there. And you thought I was a conspiracy freak. It's a conspiracy from the top down. I also found out that marijuana arrests have doubled since that asshole Clinton took office—about three-quarters of a million people, mostly just for possession. And this is from a guy who smoked marijuana himself but couldn't bring himself to admit it. Big-shot sax player. He's a real cool dude, Charlie."

I left for the kitchen to get two more beers.

Buck raised his voice. "It's weird how good people can be robbed and railroaded...while these assholes from top to bottom are getting something out of it. Clinton even thinks he's getting something out of it...he thinks his stand against pot disassociates him from his flaky past, but it doesn't. It just shows what a fucking hypocrite and liar he is. The Great Pretender. He says his critics didn't vote for him anyway. One-box Willie. Big joke. He demands a recount. As far as I'm concerned, he's a traitor to the country. He didn't want to serve when he was supposed to, he didn't support our troops, but now he's the Commander-in-Chief and big-shot President who's proven to the whole world that he's above the law. Lock 'em up and throw away the key, unless they're politicians. Our so-called trusted officials simply let him off the hook. About as slick as O. J. Not much difference at all. Both guilty as hell. The whole system is rotten from top to bottom and it's getting worse fast. All I know, Charlie, is I'm not going to stand by and let a bunch of fat cats get even fatter at Victor's expense. Oh no, I'm not going to stand by on this one. I won't stand by and let him get railroaded. Thanks for the beer."

Buck started to relax, then his energy level suddenly shot back up. Excitedly, he said, "Look what I just bought!" He reached into his front pocket.

"What is it?"

"I stopped by Radio Shack on the way here to do a little snooping...might as well get in the mood, huh? It's a long-play, voice-activated miniature recorder. Nothing fancy, but it'll record about an hour of talking. Schruder lives by himself...so that'll help."

"I'm as interested in what kind of files he might have at home as hearing what he has to say," I said. "I wonder if a small Polaroid would be useful?"

"Forget that—I've got a digital camera that shoots in the dark, and I can make my own prints right from my computer. You should get with the times, Charlie. When do you want to make a go for it?"

"Probably the sooner the better," I answered. "Poor Jade. I'm going over to see her."

"Tonight?"

"Yes, after you leave."

"I mean the hit on Schruder's place."

I felt like bypassing Schruder and going straight for Patch's throat, but I didn't know if he had anything to do with Victor's case directly. Messing with a U. S. Senator would be far too risky this early. For one thing, there'd be too much publicity...unless, "Hey, Buck, if we grabbed Kimberly, do you think there's any way Patch could be stopped from going to the cops?"

"I doubt it," he said. "That's the first thing they always do, even if you tell them not to."

"I'm asking because, trying to get something on Schruder isn't a very sure thing. I bet we could get some quick action going by grabbing Kimberly Patch...but it'd have to be kept quiet. It'd be a sure way of getting some negotiations going for Victor's release, *pronto*."

"They'd have to give us a guarantee in writing that they wouldn't prosecute him—or us. The only thing is, Charlie, we're not even sure yet what they plan to do with Victor."

"Yeah, you're right," I said. "I'm just getting a little impatient, I guess. Well, let's get going on Schruder anyway, in the meantime. We've got to do something. We can't just stand by and do nothing."

"I'm going to start watching him to find out what some of his habits are," Buck said. "I'm getting tired of all this political analyzing crap. I'm finally ready to take some action."

"Just be careful," I said. "And remember, don't say a word if you're busted. Let a lawyer do your talking, right from the start. Never tell them shit."

"I already found that out the hard way a few times,"

Buck said, not joking.

I called Jade and we agreed to meet at her parents' house. Taking care of the hobby-farm estate without Victor was a heavy burden for her, so I wanted to help as well as comfort her.

"They were a lot rougher than they had to be," she told me. "I never thought I'd say it, but I don't like cops. No wonder young people used to call them pigs back in the '60's. They're basically a necessary evil, like standing armies. They seemed to enjoy it too much. I must be feeling a little bit of what Sarah Jane Olsen was feeling when she put those bombs under the cop cars in LA."

"That sounds strange coming from you," I said.

"Well, it's becoming ludicrous...whenever a cop dies, he's treated like a hero. They're not all heroes, believe me. Most of them are probably just into it for the power and money. Not too many *Serpicos* around. The guys who picked Victor up should be punished. It's a good thing they had guns and Victor didn't. Which reminds me, I'm glad Buck wasn't there at the time. How's he taking the news?"

"Buck? Oh, he's okay. Kind of bummed-out, of course."

Jade held her gaze. "He's not planning anything stupid, I hope, is he?"

"Not that I know of," I said, looking away.

I immediately felt terrible for lying. I wasn't in the habit of casually lying to my friends.

"You guys are planning something, aren't you?" she said. "Please don't mislead me, Charlie. There's a reason I want to know."

"What?"

"Well, we can probably accomplish a lot more if we all work together as a team."

I laughed nervously and reached out my hand. "I guess I wasn't hiding it very well, was I? Welcome to the team."

She took my hand and lightly shook it. "I feel like I've got to do something, too," she said. "I mean, besides just making useless phone calls and writing my congressman. I want to stop whatever they've got planned right away. I feel like my husband's going to be railroaded if I don't do something drastic—and soon!"

"That's the same word Buck used," I said, "railroaded. Have they set bail yet?"

"No. That's supposed to happen this afternoon. And it'll probably be huge because the new federal charges carry a maximum life sentence. I shouldn't have any trouble raising the ten- percent. Daddy can probably come up with the whole amount, but I don't want to ask him. Not again. He was pretty upset as it was when Victor got busted for growing weed on the very land he gave us as a wedding present...but I guess he couldn't resist it, the spot is so perfect for it."

"I've always been kind of curious about how he got busted—how they knew where to look. Nobody's ever figured that one out, have they?"

"No—not for sure. Buck's got an idea, though. What did you guys have in mind?"

"Something that's not legal," I said.

"What they're planning to do to Victor isn't legal, either," Jade said. "Or at least it shouldn't be legal. How can the judicial system make exceptions for double jeopardy? It's clearly unethical and unlawful in all other cases, so how is it that they can do it on a goofy marijuana charge? I know it sound's odd to say this, Charlie, but I'm beginning to see some merit in Buck's pot-conspiracy theory."

"You too?" I asked. "Anyway, this is sort of what we had planned: he bought a little tape recorder that we were thinking of planting in Joe Schruder's house. But first he's going to find out some of his patterns and habits. We also want to look through any files he might have—private, personal files, you know."

"Blackmail?"

"Well, yeah—that too, if necessary. I just wondered whether or not there might be some reference to Victor...of a not-so-public nature, if you know what I mean."

"But what if you—we—can't get anything on Schruder?"

"We have a plan B, but I'm not so sure you want to hear about it right now. It would involve some of your parents' neighbors."

"Senator Patch, probably, but who else?"

"Kimberly, but hold on. See, Buck did some research and came up with enough material—evidence—to point directly to Patch as being a major source of instigation for these stupid mandatory minimum laws, just as we thought. We think he may be getting some kind of kick-back too, but even if he isn't, he's in a good position to get the wolves off Victor's back for us...actually, *pigs* sounds more appropriate."

"Why, Charlie Pierce, you sound just like one of Minnesota's very own!"

I smiled wickedly. "Yeah, but I won't get caught like Olsen did."

"Well, just remember what Buck's always saying: 'If you can't do the time, don't do the crime.' You could get caught. You don't know how much it means to me that you and Buck are willing to stretch your necks out for Victor and I. I know it'll mean a lot to him too, when he finds out. What could you and Buck possibly have planned for Senator Patch and his daughter? I'm curious."

"Jade, first of all, you've got to remember that if you're questioned by the cops, anything you say has to go through your lawyer, otherwise—well, that's where they end up getting most people. The Miranda warning isn't as strong as it used to be...they'll squeeze you 'til you squeak if you let them. They just want to get whatever they can from you as easily as they can."

"Charlie, "I'm surprised at you," Jade said. "Is this knowledge from personal experience?"

"No," I answered, chuckling, "it's mostly from my brother, Edwin's, experience. He likes cops about as much as we do now."

Jade huffed, "Well, it's obvious they're not out to do us any favors. One of the cops who came to get Victor-McCullum was his name-pushed his head down real hard when they put him in the police car. It was just as though someone had instructed him to be extra-tough. Victor did-n't do anything to provoke it. He knew better than to resist. McCullum said, 'In you go tough guy.'"

"What'd Victor do, or say, anything?"

"No—not really. But I saw him look at the cop's nameplate. The cop saw him look too, and he didn't say anything smart after that."

"Probably just a coward hiding behind a gun and badge," I said. "About like all those heroes who waited so long to rescue the survivors in that school shooting. What the hell were they waiting for? I thought being a hero was supposed to be part of everything they do, on-duty, off-duty, whatever, including taking a little bit of a risk. Otherwise, why are they all treated like heroes when they're killed, like you were saying? Hey, did you hear a while back about how some police departments and the FBI aren't even open on weekends, even to help out in serial murderer cases? The same with weapons checks, too. I mean, what's happening to the quality of service we're getting from the *pigs* these days?"

"You're sounding very radical, Charlie. Kind of scarey."

"It's called righteous indignation," I explained, chuckling. "Actually, I'm buzzing myself up to float like a butterfly and sting like a bee!"

Inspired, Jade suddenly jumped to her feet and thrust an arm high in the air. "I say it's time we helped change the system!" she yelled.

"Yeah!" I shouted in agreement, even though I still didn't know exactly where and how to strike.

The problem was that we didn't know how far up the ladder to go. Sullivan and Tipton—at the bottom end— were already found guilty, of course. Patch was certainly guilty at the top end, but maybe not in a direct way. That would make a difference. The fact that they were holding Victor in a Federal Detention Center seemed to indicate

Schruder was involved with the feds in some way.

I told Jade, "As soon as Victor's sprung loose there'll be four of us. Against how many of them we don't know yet, but at least we're getting stronger and stronger as a team."

"And capable of doing a lot of damage," she agreed, trying to smile wickedly. But she came across looking funny instead. The expression of forced hostility didn't fit her gentle and agreeable nature. She said, "I feel like playing some Pink Floyd right now for some reason—*The Wall*."

I laughed and put on what I thought was a suitably wicked face, wondering if I looked as ridiculous as she did. It felt good to be on the verge of striking back against an unfair system, but I felt bad for wanting to share my warm feelings with Victor.

Chapter 6

Buck and Jade were due at my apartment at 3:00 P. M. It was now 2:45.

The Burnsville police had arrested Buck yesterday about a block from Joe Schruder's house and charged him with drunk driving. Amazingly, it was his first offence. He gave me most of the details. He told the cops that the breathalyzer was rigged with false settings. It was registering way too high. He then demanded a blood test, claiming he'd only had one beer. He assured them that he was going to have his lawyer look into the matter. "I should've stayed in the car," he said to me. "Some people just *look* like they've been drinking—you know, maybe like because of a swaying kind of walk. Next time I'm going to ask them if I'm actually under arrest before I get out. The way I figure it now, why help them out?"

Luckily, he hadn't aroused any suspicions about what he was doing in the area.

It was four days now since Victor had been arrested; his bail hearing was still being delayed, causing us alarm. We wanted him back right away to bring us strength and focus. His arrest was broadcast on the local news, resulting in more than a dozen calls to one TV station, mostly from curious citizens.

But one call came from a representative of the National

Organization for the Reform of Marijuana Laws, raising questions about double-jeapordy laws relating to pot cases. That was the result of a call from Buck, who's been a member in good standing since he was seventeen— roughly twenty years. The representative from NORML asked the TV station manager to run a special profile of Victor's case. To reinforce the idea, Buck called in to suggest the same thing. The station manager told Buck it was a good idea and that they'd certainly consider doing it, but they'd need several days to pull it together if they decided to run such a story. Buck wasn't satisfied and ended up calling the station manager a *biased, fucking redneck* and a *Clinton-loving democrat*. Who knows, maybe the guy is. In a way, it was good to see Buck's frustration and anger rising. Maybe some of it would rub off on Jade and I.

I heard the deep rumble of what I thought was Buck's Torino, but when I pulled the living-room curtain aside to look, it was Jade arriving in one of Victor's cars, a blue '68 Camaro Super Sport—the one with only fourteen thousand miles on it. I was surprised to see her driving it, because the car's raw power had always made her nervous before.

I opened a kitchen window and waved at her while she walked up the short sidewalk from the parking lot to my apartment. She looked up and smiled and waved back. She didn't look nervous. Coming through the door, she explained driving the Camaro. "I talked to Victor late this morning. He wanted me to take it out for a quick spin to loosen it up a little—the moving parts, you know. Boy, I sure did, without really wanting to! Guess what? Victor's bail's been set. He's getting out about five—*today!*

"Great news!" I shouted.

I was surprised to see Buck's Torino pull into the parking lot—on time and moving slowly no less. I waved at him. He waved back without any enthusiasm. "Well, I wonder what's biting his ass today?" I said, more to myself than to Jade.

"Probably that DWI."

"Yeah," I agreed, going to the front door again. "Hi Buck, we were just wondering what might be biting your ass today. Hey, guess what? Victor's getting out later today, isn't that great news!"

"Wonderful," he muttered. He glanced at Jade. "Hi Jade. Sorry, I know I should be happier under the circumstances."

"The DWI, huh?"

"Yeah...they might try to throw the book at me, even though it's only my first offence. They've been getting real serious about this shit lately. They lowered the legal limit down to .10. I demanded a blood test. I'm wondering where I'll come in at."

"Probably .11," Jade answered. "Sorry to hear about your...indiscretion."

"Ah, that's all right. I'll get over it. They'll probably end up just hitting me in the pocketbook real hard...like they did Victor. I won't have to do any county time. I learned a good lesson out of this...I'm going to start being a lot more careful from now on."

"It's not a good idea to drink and drive anyway, Buck," Jade said seriously.

He frowned. "Huh? I'm not talking about *that*, I'm talking about being more careful about getting *caught*. That was my big mistake...tipping in the wrong spot."

"Is that how you got caught?" I asked.

He answered, "Yeah—well, that's how he got suspicious, but he didn't find any cans. I handed the asshole a pop can. How'd you think I got caught, my driving?"

"No," I lied. "I thought maybe you might've been acting suspicious or something."

"Me? Hell no. I just happened to raise my hand up at the wrong time—and I came up with a brand new policy because of what happened. I'm not ever going to tip a can at or near an intersection again. I've got to remember that, no matter how drunk I drive." He looked at Jade. "Ha, ha, just kidding."

"Well, this'll surely be a good lesson for you," she said. "I wish I could say I felt more sorry for you, but I don't—in the wrong hands alcohol can be dangerous, like slow poison."

"So who's in a hurry?" Buck asked. He laughed nervously and looked at me, embarrassed. "Don't worry about me, Jade, I'll get over it. What's biting my ass? Well, for starters, I heard on the news last night that arrests for marijuana possession are at record levels. I'm not making it up. Thousands of otherwise law-abiding citizens are having their lives disrupted unnecessarily."

I laughed out loud and slapped my knee.

"What's so damned funny?" he asked, offended. "I don't think it's a bit funny. I think it's pretty disgusting how they're just pushing all these people into the prison system. Is that funny, Charlie? What the fuck are you laughing for? Is it funny that Victor's one of them? He's a victim too, you know. What's so damned funny, anyway?"

"Hey, back way off," I said, "I'm just laughing because, like, *so what else is new and up to date?* Thousands of otherwise law-abiding citizens have been having their lives disrupted because of pot for fifty fucking years, Buck. Look what happened to Freddie Fender way back when."

"Yes, and right up to today," Jade added. "Why, Oliver Stone was busted for possession of hashish just this last year. No wonder he's been making such good movies."

"You girls are stoned, right? I'm trying to be serious here. The part that's not so funny is that they're trying to cover up just how many people are locked up over weed. They're downplaying the numbers—just like they did in 'Nam. Same thing. A numbers game. Same with polls. Number games. I've never been polled in my life. Have either of you? I didn't think so.

"I know this may sound crazy, but what better way for the government to shut people like us up—the creative, rebellious ones—than to lock us up, and by so doing, deny us our second amendment rights. And I mean forever on Earth. Seriously, girls, think about it, will you? Do you think the government wants people like me running around with guns? See, it's that loose conspiracy working against us—from top to bottom, from that asshole Clinton to that asshole Tubby Tipton. Now do you see what I mean by a loose conspiracy? Even pricks like Sullivan are getting in on the feeding frenzy. And it's all tied together from top to bottom...loosely."

I said, "Yeah, I see, Buck. I just never quite put it all together like you just did. It's now plain to see. But just remember that it's only a few individuals at the bottom end we're going up against, okay? No presidents or—well, maybe a senator. But we're better off trying to work our magic at the bottom end first."

Jade agreed with me. "That makes good sense, Charlie. Maybe publicity can play a useful role later on, but I think secrecy will be our best friend for now...they can back down easier when everything's out of the public's eye."

"What about Sullivan?" asked Buck. Why not go after that son-of-a-bitch? He's up to his neck in this whole thing. Then it wouldn't be so much like we were going up against the law, either."

"Yeah—that's just it, though," I said, "Sullivan's outside the law. Which means his methods might be outside the law too."

"I'm not afraid of that asshole," Buck said. He quickly added, "as long as I have my sawed-off, 10-guage double-barrel shotgun with me. My Uncle Moe gave to me for my sixteenth birthday just before he died. He told me he figured I was big enough to handle it, but he was wrong because it knocked me back about three feet and squarely on my ass the first time I shot it—both barrels at once, by accident."

"Goodness!" Jade exclaimed. "What purpose did your Uncle have for such a firearm?"

"He got it from my Granddad. It was used mostly for show down South back during the moon-shining days...Georgia, I think."

"How interesting."

"Yeah, I'd like to see Sullivan's face if I whipped it out on him. He wouldn't look so damned cool then, I bet."

Jade jerked back in mock surprise. "Goodness! Hopefully, that won't be necessary."

Stretching himself up a bit taller, Buck said, "Hey, that's up to him."

We heard quick, heavy footsteps approaching, then someone knocked loudly on the door.

Buck immediately went over and opened the door for me. A big, powerful-looking county deputy in a crisp brown uniform stood in the doorway with his hand still in the air. He'd been caught off guard. His hand dropped down, slowing noticeably when it grazed past his gun holster. Buck's eyes had followed the cop's hand down.

"A little jumpy, aren't you?" Buck asked.

The deputy flashed a false-grin before answering, "One never knows. Is this where Charleen Pierce lives?"

"Uh, that would be me," I said, walking over to him. "What's the problem, Officer?"

"There's no problem, Ma'am, I'm just check—"

"—What in the fuck's *your* problem then?" Buck cut in. "Nobody asked you to come here, did they?"

"Buck, I'll take care of this if you don't mind, okay?" I said.

Jade drifted in close to my side. "Why, hello Officer McCullum."

The policeman was plainly surprised to see Jade. He looked back at Buck again. "Who are you?" he asked.

Buck answered, "I'm thinking that would most likely not be any of your damned business."

"I'll be the one to decide that," the cop said. "Got kind of a smart mouth, don't you?"

"Hey, it's still a free country," Buck said. "The last I heard anyway. See Lawman, I'm not like most of those other assholes out there who give up their first amendment rights just because they're talking to a cop—my second amendment rights either, as far as that goes. Why don't you go back out there and help someone commit suicide? Suicide by cop. I bet you'd get off on it."

"Sounds like you don't like policemen."

"Buck, back off, will you?" I said. "This is my place, remember?"

"Sure thing, Charlie. For you. You're right, Mister, I don't like pigs."

"Just a minute," Officer McCullum said, raising his voice. "I asked you a question."

"Fuck you," Buck said matter of factly. "Come back with a warrant. I don't talk to pigs unless it's through my lawyer, anyway."

Redness came up out of McCullum's stiff brown collar as Buck retreated back into the shadows of the living room, muttering just loud enough for the cop to hear him. "At least we're seeing good signs coming out of Seattle...well, actually, out of Eugene."

I couldn't help chuckling. "Sorry, Officer, what can I do for you?"

"I'm double-checking the ownership of that yellow Mercedes parked down there."

"Why?"

"A vehicle similar to the one down there was stolen from Minnetonka last week. I happened to see yours as I was passing by, so I thought I'd double-check its ownership. It didn't take me long to locate your apartment here with a license plate check. How long have you had the car?"

Buck's barely audible voice could be heard coming from the living room. "I wouldn't tell him jack-*shit!*"

"Your friend in there's coming very close to being guilty of obstructing justice," McCullum said. "Has he been drinking?"

"No. Overlook it," I said, "he's got war-connected problems."

"Well, he's going to have more than war-connected problems if he keeps it up," McCullum warned.

"I've had the car for about a half a year now," I said. "Is that all?"

Jade interrupted, "Do you mind if I ask you a question, Officer?"

"No, go ahead?"

"What do you have against my husband? I mean, I heard you when you put him in the squad car. Who gave you the assignment to pick Victor up? Was it Sheriff Tipton himself, or somebody else?"

"That's confidential information, Ma'am. Department business only, and I don't have anything against your husband."

She asked, "Do you know a man named Luther Sullivan?"

McCullum was caught off guard again, his face giving him away.

"I thought so," said Jade. "Well, Victor's getting out this afternoon, so you'd better lose your interest in pestering us."

"What's that supposed to mean?" McCullum asked. "Are you threatening me?"

I interrupting her by cautioning, "Don't say anything else, Jade. Goodbye Officer. It was nice meeting you—only not real nice."

Buck was ambushed down in the parking lot about two hours later, right after he got into his Torino and shut the door. Four state troopers in two maroon and gold cruisers blocked his car—front and back—and then rushed him with guns drawn.

To make matters worse, Victor wasn't released when he was supposed to be. His bail was being reconsidered on the flimsy excuse that he was a possible flight risk. It was pure bullshit, just an excuse to hold him longer while they put together—or *threatened* to put together—the new case.

Jade called me from her parents' home and asked me to come over. I'd never seen her angrier.

"It's now completely obvious," she huffed. "Police and prosecutors who make *drug* law enforcement their highest priority are strongly rewarded for doing so by these stupid forfeiture laws. They're targeting *assets*, not crime. Somebody's got to stop them before they ruin even more lives. It's becoming clearer and clearer, isn't it Charlie? Even though the so-called war on drugs is irrational, going after assets seems rational as a bureaucratic strategy, especially for law-enforcement."

"Tell me about it," I said. It's rotten and getting worse."

"At least some people are willing to fight back," Jade said. "By the way, I won't hold it against you if you want to back out."

I chuckled. "Don't worry, I have no thoughts about backing out. Remember, I was ready to do something even before you knew about it...and before it got this serious."

Jade said, "Well, that's why I'm double-checking with you now—because it's probably going to get much more serious from this point on. I want to do something right away, but I also wanted...to be sure about you."

"Hey, I know what I'm getting into," I assured her. "Hell, I know it could backfire. But at least I'd be getting whacked for a righteous cause—not really a *crime*. So I'm willing to take the risk."

"Okay, good. You're such a good friend, Charlie. Oh— I almost forgot. I just discovered something interesting over the internet. Apparently, this forfeiture business started getting out of control back in 1984—nothing to do with the book, I'm sure. Kind of a scary thought, though, huh? That's the year Congress rewrote the civil forfeiture law so that drug money could be funneled into the police agencies that do the seizing. The amendment ended up giving police a new source of income. Now they can make about as much money as they want to, limited only by the amount of zeal they're willing to put into making seizures. Of course the number of forfeitures has mushroomed. I found out that greedy cops can federalize forfeiture cases to get a bigger cut."

"Say what?"

"*Federalize* a case...it's a way for the cops to circumvent their own state laws, which usually require them to share forfeited assets with a general fund, or with school boards, libraries, whatever. In other words, they can leave the public out of the action by shuffling around a lot of paperwork—basically by conspiring with the U.S. Justice Department to share the seized assets. *Equitable sharing*, is the fancy term for it. Equitable *rip-off* is more like it. From what I understand, local cops get to keep about eighty percent and the Justice Department gets to keep the rest. No wonder some small town police departments have budgets five times what they use to be."

"Gees!"

"But what bugs me the most about all this is the secrecy involved. I don't like the idea of police departments having that much financial independence—that degree of freedom from legislative oversight. Where are the checks and balances? Apparently, some police departments are already becoming dependent on forfeiture money. I even came across an item about Attorney General Janet Reno requesting that U.S. Attorneys consult forfeiture specialists before settling cases, if you can believe that."

"I'd like to know where the media's been in all this," I said. "Why haven't they been covering this outrage?"

"Charlie, cops are beginning to think they can finance their own private operations, with no need to justify their actions...."

"That's a crock of shit," I said. "They probably figure if

public dollars aren't involved, then the public doesn't have the right to know. It's a good thing Buck isn't here right now listening to all this. The poor bastard. I wonder what angle they're going to hit him from?"

Jade chuckled lightly. "Who knows, maybe there's some obscure public nuisance law...you're probably right about him not being here right now. I don't like saying this, Charlie, but maybe we can put a plan together—and hold it together—better without his help."

The suggestion immediately made me feel uneasy. "He sure wouldn't like that," I said. "He want's to help Victor too."

We didn't say anything for a while.

She continued, "Anyway, the bottom line is that something needs to be done, and we're going to do it."

"I get the feeling it's more than just the land they're after in Victor's case," I said. "I think it could be more personal, like maybe because of his attitude."

"Maybe so," Jade said. "The same with Buck. They don't like his attitude either...and I imagine they're awfully concerned about preventing any potential defense. I'm surprised they haven't bothered you yet, Charlie—beyond asking you about your car, I mean."

"I guess I haven't given them enough reason to yet," I quipped. "What reason should I give them? Maybe I'll have to cop an attitude too."

Jade said, "Maybe they'll actually try to prosecute Victor."

Chapter 7

We knew that getting something on Schruder would be a long shot, but it was a safer shot than kidnapping Kimberly Patch. That was still an option for later, if need be.

Jade suggested I start using some of the cars in Victor's collection to keep a lower profile. I told her I'd rent a car, but she convinced me otherwise by telling me Victor wouldn't mind and, besides, the cars needed to be exercised once in a while anyway. Back at the Mastersons' estate, I hid my Mercedes under a pile of clean sweet straw in the miniature horse barn a hundred yards or so down past the llama area. I'd always liked Victor's yellow and black '71 Cuda with the 340 six-pack, but it was too flashy, so I opted for a more subdued-looking silver and black '69 442 Olds, which also had an automatic and was easier to drive.

We didn't want to risk calling or visiting Buck in jail. We talked things over and decided to go shopping for a miniature tape recorder in St. Paul. We ended up buying three voice-activated recorders from a specialty shop on University Avenue. They were even better than the one Buck had bought, being smaller and noiseless and longer playing.

I'd do the B & E, and Jade would have the less dangerous job of following Schruder to Mystic Lake Casino and keeping an eye on him and his car, a sleek new burgandy Cadillac. A call from her cell phone would pull me back to safety in plenty of time.

Jade's mother happened to have a collapsible bicycle, and it fit into the Oldsmobile's large trunk easily. I also took along the bike's tool kit and a new digital camera— Buck's previous idea. I'd have to be very careful not to leave any fingerprints behind. The rubber gloves would take care of that.

I parked the 442 Olds at the far end of a 24-hour Cub Foods parking lot about a half-mile away from Schruder's house and quickly got out and unfolded the bicycle and rode off.

Schruder—the dumb-ass—had allowed bushes to grow big up close to his house in back and the property was poorly lit, so jimmying a basement window without being seen was a cinch.

I planted the miniature recorders where I was pretty sure Schruder wouldn't find them—at least for awhile anyway. The first one I put in the ductwork behind a ventilation register in the master bedroom, not far from the phone. The second one I hid in the study, near the computer. I planted the last one in a little recess I discovered in some decorative woodwork above the front door.

I had plenty of time for snooping. I wasn't surprised to find out that Schruder was actively seeking court-ordered visitation of his grandchildren. That somehow fit into the rumors about his mean-streak. I didn't find anything at all relating to Victor's case, which left me wondering just how involved Schruder really was. Hopefully, future tapes would reveal that.

I wondered whether Tipton and Sullivan could somehow be by-passing Schruder. No, I figured he had to know what was going on. And the State Police pestering Buck was probably the handy-work of Sullivan, since he'd been a state trooper himself. Maybe an old buddy was doing him a favor, or a return favor.

I had a feeling Senator Patch was pushing a few buttons too. If so, I wasn't going to be satisfied with merely breaking into a Chief Prosecutor's home.

The idea of kidnapping a Senator's daughter somehow appealed to me. Kimberly Patch probably deserved all the excitement she'd get from being kidnapped. The idea was even more appealing to me now that I knew her father was directly responsible for some of the stupid laws like the one separating Victor from his freedom. I was beginning to feel like I was part of a family. It seemed odd to be thinking in Buck's terms, *them against us*, but if some of *them* wanted to unfairly mess with people like *us*—good average citizens, then some of us were certainly entitled to protect ourselves. That's bottom-line and common sense, simply the American way.

On the way back to my apartment to meet up with Jade, it suddenly occurred to me that a threat of violence could possibly be an easy and effective way of getting results. A threatened bombing, for example—followed by a few hints to the press about Tipton's and Sullivan's darker sides. That could bring about some good results. The pair of villains would be so concerned with damage control that they'd be stopped in their tracks, their offensive over. Well, maybe.

Then I thought about the possibility of fooling our tormentors—and the media, too—by pretending to be part of a larger resistance, sympathetic to Victor's plight and acting on his behalf.

"Wonderful idea!" Jade agreed when she arrived at my apartment.

Encouraged by her optimism, I scurried around to find a pen and some paper. "I bet they'll stop making excuses and release Victor as soon as—what should we call our fictitious group of helpers?"

Jade impulsively answered, "Why not just plain *The Helpers?*"

I smiled and pushed the writing materials at her. "Here, you write, okay? You're more literate than I am."

She scribbled "The Helpers" in large letters across the top of a clean sheet of paper. "There. That didn't take long, did it? Now let's create them."

"We should do up a practice letter at the same time," I suggested, "as though to the *Star Tribune*, explaining who The Helpers are—you know, like after a bomb scare. Do you mind if I light up a joint? It's been a long day. Night too, actually."

"No—go ahead," Jade quickly answered. "Why would I care? We're in your home, remember?"

"Just double-checking," I said, wetting my lips. I wetted the jay to slow its burning and then lit it and took a small hit and passed it to Jade. "I was just thinking, why don't we make up something like a ten-most-wanted list? We could say that Victor's case just made the list."

"Like a national list?"

"Yeah, or maybe State-wide. Victor's case probably wouldn't make a national list—sad to say. There's probably too many cases out there even worse than his."

"How about regionally, then?"

"Yeah, that's better than just Minnesota."

Jade suddenly became upset. "Damn it—society needs a *real* group of Helpers!"

"I agree," I told her, "but to be frank, a fictitious one will have to do for now. Let's get something workable down on paper now so we can pull off the hoax...if we decide to go that route, I mean. While we're on the subject, do you remember that case in Michigan a couple of years back when a U. S. District Judge put those guys away—like forever—for supposedly growing pot to bankroll a conspiracy? The conspiracy involved blowing up an IRS building and whacking a few politicians—even the sentencing Judge himself."

"Unbelievable. Yes, I vaguely remember it," she answered. "Didn't one of the guys claim they were just talking? It seems odd that the Judge didn't disqualify himself from the case...but what's your point, Charlie?"

"Well, we could pretend that The Helpers finance their activities from growing weed—it would be from real life, you know? Goofy but believable, in other words."

"Why not?" Jade agreed. "Besides, we can say anything we want to. It's believable too, because profits are shifting away from foreign countries more and more now anyway, to American growers...indoor and outdoor. We can claim to have secret plantations in every state of the Union if we want to."

"Yeah, well-protected plantations...guarded by nuts like Buck Foster."

Jade laughed and then became serious again. "Charlie, it's important that we make the bomb threat sound authentic. And the follow-up letter to the media too, explaining why the hoax occurred."

"Yeah," I agreed, then suggested, "maybe we should make it sound like it's coming from a bunch of flakes— from their point of view, I mean."

Jade laughed and then grew quiet. She scribbled furiously for a few minutes.

"How's this sound?" she asked. "After a suitable opening, I mean. 'The wrongful case against one of our comrades, Victor Stamate, has moved onto The Helpers *ten-most-wanted* list, which means that The Helpers are going to be a pain in the ass to this community until this community responds in a positive way.' Uhmmm." She stopped briefly, then continued writing. "'We believe that it is possible to build and maintain a self-empowering...resistance...through individual and small-group tactics.'"

"Good!" I encouraged her, "keep going."

"Okay, but you help me. How about, 'We are moving beyond....'"

"'We are moving beyond traditional, progressive politics—*mother-fuckers!*'"

Jade laughed and scribbled some more. "I don't think

so, Charlie. But how about, 'We are moving beyond traditional progressive politics,' then, 'however, we are not leftists or liberals. We are way past all that!'"

"You'd make a good anarchist," I joked.

She looked at me and smiled proudly. "You like the rhetoric?"

"It sounds very realistic," I said. "Keep going."

She continued, now very pleased. "Okay. Uh...how about, 'We have chosen to help Victor Stamate because his case involves outrageous legal and political corruption.'"

"Good, but a little more whacky," I suggested.

"Okay...'The Helpers cannot stand idly by while a good, upstanding member of our community is railroaded by corrupt officials. We are hereby striking back, and the ensuing battle will be financed by a profitable marijuana growing operation located within this very community.'"

"Excellent! Try adding this," I said, "'We are growing impatient because of all the injustice in America. The O. J. Simpson and W. J. Clinton cases highlight what is wrong in America. Miscarriages of justice such as these cases—and the Victor Stamate case—call for extreme actions.'"

"Wow—that sounds pretty whacky," said Jade. "But we need to say something about the madatory minimum laws too. How about, 'You should blame unfair mandatory minimum sentencing laws for this...disruption of social order. It is up to *you*, the people of this community, to help undo the harm—'"

"Oh, oh, oh!" I interrupted. "Let me add this thought before I forget it. 'When a society is built on violence, violence is one of the few things people understand...and take seriously."

"Good," Jade said. "You must've studied Marxism or communism or something, huh?"

I laughed. "No, it's just that extreme times call for extreme measures."

"I'll write that down too!" she said, laughing along with me. "And I'd better hurry up, before I forget!"

She scribbled furiously for another minute while whispering under her breath. "Okay—that should about do it. Anything else?"

"No, that's good," I said. Then quickly I thought of something else. "What about the media? Maybe we should direct some blame at them, too."

"You're right, Charlie. How about, 'We hold you, the media, partly responsible for what's wrong, because you're often off-base, or focusing on wrong subjects. You ignore pressing issues. Also, you're partly to blame for all the shootings going on. You need to dig up and expose political and legal corruption. You need to begin representing *all* citizens more responsibly.'"

I said, "Okay, there, now we just need to put something whacky in at the end...like something Buck would come up with. How about, 'And stop being so anti-gun. Who's trying to dismantle the system anyway, you or us?"

"And just for Buck, I'll add a post-script," said Jade. "'Remember that the Second Amendment protects the first one. Who's going to help you when the citizens are all disarmed? You'd lose your voice, so wake up!'" She chuckled and looked up at me. "Does that sound nutty enough?"

"Just about perfect," I answered. "Now, how about the

actual bomb scare?"

Jade looked at me shrewdly. She paused, then suggested, "How about the Bunyan County courthouse?"

Victor's expensive lawyer, Otis Franklin, was furious that his client hadn't yet been released on bail. Though not able to get his immediate release, he did file a motion to dismiss the indictment based on timeliness issues. He also filed a motion to inspect whatever evidence the Feds had against him.

Jade and I concluded that the noose around Victor's neck was tightening way too fast, so we went ahead with the bomb scare. We watched the commotion outside the courthouse from my apartment, live, on the noontime news over a few glasses of champagne.

Sheriff Tipton had to move all the prisoners because the jail was connected to the courthouse. Buck didn't seem to mind all the excitement. I suppose the commotion was a nice diversion after spending two days locked up for threatening Officer McCullum. Of course Jade and I knew the real truth. We would go to court if necessary.

Buck saw the news camera and waved as he was hustled away in belly-chains and ankle-bracelets, along with about two dozen other inmates dressed in bright orange jumpsuits. They were being loaded onto a big dark-blue bus. He smiled broadly, looking up through the tree branches at the bright July sun. Without knowing it, he gave us a good shot of his face, broken-off tooth and all.

I said, "What an idiot...he's actually enjoying it. Other prisoners are trying to hide their faces, look."

"I wonder if he suspects we're behind it?"

"I doubt it," I said. "He's too busy enjoying all the official chaos...this is *really working*, isn't it?"

"Like clockwork. Look at them running all around! Charlie, are you absolutely sure you didn't leave any fingerprints behind in the phone booth? Maybe palm-prints, or—"

"—I didn't even take my gloves off."

"Good. Well, I'm positive nobody saw you...and there weren't any cameras around. You wouldn't have needed the wig. How did the accent go?"

"I was nervous as hell, but those three years I spent in Texas weren't for nothing, as it turns out."

"Guess how long it took for the mobile crime unit to show up at the phone booth?"

"I'm guessing less than five minutes?"

"Two and a half."

"Wow! They really take this bomb-scare shit serious, don't they?" I exclaimed. "I hope the media does too. When should we send the letter out?"

"How about later this afternoon, from Mankato or St. Cloud—somewhere close enough for it to be delivered tomorrow or the next day."

"Sounds good to me," I said. "I'd just as soon get away for awhile anyway, just in case anyone comes calling. Like that bastard, Sullivan, for instance."

"No kidding. Well, how about we take the Chevy SS to Stillwater. We'll take the top down and enjoy the sun. We can get lost for *hours* shopping there...and we'll eat dinner there too, okay? I'll buy."

"Sounds good to me," I said. I took out a joint and lit it and took a long drag on it, then held it out to Jade. "I could definitely go for a road trip right about now," I added, trying to hold the sweet, pungent-smelling smoke in.

Jade took the joint gingerly and took a small puff, Slick-Willy style.

I joked, "Jade, it might help if you inhale a little more—all politics aside."

"Actually, Charlie, I've got zero tolerance going right now," she joked back. "Maybe I should've just said *no* in the first place."

I disagreed with her. "No—believe me, it'll do you some good. It'll lighten you up after all the stress of this morning."

"I'm just glad it's over with," she said. "It looks like it might work. I hope it does. When do you think we should check on the tape recorders?"

"I'd give it a couple days, at least, " I answered. "For one thing, I don't want to be anywhere near Schruder's house for a while, especially after today. For another thing, he lives alone and he's gone a lot, which means it'll probably take longer to get anything...for the tapes to fill up. I don't want to go back in too soon."

"I'll have to be more patient," Jade said. "Anyway, I'm satisfied for the time being—at least I feel like we're finally getting somewhere in all this craziness. At least we have some hope now. I just wish there were a *real* group of Helpers...to help others."

"It'd take more people like you and me getting pissed-off first, but who knows, the time may come. I don't think we're that far ahead of most Americans on this one."

"No, we're simply ahead of our elected officials," Jade said sourly, "except for a small handful of brave souls, like the Governor of New Mexico, and maybe Ventura—although he hasn't said much about legalizing marijuana since he campaigned saying we should consider it."

"It'd be too easy to attack him as being pro-drug," I said.

"I know, but I hope he doesn't let the young people down who put him in office. I wonder what's going to happen with medical marijuana here in Minnesota this year. I still can't believe the nerve of that U. S. District Judge in California—sentencing a veteran with PTS to prison after the people of California voted for medical marijuana. That's just what the Federal Government had been threatening all along, too. The nerve!"

"Speaking of medical marijuana, here Jade, you need another hit," I said. "And by the way, it's not the government, it's individuals in the government, remember? In that California case, it was just one judge. Let's not make that mistake."

Jade smiled a bit wickedly, then with determination said, "I know...that individual judge should be punished, the same as certain individuals around here should and will be if we have anything to say about it."

I turned the TV off and we left for Jade's house to pick up the blue '68 Camaro SS convertible. It was a beautiful, powerful machine, having original wide-oval tires on Crager mags and lots of hand-polished chrome.

Chapter 8

Early the next morning Buck called and asked me to pick him up. I called in to work sick—something I hadn't done for months—and arrived at the county lock-up just as he was having his personal effects returned by an enormously fat and bored cop sitting behind a low gray counter with a swinging gate. "—and make sure you count your money," the cop finished instructing Buck.

"Believe me, I thought of that before you did," said Buck smugly. He saw me. "Hey Charlie! Thanks for coming so soon!"

"The traffic was light," I said. "You look a little happier than usual to see me."

"Yeah—well, I figured I'd start the day off with a smile and get it over with," he joked. "Let's hurry up and get the hell out of here before I get into trouble over some other concocted bullshit."

As if on cue, the fat cop mumbled, "Sir, I'm requesting that you watch your language in the presence of a lady, please... it's a old law."

Buck mocked surprise. "Hey—since when did you get so polite?"

"Come on, let's go, Buck," I said.

But he grinned mischievously instead and said, "Officer, you seriously—I mean, *seriously*—should consider getting into a regular exercise program." He turned to leave and took a few steps, then added over his shoulder, "A little bit of exercise never killed anyone, you know."

"Hey, no use taking any chances," the fat cop mumbled. "You have a pleasant day now, Sir."

We walked down the short corridor leading back outside. "No wonder they have him working in there," Buck said. "Besides being grossly overweight, he's also too polite to be a real cop."

"He wasn't being polite," I said. "He was being a smartass. Can't you tell the difference? Do you really think he wants you to have a pleasant day...Sir?"

We got into the 442 Olds and headed for some coffee, then left for Buck's shack on Normandale Lake. He was worried about Rosie O. and the babies, even though I'd agreed to take care of them.

"A bald eagle!" he repeated for the third time. "I couldn't believe it either...it came swooping down low over the lake and made a bee-line for the babies. I saw one flying up high over 494 about a month ago, right about directly over the Mall of America...probably because of the Minnesota River being so close...and the Mississippi. You ever see seagulls flying over by your place, Charlie? Go ahead, Girl—what the hell you waiting for? Light one up. So of course Rosie was running around, going crazy, kicking and squealing—protecting her babies, you know. She's a good mama. She scared it off before I could. I've got national pride and all that, Charlie, but if came down to Rosie or just that one bald eagle...well, I'd be in trouble again. I'm thinking about changing her name again because of her unselfish heroism.

She deserves a better name than Rosie. Let me know if you think of anything fitting, okay Charlie? She's definitely a good mama. Good instincts. Off the subject a little, you wouldn't believe what I heard in jail about Victor's little problem."

"You shouldn't have mouthed-off to McCullum," I said. "Why don't you slow down a little bit. You seem to be talking awfully fast. You might want to lay off that coffee until you've had something to eat. What did you hear about Victor?"

"That's all right," he said. "The pot'll calm me down some...either that, or it'll make me even more excited. Wow Charlie, what's a nice girl like you going with a joint like this?"

"Last year's homegrown," I said matter of factly. "What'd you hear about Victor?"

"First I want to tell you something else."

"What?"

"I've had plenty of time for thinking lately, and I've decided to—you know—give my career another try."

"What career?"

"Come one, Charlie. You know what I'm talking about."

"You going to start raising even more swine?"

"Come on."

"What? Oh, you're talking about that stand-up stuff again, aren't you? I wouldn't do it, Buck," I said, "you're liable to get killed next time. What'd you hear about Victor now?"

"Forget Victor a minute Charlie, will you? I'm not asking you to choose between friends or anything, but I've been locked up for *three fucking days!* The least you can do is listen to me for a minute."

"Sorry," I lied. "Okay, go ahead."

"Listen, I've thought up some good new jokes. Well, actually, some of the guys in jail helped me...and I've refined some of my old ones. I just have to have more confidence, that's all."

"Yeah," I said, "then you wouldn't feel the need to drink so much before you go on stage, huh?"

"Well, I thought long and hard about that one, too," he said seriously, "and I came to the conclusion that I don't want to attribute my success to liquor, anyway. A lot of artistic people are guilty of doing that—you know what I mean? Are you following me, Charlie? In other words, I'd rather know I did it myself. Plus, then I won't have to worry about losing my cool because of some fat bitch in the audience."

"Good, clear thinking," I said.

"There's a few other things I thought about, too—long and hard."

I glanced at him suspiciously.

"What?" he asked me, looking innocent and puzzled. He took another hit and held it, then gasped to add some fresh oxygen. "Anyway...I'll tell you...all about that...later on." He coughed and filled the car with smoke. "Whew! Where did you get that?"

"I already told you, last year's homegrown—it's not store-bought."

"It's good," he said. "Anyway, to finish what I was

telling you, I'm joining the NRA right away—no more bull-shitting around about that. Also, I'm going to contact High Times. That NORML thing didn't work out very well...they were way too damned sensitive at the TV station, for one thing. Also—what else? I already told you about the comedy thing...uh...."

"About Victor," I reminded him.

"Damn! My tolerance sure went down in only three days! At least something good came out of my being out of commission for awhile. What were we talking about now?"

"Victor—you heard something about Victor!"

"Hey, don't get so excited." He leaned back away from me. "Okay, Victor...I might name one of the babies Victor...maybe Charlie too. How would you like that? How'd they look? Have they put on much weight?"

"Fuck the damned pigs!" I yelled, stomping on the accelerator. The Oldsmobile's tires screeched sharply and I lost control and slid sideways back and forth on the pavement several times before I finally straightened it out. "Damn it, now look what you made me do! You and those stupid pigs—why don't you get a horse or a cow or something? Damn! I'm tired of hearing about your stupid pigs."

"Pigs aren't stupid, Charlie," Buck said slowly, in a low voice, obviously offended."

"Okay. Sorry Buck. Pigs are nice. Now, about Victor."

"Oh yeah. I might've found out who snitched him off back a couple of years ago, and you're not going to believe who it might've been—if it's true, that is."

"What're you talking about? Who?"

"Victor."

"You're going to have to lay off that pot, Buck."

"Victor," he repeated. "Don't you remember? We were talking about Victor. Damn, you're the one who should lay off it, not me. We're talking about Victor. He was set up, supposedly so someone else would have some goodies to give to the cops...so they'd leave *him* alone. You get it? In other words, someone paid someone else for information so he could have information to give the prosecutors so he could get a better deal...with the prosecutors. Are you following me?"

"No," I said. "Say it a different way."

"Okay. Just give me a minute to get my thoughts together." Of course he didn't wait even a second. "In other words, someone made some money by telling someone else about Victor's plants, so that person could use the information to get a better deal with his prosecutor."

"That's what I thought you said."

"It was supposedly someone with the last name of Pierce. Possibly your brother, Edwin. So I heard, anyway. It's probably not true. Do you have any cousins in Savage, living over toward Edwin's house?"

What a blow. I told Buck I didn't think so but that I'd check into it.

"I talked to someone else who did some county time with your brother. The guy said Edwin was really weird, like when he was a trustee, he'd walk up and down the hallway butt naked. He also used to blow marijuana smoke through the cell-doors for inmates to inhale. Weird, huh?"

I waited to tell Buck what Jade and I had done without

him. I didn't feel comfortable talking to him about it, especially after what he'd just told me about my own brother. I was a little worried that he didn't trust me the same— guilt by family association. I stopped talking for a while and just drove the Oldsmobile smoothly, spaced out.

I wondered how Edwin might've known about Victor's plants. Could I have foolishly told him?

Buck finally broke the long silence by asking me about my job. Then he asked me what I'd been doing for the past few days. "Just working and hanging out with Jade," I told him. I quickly gave him the details about why Victor's release from custody was still being held up, and of course he instantly became angry, in spite of his buzz.

He spit out the window. "The dirty, fucking bastards!" He spit again.

I was appalled and told him so.

He looked at me defensively. "Sorry, I couldn't help it...bad taste in my mouth."

"Well, watch out for Victor's car, will you?"

"Don't worry about it, it was a good, clean spit."

I decided to tell him about the tape recorders. "Hey, would you like to drive down to Burnsville with me tomorrow night?"

"I don't know, what do you have in mind?" he asked.

"Re-visiting the inside of Schruder's house."

He studied my face, quiet for a moment. "I'm not surprised," he said. "Just couldn't wait for me, could you? Was Jade in on it too, or just you?"

"Both of us," I answered. "You didn't miss much. She covered Schruder at the Casino while I planted some recorders. It wasn't a big deal. Now we need to go back and pick them up. Jade said she'd cover Schruder again." Knowing his ego was bruised, I added, "Why don't you come with me tomorrow night? We're still a team, aren't we?"

"I'd rather cover Schruder," he said.

"Why, so you can drink and gamble like a fool right along with him? Forget it, Buck, that's Jade's job. This other part is more important—more dangerous, anyway. I need your help in case something goes wrong."

"Nothing went wrong before," he pouted. "You guys got along just fine without me before."

"Yeah—I was lucky too, I said. "Plus, I had to ride in on a bicycle. This time, you can drop me off and monitor the area with one of Victor's cars and a cell phone."

"Yeah? One of Victor's cars?"

"Well, I hope I'm not speaking too soon...I'm assuming Jade wouldn't want you to use your own car."

"Which ones did you get to drive so far?"

"It's not important," I said.

"I'm just curious."

"Just the Olds here, and the '70 Challenger. We took the '68 Camaro to Stillwater yesterday. Jade drove. Feel better, now?"

"Fuck you, Charlie."

"Hey, it wasn't my fault you got hauled in, was it? You're the one who couldn't keep your big mouth shut. Just because you got locked up didn't mean we were going to stop—"

"All right, all right...forget it," he said, putting up his

hand. "Do you think she'd mind if I take the Cuda?"

"Da, I think so," I said. "It's stands out like a big yellow hornet, for one thing."

"What's the other thing?" he asked. "You worried about me being able to handle it? Don't worry, because I wouldn't drink much at all if I had one of Victor's cars out. I'd treat it with kid gloves."

"I believe you," I said. "Like you wouldn't even accidentally spit on it or anything, right?"

"Fuck you, Charleen. How about one of the Mustangs, then? I like the black fastback with the 351 Cleveland in it. What year is that, a '70? Or that red Cyclone...that's got a 351 Cleveland in it too, I think."

"Don't get your hopes up too far," I cautioned him. "I only said Jade probably won't want us to use our own cars...I didn't say anything about you getting one by yourself, or you getting to pick out whatever one you want, or anything like that. Give me a break, will you?"

"Sure. Anyway, I wouldn't ask to use the GTX."

"That's noble of you," I said. Let's change the subject now. And not to Rosie."

"You want to hear some of my new stage jokes."

I rolled my eyes up. "Sure, why not."

"Well, do you, or don't you? I'm not going to waste my time if you're not in the mood to hear them. Maybe you'd rather hear about something else I've had a long time to think about. Like about all the damned drug testing they're doing now? They're not satisfied with piss-testing anymore...now there're moving into hair testing. Yeah, I'm serious. What are you looking at me like that for? I'm not buying any more beer from Budwiser. They hair-test all their employees. Plus, I'm going to send them a nasty e-mail. What hypocrites!"

"Go ahead," I said.

"Okay. What? About the jokes or the damned hair testing?"

"Whichever you prefer," I said.

"You really don't want to hear my new jokes, do you? What a bitch."

"Hey—don't get personal," I said. "I've got a lot of stuff on my mind. Like picking you up and taking you home, stuff like that."

"Yeah, sorry about the bitch," he said. "Bastards! What could be worse? Here's these assholes making a mint by taking away our freedoms. The idea is already bad enough anyway, but to make a bundle on it, too? They should be punished. You know they should be, Charlie. Think about it, will you? Where in the hell is the ACLU when you need them? Are they even still around? You never hear anything from that Nader guy anymore, either. What the hell's going on? Testing kits for parents to use on their kids. What are we doing? What kind of message are we sending our fucking kids, Charlie? Like, don't think anything of it, right? It's just normal, everyday intrusion, right? Forget it! I'm doing something about it—and I'm also joining the NRA right away. The only way to stop all this crap is to mob up and take action."

"Right," I said. "That's what we're doing, taking action."

"I mean *more* action," Buck said. "On a lot of fronts,

because there's a few other things that's been pissing me off too that I've had a lot of time to think about."

"I'm not surprised," I said. "An idle mind is the devil's workshop."

"Yeah, I suppose. I'm talking about fighting fire with fire, Charlie. That reminds me...I'll tell you later about what the local Indians here have coming, okay?"

"Sure."

"Also, I'd like to discuss compulsory service with you— how it relates to gun control, you know?"

"Don't forget that one."

"And I decided I won't talk to you about abortion any more."

"Suits me fine," I said, concentrating on my driving.

"I've also thought long and hard about all this tobacco settlement business, about how the true victim's are being left out—the victim's survivors, you know, like me. My dad died the same year the warnings came out. Lung cancer. Left six kids."

"Sorry to hear about it."

"Yeah," he said seriously, "and it's becoming more and more evident to me just how much conglomerate journalism is manipulating the media—they're a major part of the conspiracy. You know what I'm talking about, Charlie— the pot conspiracy. The media's somewhere about in the middle, manipulating all kinds of shit. A lot of Democratic propaganda, mostly. I suppose you heard about all that political name swapping? Yeah, some asshole Democrat accidentally sent some of their crap literature to a Republican off a TV donor list. I'd say that's a smoking gun."

I turned onto Buck's long driveway and punched it, getting a little squawk from the Olds' back tires. I'd had about all I could take of Buck Foster for one day. And here he hadn't even started drinking yet. "I can't stay," I said.

"That's all right," he answered. "I've got stuff to do, anyway, like feeding Rosie and checking out the little ones. Let me off close to the pen there, will you? Thanks for the ride—and for taking care of Rosie and her puppies for me. Did I tell you I might change her name again? Let me know if you have any good ideas, okay?"

"Something's wrong with you if that smelly sow is the most important thing to you right now," I said, "after being locked up three days."

"Having a stiff shot of cinnamon schnapps—that's the next thing I was going to do after checking on Rosie. Hey, you're getting to know me pretty well, Charlie."

"Too well," I said. "See you tomorrow afternoon...late afternoon. I might even let you drive a little bit if you haven't been drinking too much—and if I'm in a good mood."

"Ha!"

"That's for calling me a bitch," I said. "Bye Asshole—don't bother telling Rosie hi for me."

He got out and was just about to slam the car door when he remembered it was Victor's car, not mine. He grinned at me, then pretended to wipe spittle off the side of the car with his sleeve. At least it looked like he was pretending.

Plans changed and Buck and I ended up meeting with

Jade at her parents' home later that night. She wanted us to stay with her until Victor's problem was resolved. Not only would it be safer for her, we'd help her out with the chores. I'd stay in the huge log mansion with her and Buck would *camp out* a hundred yards to the west in one of the three rustic guest cabins. She specifically asked him to leave the deer on the property alone.

"Not the right time of the year, anyway," he told her. Then he pressured her into agreeing to at least let him bring his bow over for target practice. I reminded him to leave his guns at home. He told us that the estate's layout was perfect for setting up a perimeter of defense. The hilltop had a lot of large trees for cover, if necessary, and the grounds were somewhat protected by a fence and a wrought iron gate that was normally used only for giving unwelcome visitors the impression of a desire for privacy. We weren't going to be that polite though. We were going to start locking it.

The following night, I exchanged the tiny cassettes with fresh blank ones. It was as easy as planting the recorders the first time I went in, even easier.

Buck was impressed with my criminal skills, and he was practically overjoyed to be behind the wheel of the black '70 Mustang. The nearly chromeless fastback blended in with the night—which was his main reason for choosing it, he reminded me. "Just like Zorro's horse. It'd never keep up with my Cobra Jet on the open stretch, though. Short twists and turns, yeah, then I'd leave it behind."

"In your smoke, right?" I said, needling him.

"Damn right in my smoke—and not from the engine either, from my tires!" He slowed down to cross 35W, then punched it just short of getting rubber. We were headed back east toward the estate to meet up with Jade again, who was returning from the casino. Buck punched it again in third gear going about fifty and got a little squeak. "I have to be careful," he reminded himself out loud, "we're carrying—and I mean more than just a few doobies or beers."

"I can hardly wait to find out what's on them," I said. "Are you sure they'll play on the recorder you bought last week?"

"They take the same size tape, I already told you that," he said. "Here...why don't you fire this up?"

"You sure you want to smoke right now?"

"Why not?" he said. "I'm practically risking my life for Victor. He won't mind us smoking in his car. We'll leave the windows cracked and then roll them down all the way for a while after it's out. Here—and I haven't had much to drink. I was careful about that."

"What the hell," I said, pushing in the Mustang's cigarette lighter. "It's only got seven thousand miles on it...might as well break it in."

"Shit, Charlie, who are you trying to kid? Victor's probably already broke it in. Here, put this tape in...it's The Blues Brothers, *Briefcase full of Blues*. What do you think he does when he takes these cars out for his Sunday afternoon drives?"

He became uncharacteristically quiet as he managed to both drive and bogart the joint. Finally, he passed it to me.

"You know," he said, "I never told you this before, but I actually went with a librarian for awhile once, a long time ago. Before I met Beth Ann. She was a real trip."

"Maybe you should've married her," I said.

"I don't' think so," he answered. "A good marriage may last forever, but a bad one seems to. She was always playing mind games with me."

"Like what?" I asked him naively.

"Oh, stupid shit. Like, she still lived with her parents, see, and this one time she called me and said, 'Come on over, nobody's home.' I got there, and sure enough—nobody was home! Dumb bitch. She thought it was real funny. That was right after we had our last big fight. She was always going 'sshhh.' A librarian to the core. Believe me, we weren't compatible. Plus she didn't like me smoking dope either. That was the last straw."

I laughed. "You're making that up, aren't you?"

"Serious as a heart attack," he answered.

"Practicing part of a new stand-up routine on me, right"

"Nope."

"Bullshit."

"Well, I've got one for you, then," he said. "You know why God made man before woman?"

"Why?"

"Because he didn't want any suggestions. See, women should be obscene, not heard."

"Oh, yeah, I get it," I said chuckling, "you want me to sit here and suffer without complaining while you practice your new jokes on me, right? You want me to be a guinea pig with a huge funny bone, right?"

"Basically, yeah," he said. "What's wrong with that? I put together part of that last one from an old Groucho Marx line. A couple of chuckles won't hurt you, Charlie, or even an outright belly laugh or two. What's wrong with that? Would you rather I start bitching again? I hope not, because it suddenly dawned on me in jail last week that I'm probably better off thinking about funny stuff instead of being pissed-off over stupid shit all the time. Who knows, maybe I can even make a few nickels on the side...what do you think? Charlie?"

Chapter 9

I pulled up to the gate and stopped. "Jade should be back in a couple of minutes," I said. "Here, she gave me a key...would you mind unlocking the gate?"

"No problem," Buck answered. "Do you think she'd mind if we start listening to the tapes before she gets here? I'm real curious."

"I hope not," I replied, "I'm a little curious, myself. We should wait at least a few minutes, though, don't you think?"

"She won't mind," Buck said. "I know her type...very understanding and forgiving. The exact opposite of you."

He unlocked the gate and smiled and waved. I saw a flicker of movement in the rear-view mirror and realized too late that he was waving at Jade, not me. He saw me wave and—without raising his voice—mouthed, "I wasn't waving at you, Dumb-ass." He got back into the car and we began coursing up the long red brick driveway to the house. Jade would re-lock the gate.

"I kind of wondered why you were being so friendly," I said.

"Don't take it personal."

"It's hard not to take it personal when someone calls you a dumb-ass, Asshole."

"Okay, we're even now."

He parked slightly downhill away from the house, where the Mustang could rest comfortably in a large shadow cast by the huge log home. Looking back up, the young white pines silhouetted by the house lights at the top of the hill were soft and fluffy and beautiful. I was in a good mood. I felt hopeful. I decided to avoid quarreling with Buck, especially around Jade.

"I hope we get something on Schruder," I said.

"The bastard. What raw fucking nerve."

"Buck, we don't even know how involved he is yet."

"It doesn't matter. He's the one who fucked with Victor the first time around."

"He was doing his job, basically. Because of someone snitching him off—I know, I'm going to check into that. But Schruder didn't seem to go after Victor real tough. He ended up with a pretty light sentence, after all. I don't think Schruder's the one who instigated this double-jeaopardy crap."

"Well, we need to find out," Buck said. "I don't want to mess with him unduly if he's not guilty. I'd rather go right to the source. It's too bad people have to distrust each other so much, but I guess it's our best defense against betrayal. You know what I mean?"

I figured he was referring to my brother, Edwin, and possibly to me too. I quickly changed the subject. "Doesn't Luther Sullivan scare you?"

"Fuck him. What's he going to do? Anyway, I've got my ten-gauge waiting for him—and my bow."

"You do? Since when?" I asked.

"Since I went to get them earlier today. I hope the

German beer guy came by this afternoon like he was supposed to."

"I asked you to leave your guns at home."

"Yeah, I remember. Well, I didn't do it...so what? I brought along a fresh bottle of schnapps too, partly so I can put up with you better."

"Oh, I see. You're already blaming me for your binge-drinking tonight. Well forget it, Buster. I pay my own dues for my own drinking. You're on your own. Just do me a favor and don't get too obnoxious tonight, okay? Otherwise, you can stay right down at your rustic little campsite."

"Fuck you, Charlie. I've got the run of the place. I might even practice with my bow some tonight, as a matter of fact. I won't make a bit of noise, either, unless one of my arrows accidentally zings off something and goes somewhere it's not supposed to—like in your ass, for instance. It'd make a good, big target—that's for sure."

I put off my idea of not quarrelling with him. "You didn't talk about my ass that way a few weeks ago."

"Why do you keep bringing that same old shit up? I told you I was drunk—and sorry—at least three times. Aren't you supposed to drop it now? Isn't that like a rule of etiquette or something?"

"As a matter of fact—if I recall correctly, you said I had a fine ass. Those are the words you used, my good friend, Buck Foster. Fine ass...yep, something I already knew anyway, by the way. You certainly weren't the first guy to tell me that."

"Probably not," Buck huffed. "I bet you were a real

dick-tease in high school and college, too, protecting that precious stuff, huh? Probably afraid of wearing it out."

"Saving myself for the right guy was more like it," I said. "Something you wouldn't understand. There's Jade. Will you quiet down now and leave me alone?"

"Okay, but as usual, you started it—you may as well recall that later, too."

"Whatever."

"See, you always have to get in the last word, too."

"Gees!"

"See? Hi Jade! We were just reminiscing about the good old days back in high school. Charlie claims the boys used to tell her she had a fine ass. I was just about to ask her whether or not she had her pants on when she was getting all those compliments."

I decided it was better to laugh it off than to kick him. Jade laughed too, but not until I did.

We grew excited as we made our way to the den.

"Did Charlie tell you I turned over a new leaf?" Buck asked Jade.

"No. Why? What happened?"

"Nothing really happened...I just had a lot of time to think. Clearly, you know, like a Budda in a ten-foot cell."

"Well, how have you changed?"

"He hasn't changed yet," I interrupted. "He's still mulling over the details."

"Butt out," Buck said. "Actually, Jade, I'm thinking about making another go at stand-up. I can be pretty funny at times, you know, when I'm not pissed-off and bitching about some social injustice or another. That's what I mean by turning over a new leaf—concentrating on the positive instead of the negative."

"That sounds wonderful," Jade said. She sat down and studied the first tiny cassette. "This one is either full or it hasn't recorded anything at all yet."

Buck glanced over at me for support.

"He's serious this time, Jade," I said.

Buck smiled at me and nodded his head in thanks.

"Okay, we'll have to be real quiet now," Jade said, finger poised.

"Uh, can you wait just one second, Jade?" Buck asked. "I mean, I just wanted to tell you one last thing. Thanks. I decided I'm going to start being more professional about my habits. I'm talking about a quality decision here, Girls. By that I mean no more heavy drinking on the job...just a few nips to chase away the nervousness, that's all. Hey— there's nothing wrong with a little bit of sobriety in moderation, right? And I'm going to start dressing a lot better too."

Jade smiled as patiently as she could. "Well, you know what they say about clothes making the man...."

"Exactly," he said. I mean, look at it the other way around—how much influence do naked people have in society?"

Jade laughed, her finger still poised over the cassette player.

"I wouldn't say that," I cut in. "Look at the movies and advertisements these days. Are you through now, Buck, so we can listen to the damned tapes? Actually, we're not here to discuss your next career move anyway, remember?"

"Fine," he said. "One, fuck you, Charlie. Two, Jade, go ahead and push the damn button."

The first tape was from Schruder's bedroom, and it was blank. Not even a phone call.

The second cassette—from above the door—contained several unimportant greetings and one that was unmistakably the voice of Luther Sullivan saying, "Good Afternoon, Joe." Schruder then asked Sullivan why he'd "come back." Nothing else on that tape. Obviously, the two men had quickly moved away from the door.

The third tape caught a great deal of Chief Prosecutor Joe Schruder's assisted suicide in chilling detail.

I said, "Oh shit. Play it again, Jade."

"Hey—that's pretty funny," said Buck. "Here Schruder's dead as a door-nail in the garage, and you're creepy-crawling through his house...how does that make you feel?"

"Creepy."

"At least we're pretty sure you won't get caught," he said. "No witnesses—except for me. No fingerprints...nothing like that."

I asked, "Don't you think they're more likely to search his house and find the tape recorders right away now?"

"It won't matter," Jade said. "They're common enough, and I paid cash for them, remember?"

"Yeah, okay," I said, swallowing hard. I imagined Joe Schruder's body slumped over the wheel of his shiny new burgandy Cadallic. "His car must've finally run out of gas."

Buck wasn't the least bit fazed by Schruder's death. "Well, the son-of-a-bitch had it coming, I suppose. A hell of a way to go, though. Kind of different, huh?"

"I can't believe we already have the goods on Sullivan," said Jade. "We need to make another copy of this right away...let's listen again."

The recorded conversation between Schruder and Sullivan lasted about twenty-five minutes. It began with a minute or so of nonsensical pleasantries, then Sullivan pulled a gun on Schruder, getting right down to business:

"Meet Dr. Jack, Joe...it's a .44 Bulldog, and believe me, his bite is much worse than his bark, especially while he's wearing his silencer."

"Put that away—what in the hell are you doing?"

"You had your chance, Joe. I warned you that I don't take no for an answer. And just so you don't get any silly notions, I'm letting you right now that I rarely change my mind once it's made up."

"What are you talking about? Put that away Sullivan."

"Not until you've rewritten your will and committed suicide—something you're vaguely interested in accomplishing anyway, so I hear."

"This is outrageous! Get out of my house before I call the police!"

"You've got a choice, Schruder...it's either Dr. Jack here, or a nice, peaceful, non-violent death scene. With all the violence these days, you don't want to add to it, do you? Who would find you? No, you'll want to go more gracefully. Dying is the last thing everybody does, but for some people it's the first thing they do correctly. Do this correctly, okay Joe? You really should be a better sport about this."

"I no longer want to die—leave me alone! I've had lots

of problems...family problems."

"I know all about—"

"—I want to see my Grandchildren!"

"It's too late for that, Joe. You need to focus your mind on the business at hand. You were warned...you should've signed the papers."

"I told you, Luther, the Stamate case is too hot right now. It's high-profile—on the news and in the papers. Senator Patch would be all over my ass...."

"You didn't even check with him."

"How do you know that?"

"I've got my sources. Now get a pen and paper, and keep your hands where I can see them. I won't hesitate to splatter you all over your nice room here...you should be more concerned about cutting down on all the blood and violence. You should be thinking of others right now."

"Please, Luther. I've had a lot to deal with. My mind isn't quite right...the casinos have almost ruined me. Hasn't anyone in your family ever suffered from mental illness of one kind or another?"

"Yes, about half of them...but they seem to enjoy it for the most part. You're a nuisance to everyone around you—your former wife, your children—"

"—Not to my Grandchildren! I want to see Billy and Josephine!"

"Stop that damned whining."

"What're you going to do?"

"I'm not going to do anything—except hold this gun, and maybe shoot it. You're going to do everything. Now get a copy of your old will out. Then you're going to start writing."

"Please, Luther, let's reason this out. I've got a little bit of extra cash in the house here—about forty thousand. You can have it."

"It's already mine. And I've got plans for all your other assets too. Your ex-wife and children are going to inherit everything you—"

"—No! I won't do it!"

"Okay, fine, where do you want them to scrape you up? In here? No Joe, a quiet, dignified death in the garage would be much nicer. You have that option as long as you don't make any stupid moves. Otherwise, it's right here...and right now."

"Okay! Okay. Wait. Slow down. Let me think."

"There's nothing to think about. Stop talking. You either do what I say, immediately, or Dr. Jack here is going to leave you completely speechless. Maybe you'd prefer it this way—you won't feel a thing."

There were only respiratory noises and sobbing for the next several minutes, along with the sounds of a drawer opening and papers being shuffled around. Then:

"That's good, Joe. You did a good job. Don't sign it yet though, because you've got to make room for a couple more things...donations."

"What are you talking about? I'm finished."

"I want you to add a couple of charitable contributions."

"I don't want to. I want everything to go...to my family."

"No. You've been very selfish, Joe. I want you to pick

out a charity to donate fifty thousand dollars to."

"Fifty thousand dollars!"

"Yes, and I'll pick one out too. Another fifty thousand dollars. A hundred altogether. Don't worry, your next of kin will end up with ten times that, even after your funeral expenses."

Another long pause.

"Have you picked one out?"

"Yes."

"Well then, write it in."

"Don't you want to know what it is?"

"Not really."

"The national debt."

"Good thinking, Schruder. Now I'm *very* sure no one's going to miss you. Write this down: *Mid-west Strippers, United.* It's a legitimate, tax-deductible organization. I set it up myself a few years ago to help my girls out...you know, with family emergencies, that sort of thing. It's a good fringe benefit for them. A very good cause. The public will appreciate your concern for my girls, Joe, even if your ex doesn't. Hurry up now, I don't have a lot of time."

There were the sounds of papers being rustled again, then more sobbing noises. Finally, we heard a door close.

The Chief Prosecutor for Bunyan County was found two days later, on Monday. The cause of his death was determined to be suicide. No one was surprised, not even old Mrs. Ricks, the nosy neighbor who first called the police hinting that something was probably wrong. Joe hadn't told her he was going away for the weekend, for one thing. According to the late night news, the police had broken through the back door about mid-morning when Schruder didn't show up for work.

We thought about going to the police with the tape right away, but we were concerned about the possibility of it backfiring. More than likely, Victor's problem would go away now with Sullivan's arrest, but what if it didn't? What if Schruder's successor decided to push the case in spite of the adverse publicity? There were still too many unanswered questions—and worse still, the cops would surely start digging into how the tape was made. I didn't feel like being martyred unnecessarily.

Jade turned the TV off and suggested that we go to the media. Again. We still hadn't told Buck that we were responsible for the bomb scare. And we didn't tell him about the follow-up letter to the *Star Tribune* either. Partly to protect him, but partly not.

The paper had made a reference in Sunday's edition about receiving a strange letter relating to the bomb scare, but they hadn't gone into detail—only that the letter was turned over to the FBI. Buck was reasonably curious, but he apparently hadn't put two and two together. Jade and I decided to keep him in the dark about it.

We were excited about the prospect of Victor's soon release, but we were stumped and frustrated about exactly how to speed it along now.

"I know one thing," said Jade, "the media can't ignore the murder of a Chief Prosecutor."

"They can if politics are involved," said Buck. "As long as they've got that asshole liberal bias going. Fucking

Democrats. The majority of the media is simply pulled around by the nose—by Democrats. That's the only reason Clinton's still in office. One-box Willie. Mr. Cool Sax Player, joking about a re-count. What an asshole—and *Congress* is the big, shitty butt!"

"Let's not get sidetracked," I said.

"The media is full of shit," Buck continued. "I wouldn't count on them for anything. What have they done lately to help separate hard drugs from soft drugs? Not much. They talk about hard drugs and then flash a picture of a bright green marijuana leaf right along with all the powder and rocks and shit. That has a big impact on the average stupid citizen, and it's total bullshit."

"Okay then," Jade said. "I'm sorry I brought the media up. Let's forget about them for now."

"They're letting all this injustice happen," Buck went on. "They carry a lot of the blame. This whole thing—you know, the conspiracy—is a political issue that the media can do a hell of a lot more about, that's for sure."

"I agree," Jade said. "They just don't understand the ethical and moral dimensions of today's society—they obviously don't see all the wasted money and ruined lives."

"Oh, they see all right," Buck said vehemently. "They just don't want to help separate hard drugs from soft drugs. The same with medical marijuana. Same reason—because it'd go against the grain of that hypocrite, Clinton. Shit flows downhill. See, a lot of this is directly Clinton's fault, because he helps set the national mood. He's rotten through to the core—a recidivist liar. He pretends to be cool, you know, with the sax and shades and all that shit, and then his administration slams the hell out of pot smokers, even veterans using it for medicinal use! And he's the leader, the head. He's supposed to be representing the Boomers. Ha! You know how a fish rots, Girls?"

I knew I was about to find out. "We're not getting anywhere here," I answered. "Let's forget about Clinton and the media and just move on, okay? I agree, they're all rotten."

"From the head down," he said. "That's how they rot. And that's how our country has been rotting for the past seven years now—from the head down. Clinton."

"Do you mind if we make some kind of decision here?" I said. "I want to go to bed pretty soon. I'm getting tired."

"Me too," Jade said. "Maybe we should sleep on it. We need to think this out with clear heads. The main thing to realize for now is that we're holding the trump card."

Buck suddenly shouted, "This is hilarious!" He slapped his knee. "This is going to be fun, fun, fun, no matter how you look at it! I'm not the least bit tired. As a matter of fact, I think I'm going to have a couple of hits and go out and practice for awhile."

Jade and I both frowned at the same time. He quickly raised a hand. "Not to worry, Ladies—not around any of the animals."

Chapter 10

We agreed to stay at the hobby farm estate for the entire morning to put our heads together about the tape. I thought sending a copy to the media right away would be a good idea. It'd hopefully get Sullivan off the street and away from us. But then again, if it backfired, Sullivan could become even more dangerous to us...and that wouldn't help Victor at all.

Jade and I were making breakfast. We thought Buck was still tending the livestock and doing other chores when he startled us by coming up through a back basement door. We both whirled around to see him standing only a few feet away from us in the brightly-lit kitchen. "Sshhh," he whispered, "...cops at the door! Sheriff Tipton and a State Boy...they should be at the front door right about now...they walked in from the gate."

Buck was dressed in camouflage from top to bottom and holding a beer mug in one hand and his hunting bow in the other. A quiver-full of razor-sharp broadtip hunting arrows was slung dangerously across his back.

At first I thought he was joking. I was about to tear him a new ass for startling us when I saw the look on his face— which took longer because of all the green and brown camouflage paint he'd smeared on.

"Shit. *Fuck!*" he whispered hoarsely. "What should we

do?"

Jade said, "Let me take care of it...no problem. You guys just stay back, okay? I don't know a thing."

"You don't have to go to the door," Buck whispered. "Why don't you just wait for them to leave?"

"They'd just come back later."

"So what's wrong with that?"

"I'd rather get it over with," she answered. "Plus, you can smell this bacon frying a mile away."

Buck suddenly cocked his head sideways and looked up slightly, signifying that a light had come on in his brain. "Why haven't they rung the doorbell yet?" he wondered aloud. "Shit, I've got plenty of time."

Jade looked puzzled. Buck asked her where the sugar was kept. It only took me two seconds to figure out what he wanted it for. A mischievous grin slowly spread across his face, confirming what he had in mind.

I grinned too, and advised him not to overdo it. "You want them to at least get a few miles away before it starts acting up."

The doorbell rang.

Jade studied Buck for a moment. "It's in the pantry, there," she said, pointing back to where he had just entered the kitchen. She suddenly looked angry. "Believe me, this won't take long. I'll be right back!"

"Keep them at the door for at least two minutes though, will you?" Buck asked her in a whisper.

Now she was puzzled and confused as well as being mad as hell as she left to face the cops. "Just don't do anything...you know. Just be careful," she advised him. "Don't do anything you might regret later."

I watched him pour about a cup of sugar into a front pocket of his camouflage pants. He whispered to me, "I wish there was some pancake syrup or molasses around—I heard it works better for some reason. Anyway, try not to worry about me, Charlie," he said. "I'll be right back!"

What an asshole, I thought to myself. *Just can't resist fucking with cops.*

I crept through the house to a window where I could see part of the driveway leading to the gate and still listen in on the conversation at the front door. I caught a flash-movement out of the corner of my eye. It was Buck low-crawling with his bow. I watched him slither across the driveway near the gate, then, like a greenish-brown ghost-lizard, he instantly vanished, blending in with the brush and trees.

I heard Tipton's voice, loud and aggressive, introducing a Captain Rogers to Jade. They both asked her questions about the bomb scare and the letter to the press. "Naturally, you'd be one of the first suspects we'd want to talk to," Tipton said. He was breathing hard from the short hike up the driveway.

"*Naturally*," I heard her say sarcastically, then she added, "Well, Sheriff, sorry to disappoint you, but I don't know anything about any of that, except what little I read in the paper. But if someone's trying to help my husband, then I'm glad."

"Now Mrs. Stamate, this is getting to be real serious fast," the fat lawman warned her.

"It's *been* serious to us—to me and Victor!" she retorted

angrily.

"Well, don't blame me," Tipton said. "He brought it on himself."

"No he did not bring it on himself!" she screamed. "And I *do* blame you—you and that evil flesh-peddler, Luther Sullivan. Victor's case is over—it's been over for close to two years now, and you know it! What were you supposed to get out of bringing it up again, Sheriff? Whose idea was it anyway—yours or Sullivan's?"

No one said anything for a while, then Captain Rogers spoke up. "It wasn't their idea...it was mine."

"*Yours?*" Jade asked him incredulously.

"Yes, Ma'am, I'm the liaison—the field officer if you will—between the State of Minnesota and the Federal Government."

Jade became animated. "And exactly how did *you* get involved?" she asked the Captain in a huff.

"I'm not a liberty to discuss that."

"I'll just bet you're not," she snapped.

"What are you insinuating, Mrs. Stamate? Are you withholding information? Is there something you're not telling us?"

"Believe me, *Captain*," she answered, "there's a whole lot I'm not telling you. And you can mark my words on one thing: all this nonsense will be over with sooner than you think."

Don't say anything else, Jade.

Sheriff Tipton said, "You wouldn't want to be charged with obstruction of justice now, would you, Little Lady?"

"No more than you'd want to be charged with corruption, Fat Pig!" she shouted back.

Captain Rogers cut in. "What are you suggesting, Mrs. Stamate?"

I grimaced and walked up beside her. "Breakfast is ready, Jade," I said. "The eggs are going to get hard."

"Thanks!" she hissed through clenched teeth, not sounding at all grateful. "I'm extremely hungry, too!"

"This will only take a few more minutes," said Captain Rogers.

Jade said, "Didn't you just hear my friend? 'The eggs are getting hard.' I don't know anything...stop bothering me now. Go away."

"We're just trying to get to the bottom of this," Tipton said softly, soothingly.

Jade's dark Spanish eyes flashed. "Then go talk to Luther Sullivan! Go away! You both already know exactly what's going on anyway, except for the truth about Schru—"

"—The eggs, Jade," I said, pulling on her arm. But it was too late.

"It's a riddle...go figure it out!" she screamed into their faces.

"What the hell are you talking about?" Tipton asked, frowning. He was sweating profusely. The fat on his forehead bulged out pink and uneven. He looked questioningly at Jade, then at Captain Rogers.

"Nothing," I answered for her. "She's just pissed because you guys are trying to railroad her husband over bullshit, that's all."

"What're you hiding?" Captain Rogers asked Jade.

"Come on, let's keep the conversation going...let's share the knowledge, okay?"

"Okay, *Smart Ass*," she shot back, now completely out of control. "Sullivan's going down for murder—and right now I'm wondering what kind of charges you two clowns are going to face. Charges you weren't counting on, that's for sure!"

Tipton's big brown hat with the heavy metal badge suddenly flew off his head and stuck to the log doorjamb in front of him. It was just as though a ghost had suddenly slapped it off his fat head.

"Ha! Ha! Ha!"

I leaned over sideways to see Buck. He stood about ten yards beyond the two cops and released another arrow, then quickly reloaded. The arrow stabbed into the same log farther down, about three inches above the State Policeman's head. Rogers quickly ducked down and peered back up it. The arrow was still quivering. It was too late to go for his gun because Buck was now only a few yards away and his bow was drawn back with an arrow pointed directly at the State Trooper's chest. Captain Rogers' hand froze near his holster.

Tipton put his fat arms up in the air and began waving them around in little circles. He looked a little bit like he was trying to do the twist. "Don't shoot! Don't shoot!" he screamed in a high-pitched, squealing, pig-like voice. He changed to a sort of sloppy tap dance.

Buck stood like a statue, unflinching. In more ways than one, he looked like a dummy in a sporting goods store. His eyes were fixed on Rogers' hand.

"Looks like a good case of self-defense to me," he said. "Move your hand away, State Boy. Slowly...very slowly and carefully. And don't you get any ideas, Tipton," he added. "I can load up another one of these arrows and put it straight through your throat in just over two seconds. Matter of fact, I was just out practicing. Fat neck like yours, it'd go through as slick as greased lightening—know what I mean, Fat Boy? Hey—Charlie, Jade, you know something funny? We've got a State Boy here, and a Fat Boy. Two boys trying to do a man's work. I'd say that's pretty funny."

He taunted Rogers further by saying, "Go ahead—go for it, Hero. That's one of the problems with cops these days—not enough heroes. I didn't see any heroes in that big school shooting...just a bunch of cowards waiting for the dust to settle."

"Take it easy, Buck," I cautioned.

"Hey, I'm perfectly in control," he answered. "Don't worry about me—I won't get hurt. I just wish I could say the same about these guys...but it's up to them."

"Don't be stupid," Captain Rogers said. "Put that down."

"Hey, something else funny!" Buck exclaimed. "That's about what Schruder said to Sullivan just before his...how can I say this delica—"

"—His assisted suicide," Jade cut in. "That's why he's going down for murder, like I just said."

"See, at this point we just don't give a fuck," Buck said, continuing to hold the razor-tipped arrow back. "Get it? Gees, I hope my fingers don't slip. Charlie, would you mind going to get my shotgun? Make sure it's loaded."

Jade became even bolder. "You've forced us to meet you on your own terms. Only we're more honorable than you, because we're motivated by loyalty, not *greed*."

"Big shots," Buck said. "Just no heroes. Rather have fun macing the shit out of students, like in Denver. Or clubbing folks and shooting them with rubber bullets like at the Battle of Seattle. Or just out fucking with people going to yard sales—that sort of thing, right Tipton? Wasn't that you told me once you'd outlaw them if you could? My arm's not even getting tired."

Hoping to defuse the standoff, I said, "I think it might be a good idea for you cops to leave now. I know, the situation here stinks. But you really should go do some sniffing somewhere else for awhile."

"Yeah, like around Sullivan's nasty ass," said Buck. "That's where it really stinks. Now get moving...and keep your hands out where I can see them until you get to your car. And don't come back, because I might be in the woods waiting for you."

Rogers whispered into Tipton's ear, then—arms outstretched—the two men turned around and walked back to the gate.

"Nice one, Guys," I said sarcastically. "We're a real team, huh?"

"Gosh, I'm sorry," Jade said.

"Never mind that for now," Buck said, keeping his eyes on the pair of cops. "We need to think about getting the hell out of here as soon as possible!"

Jade said, "I don't think those two are going to do anything until they check back with Sullivan...or Patch."

"Probably not," I said. "They'll want to know what's going on before they step any deeper into the shit."

"Yeah, but we can't take a chance on that," said Buck. "They could be calling in forty thousand fucking pigs right now—and I just threatened a couple of them."

Jade asked, "Then what do you suggest?"

"Just that we hurry up and get the hell out of here...and not by car, either. I don't know about you two, but I'm gone. It's probably best if we splint up for awhile, anyway."

"I'm going to stay," Jade said.

"Fine," said Buck. "It's up to you. But as for me, I just got out of the pokey, and I sure don't want to go back again any time soon. Don't worry about me...I'll be in touch. How about you, Charlie? What are you going to do?"

After getting permission from Jade, Buck went down into the den to get a refill of beer and came back two or three minutes later, belching loudly. He acknowledged Jade with a little smile and nod of thanks as he swept past us.

"I guess you weren't in that big of a hurry," I said, trying to sound more disgusted than I actually was.

Jade and I watched him head down the paved trail toward the cabins, toward his *campsite*. Foam from the cold beer sloshed onto his camouflage shirt and splattered down onto the hot pavement. Steam from the beer rose up off the pavement. A warm breeze quickly dispersed it. He was probably stopping to get his dope and a few things before *escaping*. I figured he'd probably run hard and long, then change clothes and hitch a ride somewhere.

Jade ran back inside to phone Otis Franklin, Victor's lawyer.

"Wait a minute, Jade!" I shouted after her.

She paused. "Listen," I said, "we're up to our ears in illegal stuff—right along with Buck. It might not be such a good idea to involve Mr. Franklin just yet. I mean, I think we can handle this ourselves without anyone else's involvement. Besides, even if you called Franklin, Sullivan could still be after us in a matter of hours...or minutes even. Who knows what it's going to take to stop—"

"—Hey, you know what?" Jade interrupted. "They may not even tell Sullivan what they just heard from us. Maybe they'll be smart and break with him right away...so they don't go down even harder themselves. Maybe they've already turned on him!"

"I wouldn't count on it," I said.. "For one thing, they don't know about the tape yet...the proof."

Jade suddenly looked embarrassed. "Thank goodness for that."

"Don't worry about it," I said. "I was getting pretty pissed, myself."

"I feel like such a fool right now. This is all my fault."

"Bullshit to that notion," I said. "It's *their* fault—and maybe it's better that it's coming to a head sooner than later, anyway."

"Thanks for saying that," Jade said. She took in a large breath and let it out slowly, letting her emotions settle. "You're such a good friend, Charlie. What should we do?"

"Well," I said, "obviously, our first priority should be protecting ourselves from Sullivan."

All at once she looked older. Alarmed, she asked, "Well, how can we do that?"

I suddenly hated Sullivan. Though I didn't believe in the death penalty, I felt like killing him, not just for everything he'd already put us through, but because we now had to hide from him too. "Buck was right," I said. "We have to get out of here. Does your father have any handguns that you know of?"

"Just an antique revolver," she answered, "but I don't like guns. I was supposed to see Victor today, Charlie. And what about the plants and animals here?"

"Buck did a good job of keeping everything up," I assured her. "Everything will be fine for a few days. We'd better take the gun with us."

"I don't know...we don't even have a permit for it. I don't know if there's any bullets for it, either." She started crying.

"Don't worry about it," I said. "We're in this together, with or without the gun."

"We'll take it with us, just in case, Charlie," she sobbed. You're such a good friend."

Of course she didn't know about my earlier thoughts of her husband. I promised myself that I'd try not to think of him that way again.

I reached into a front pocket of my jeans and took out a crumpled joint and wet it and reformed it, then dried it under my lighter and lit it. I offered it to Jade, smiling and chuckling nervously. "Here."

I suddenly remembered my Mercedes under the straw in the barn. "They didn't see my car here," I said. "It's still in the little barn. What do you say we grab what we need for the next few days and split...maybe go to Eau Claire or Des Moines? It's not going to be safe in this neck of the woods for a while—that's obvious."

"What about Buck?"

"I guess he's on his own. Maybe he shouldn't have shot those arrows."

"We shouldn't just leave him."

"Maybe we'll spot him on the way out," I said. "If not, we'll just have to try calling him later on. I think I have his cell-phone number. There's basically nothing else we can do for him right now. Come on, let's hurry."

"We got 'em, but they're expensive Ma'am," the old man behind the counter at LaCross Gun and Tackle told Jade. "A box of fifty will cost you almost a hundred dollars."

"You don't carry a smaller box?"

"No Ma'am, and you'd be hard-pressed—lucky, actually—to find 'em stocked anywhere else in Wisconsin. Please let me know, now, if you ever want to sell that piece."

I looked at Jade. We both smiled.

"No—seriously," said the old man. He peered over the top of his glasses, "I'd like to buy that piece for my own collection—believe me, a .44-caliber Colt in that year and in that condition is hard to come by. It's almost like a couple of Colts Sam Walker had—he was a Texas Ranger, you know."

"It's not for sale right now, but I'll remember," Jade said with a silly smile on her face. She elbowed me.

The man took his wallet out and extracted a business card with tiny silver and gold handguns emblazoned all around the edges and handed it to Jade as delicately as he'd just fondled the revolver. "Thanks for bringing it in and letting me see it. Make sure you keep it locked in that nice box, now, just to be on the safe side. Rosewood?"

"Yes," I answered for Jade.

I'd tried reaching Buck from pay phones three or four times before finally connecting with him just after passing Mankato. "Don't tell me where you are, okay?" I'd told him.

He'd been offended. "What do you think I am, stupid?"

"We've already covered that plenty of times," I reminded him. "Is everything all right? Don't tell me where you're going or anything."

"Knock it off, will you? I took care of Janet, that was the main thing."

"Janet?"

"Yeah, I changed—oh, never mind. I'll tell you about it later on. I couldn't mind up my mind on Hillary or—"

"—Later on is a good idea!"

"Hey—relax, will you? Listen, do you remember that place where the fat lady sneaked up behind me and belted me off the stage?"

"Yeah."

"Well, I called there—from a pay phone, don't worry—and begged and begged until I actually ended up landing a gig there. Tonight! Yeah, I'm serious. Someone cancelled at the last minute—left the dude hanging. Said he'd give me another chance since it's been over a year ago. Said he wasn't opposed to giving fellas with damned good potential another chance. 'Damned good potential,' he said. He even laughed it off."

"No shit."

"Yeah. Why don't you meet me there, give me a little support, you know? I mean, as long as you were just heading out...somewhere...anyway."

"What time's the gig?"

"Not until ten. And get this, no brats in the audience, guaranteed. Cash money on the barrel-head, too."

I didn't come right out and tell him "no," so he knew we'd be there.

Jade put the plump .44 shells in the glove-box and gingerly re-wrapped the rosewood gun-box with a large pink and blue beach towel and placed it back into the Mercedes' trunk, then we left to get something to eat and find a hotel for the night. We ended up having fresh crappie and we got a room with a great view of the Mississippi River.

We still had over an hour to kill, so I showed Jade how to load and unload the beautiful old six-shot. I also taught her how the safety worked. I didn't tell her what tremendous power it packed, nor about the fist-sized hole one of the bullets would make coming out the other side of a person.

"The man in the gun shop said it looks like it's never even been fired," Jade said.

"Well, maybe you'll be the first one to get to shoot it then," I kidded her.

"It would really blow Sullivan away, wouldn't it?"

"That's for sure!" I agreed.

Chapter 11

Buck knocked on our hotel room door five minutes early.

I jammed the silver barrel of the big .44 down into the front waistband of my jeans—unloaded, of course, wondering what kind of reaction I might get out of him. We were all happier than usual to see one another, I suppose because we felt safe, having temporarily escaped our problems back home.

"Damn, Girl!" Buck exclaimed. He leaned back out into the hallway and shot a glance up and down both sides, then quickly came in and shut the door and whispered, "Wow, where'd you get that? Can I see it?"

"Nice, isn't it?" I said. I took it out of my waistband and handed it to him. "It's unloaded, but be careful with it anyway—it's Jade's father's. It's old and worth a lot. I mean a *whole lot*, Buck."

"Nice," he said, taking it. "You sure it's unloaded?"

"Of course," I answered. "Damn, didn't you just hear me? We're trying to help one another here, not kill each other. You been drinking, or what?"

He immediately began twirling the heavy, valuable weapon around on his finger, first making it spin forward, then backward, back and forth, back and forth. He suddenly squatted down low and—arm outstretched—pointed it toward the single large window overlooking the wide river. "Blam! Blam! Blam!" he whispered loudly. He spun the pistol forward and backward again and pretended to palm the hammer a single time. "Blam! Gotcha, you son-of-a-bitch, Sullivan! He just as quickly changed his deadly serious face to a pleasant one again by smiling broadly. "I got him, the son-of-a-bitch. That'll teach him to fuck with *me*." He handed the gun to a startled Jade.

"Wow! That was great!" she said. "Where did you learn to do that?"

"When, not where," he answered, looking a bit embarrassed. He chuckled good-naturedly. "I went through a lot of gun and holster sets when I was a kid. Roy Rogers, Gene Autry, Buck Owens, you name them. But I always liked Zoro the best. I'd like to put the mark of Zoro on Sullivan's chest right now. Swush! Swush! Swush!"

"Buck, do you mind if we don't talk about Sullivan for a while?" Jade asked. "Just for tonight...as a favor to me? I'd like to try to relax for a change."

"Me too," I said. "You feel like going over your routine, Buck? How are you doing? Nervous, or have you been hitting the bottle?"

"Thanks for reminding me," he said, taking out a small pocket flask. "Actually, I've got it down pat." He held the little flask up. "I bought it in Stillwater. It's antique. How about a shot of cheap schnapps?"

"What kind?" I asked.

"Wild blackberry. Probably no such thing—just flavoring, but it sounds good. Tastes pretty good, too, actually. I only had one little nip so far."

"Oh yeah, what're you, pacing yourself? I'll try some, thanks."

"Go easy on it," he warned, "it's a hundred proof. Oh— that reminds me, there's a book I wanted to show you. I'll be right back."

He went to his own room across the hallway and quickly came back with an old, dusty-rose colored hard-cover book with splash marks and stains all over its cover and edges. The browned pages were uneven at the long edge, and the entire book was actually warped. Someone had apparently once driven a large nail or spike into the center of the book, as though it'd been nailed to a wall. Buck read the title deliberately slow for effect: "'*How to Drink and Stay Healthy.*' And, no," he added quickly, "before you ask, I didn't put the hole in it. I got it at a yard sale. Excellent book...only a quarter, I think."

"Whatever helps," I said sarcastically. "Its ugly. Put it away, I don't want to see it, yet alone touch it...or hear what it says. It looks like it's been in an old outhouse."

"It's the message that's important," Buck said.

"Yeah, maybe, unless the message is death from the germs all over it."

"It mainly says to get a lot of extra fluids, and to keep your immune system up—and of course, not to overdo it. It was written in 1941, right during the war. This guy—Dr. Sage—claims most people can cut down on their drinking better than completely quitting. And now they're saying the same thing again—after all these zero-tolerance years. You know what I'm talking about...the twelve-step stuff. Now this is my kind of guy. See, he knew the truth way back then even."

"That must be why that book is still around," Jade said.

Buck gazed at her a few seconds, not quite sure how to take the comment. "Anyway," he said, taking a big—but apparently not unhealthy—drink out of the handsome metal flask, "I'm on the road to recovery!" He broke out into a knee-slapping laugh and had trouble screwing the top back on the flask. "Don't worry," he said, "I'm going to pace myself tonight—I'm not going to blow the start of a brand new career. No Ma'am!" he yelled, jumping to his feet at attention and saluting me.

"You had anything to eat yet tonight?" I asked.

"No," he answered. "Too nervous...but I'm feeling better now."

"You should get something to eat," I advised him. "It'll help regulate that schnapps. I bet it even mentions that in your book there, right?"

His eyebrows shot up in surprise. "As a matter of fact, you are correct as usual, Queen Friday!" He bowed and started to lose his balance, then quickly took a small side-step to catch himself. Laughing, he said, "Just that joint I smoked a couple minutes ago. You are correct as usual," he repeated. "That's what the sage, Dr. Sage, says: 'You have to eat something.' I'll eat something on the way to the club. What time is it, anyway? We've got to leave pretty soon."

Jade asked, "How are you ever going to remember your lines?"

"The lines aren't a problem," he answered. He grew serious. "The biggest problem for me has always been having to deal with...*fat-ass women* in the audience. If they can't take a joke, why don't they just stay home? The same with leaving their damned kids home too. Who takes kids to night clubs or strip joints, anyway?"

I said, "I think that woman with the kid was the manager's sister. And people don't come to nightclubs to be personally insulted, Buck...they come to be entertained."

"I'll entertain 'em tonight, that's for sure," he joked. "Especially the fat gals. Only this time, I'm waiting 'til the end of my routine. I've got a new fat-gal joke—want to hear it?"

"Why don't you save it and surprise us," Jade suggested.

Again, Buck wasn't quite sure how to take her comment. "Okay, anyway, I've got to get going, " he said. He quickly got over it and grinned mischievously. "I'll give you a hint though: it's about a fat lady losing her underwear— you know, while she's wearing them."

Jade immediately said, "Oh, no, no, no—don't use that one, Buck."

I agreed with her. "Leave the fatties alone, Buck. You never learn, do you?"

He replied, "Yeah, I learn all right...that's why I'm working it in at the end tonight. You guys worry too much. Way too much."

"Ladies and Gentlemen, tonight *Effie's* has the privilege of welcoming back one of our favorite comedians. He's been away for awhile, due to personal problems. All the way from the Twin Cities, Mr. Buck Foster! Give him a big hand, Ladies and Gentlemen! Buck Foster!"

Buck leaped up onto the small stage with an amazing

degree of vigor and loose-limbed grace and strode confidently over to the spotlight and mike. I don't think he was even aware of the sparse hand-clapping. He was beyond that, well into a personal dementia of his own. It was obvious. His eyes were glassy from the pot, yet they were oddly bright, not yet bloodshot from the alcohol. He was still climbing up and up before the great fall.

Jade and I sat down with four large plastic cups of beers—no bottles or cans allowed—at a table very close to the stage, just in case Buck needed help of one kind or another. Jade didn't like the atmosphere. She was nervous and uncomfortable. Buck had gone over a few lines on the way to the club—actually, a shit-hole strip joint—and it sounded pretty good. I figured he'd be okay as long as he stuck to the script. Jade was less optimistic. "I just hope he doesn't fall off the stage and get hurt," she whispered to me, laughing.

I joked back, "Yeah—and I hope we're not sitting too close to the stage. But my greatest fear is that he'll lose tract of time and drag it on and on, or maybe start ranting and raving about Clinton or his pot conspiracy theory." I laughed loudly. "And if he leaves the stage early, I bet it won't be from falling."

Buck saw us laughing and waved. "I'm glad to see that some of my best friends are here tonight," he said. A few people behind us started clapping. I started to turn around, but decided against it and began clapping along with them instead.

"Sorry I've been away so long," he began. "Yes, I've had personal problems, as the man was just kind enough to mention. You know how it is though...laugh and the world laughs with you, stub your toe and the world laughs whether you do or not. I won't bore you with all the details of what I've been going through...it's not that funny, especially to me. But just to give you an example of the bad luck I've been having...I went to visit Salt Lake City last month and I got mugged by a Mormon! I swear it's true...it was in all the papers!"

Jade and I forced ourselves to laugh, even though we'd already heard the opening in my car on the way over. Several other patrons laughed lightly, politely.

"Has anyone noticed how much hair I've lost since the last time I was here?"

I raised my hand and he pretended to scowl at me.

"It was just a rhetorical type of question, Lady, not a real question," he said. He leaned forward drunkenly and laughed. "You know what though? The idea of losing my hair doesn't bother me a single bit. See, some people don't mind losing their hair. Others do. Men don't seem to mind it nearly as much as women do."

A few more polite laughs. No boos yet.

"I don't know if you've noticed, but I'm looking a lot older too."

I entertained the idea of raising my hand again, this time unplanned, but I quickly decided against it.

"Age is only a state of mind, right? Well—that's provided you have one left. I thought maybe I was going crazy—you know, from all my problems, so I called this psychiatric hotline. I got their menu. It said, 'If you are obsessive-compulsive, please press one repeatedly...if you are codependent, please ask someone to press two for you...if you have multiple personalities, please press three, four, five and six.'"

There was some laughter and light applause. His routine seemed to be picking up.

"It was a weird menu, folks. It said, 'If you are paranoid-delusional, we know who you are and what you want...just stay on the line so someone from the U. S. Government can trace the call. If you are schizophrenic, listen carefully and a little voice will tell you which number to press. If you are depressive, it doesn't matter which number you press. No one will answer.'"

The applause and laughter increased. He was becoming more confident, holding it together very well.

"Now, folks, you don't mind if I tell you a few what I call *fat-gal* jokes, do you?" he asked the audience. "Because if anyone does, just let me know right away, and I'll—"

"—Hey!" A woman's deep, raspy voice suddenly boomed out from behind us. "Hey! I thought I recognized you, you dirty son-of-a-bitch!"

The next thing I saw was a foam-spraying missile flying over our heads, and we were misted with a light shower of beer. The plastic cup somehow held most of its contents, and it hit Buck right in the nuts, drenching his trousers. He immediately doubled over. Several patrons subdued the furious woman before she could reach the stage. She managed to knock over three tables and about a dozen chairs before two security men quickly escorted her out of the club, holding her tightly at each elbow. She lurched backward several times on the way to the door and yelled over her shoulder, "You just wait, you bastard! I'll be waiting for you outside! You won't get away this time!"

"Oh shit," I said to Jade. "I'll be right back."

I hopped up onto the stage and helped Buck keep his balance until he could straighten up. He grabbed hold of the mike-stand for support. "Thanks," he said to me, then mumbled into the microphone, "Damn, you guys need to screen your customers better...well, this proves that I'm not the only one out there with problems."

The audience of fifty or so stood to their feet and applauded. Buck shuffled around uncomfortably for another minute or so in spite of the alcohol's pain-deadening effect. He managed to recover, then went on successfully for the next ten minutes or so, ending his routine by reciting one of his favorite childhood poems:

The night was dark,
the sky was blue,
around a corner,
the *shit-wagon* flew.
A bump it hit—
a scream was heard,
the driver was killed
by a flying turd.

The audience clapped good-naturedly and rose to their feet again.

"Thank you and good night, Ladies and Gentlemen!" Buck shouted, arms outstretched. He stumbled about the stage and threw kisses while loosely holding onto the mike stand for support. "And always remember," he said, "love may make the world go around, but it's laughter that keeps us from jumping off! Thank you! Thank you, Ladies and Gentlemen. *Most* of you were very kind. Good night!"

The security detail at *Effie's* ended up banning Buck's tormentor from the club for a year. Buck collected his seventy-five dollars and assured Effie that he had no intentions of filing assault charges against the "fat monster" who had hurt him—again. "Just a hazard of the trade, I guess," he told her. Effie promised him some future gigs, along with a warning not to drink quite so much the next time.

We made it back to our hotel rooms just before midnight. Jade and I felt like staying up to strategize, so we invited Buck to our room. I immediately got after him for overdoing it with the schnapps, and he defended himself loudly.

"Bullshit, Charlie, I was mostly just high on weed. You saw for yourself how well I did."

"Sshhh. Keep it down, will you?" I warned him. How would you've done without drinking?"

He frowned and appeared perplexed. "Say, just what are you getting at, anyway? Leave me alone...I thought you wanted to talk about that asshole, Sullivan?"

"We do," I said. "I'm just reminding you of something you said last week—about not wanting to attribute any success you have to drinking. Remember? It seemed to make good sense to you at the time. How do you feel about it now? I'm just wondering."

"Why don't you lay off?" he said. "I did real well

tonight."

"Yeah, but how much did the schnapps help?"

"Fuck you, I'm going back to my room," he said in a huff. "I'm tired anyway...and besides, my balls still hurt. I think one of them is swelling up."

"I'll bet there's something else swelling up too," I said, teasing him. "And I'm not talking about your big head, either. I'm talking about the other one. Thinking about your fat friend at Effie's, aren't you? Come on, admit it."

"That's it—I'm out of here," he said, scowling. "I hope Sullivan sneaks up on you tonight and rapes the shit out of you before finishing you off."

Jade laughed. "Come on, Buck, she's just ribbing you. Stay for awhile—for me, okay? Charlie, leave him alone...he's had a stressful night."

"Okay," I said, trying not to laugh. "Sorry."

Buck said, "No, you're not sorry. But I'll stay for Jade. Let's hurry up and get this over with now, because I'm really slumping. Matter of fact," he said, reaching into his shirt pocket, "I need a couple of hits to pick me up—plus it'll help me think more creatively, too."

"Oh, you mean like how alco—never mind," I said after seeing his red-eyed stare.

"You know what, Charlie?" he said. "You just reminded me of something that's really been pissing me off lately. About the Government, I mean. I honestly think they're afraid of creative thinkers. Maybe that's part of what's behind the conspiracy...you know, to silence pot smokers. Like freedom of thought is dangerous to the Government. McCarthyism, that sort of thing. They're still afraid of what people might think and say. Pot smoking really opens up the channels of discussion and dissension. Are you following me?"

"I'm following you, Buck," said Jade. "But you don't have to worry, because free speech is protected here in America."

"Yeah, for now. But as soon as the Second Amendment is shot to hell, the First Amendment won't be as strong...they'll go after the free-speechers next. That's when the assholes in the media will see that it's too late, and they were the ones who helped cut their own throats by supporting gun control. See what I mean? Besides, there's already huge loopholes in the First Amendment."

"You're certainly right about that," Jade agreed. "There's already exceptions for imminent lawlessness and for endangering national security. Those are pretty broad terms, Buck—making for a lot of room on the slippery slope. I'm referring to public safety as the excuse."

Buck was surprised. "You been thinking about this stuff, too?"

"Sure," she replied casually. "I thought everybody did. You think about the future of our freedom too, don't you, Charlie?"

"Not that much," I admitted. "I figure we'll be okay during my lifetime, and my kids' if I ever have any."

Suddenly full of self-righteousness, Buck said, "That's damned selfish of you, Charlie."

"What's it going to matter after I'm gone?" I answered him flippantly.

"I didn't think you were that selfish," he said. He stared

at me a long time, appearing to have genuine pity for me. "What little freedom we have left was paid for going back hundreds of years," he told me, "by folks looking out for you and me...way into the future. Can you dig that?"

"Let's not get into gun control again right now," I said.

"Okay, let's get into the compulsory service issue, instead then," he said, raising his voice. "That's the problem...and do you notice the gender bias? Girls don't have to register for the draft. What a steaming crock of horseshit! Everybody should have the equal opportunity of serving, then all citizens would have a better grasp of what the flag and freedom is all about. Women have been getting out of the heavy shit for too long now. Always bitching about guns without even knowing what the Second Amendment is all about. No respect for soldiers or history! Women serve in Israel, don't they? Instead of paying big bucks to volunteers, we should make everybody sacrifice and serve equally. It'd save the country a bundle, and everybody—including you—would have more respect for what *some people* have had to endure all these years. I'm talking about facing horrible deaths in the trenches, stuff like that. People like you, Charlie, and Rosie O'Donnel have just been skating by, talking about stupid shit, bitching about unimportant crap, not at all interested in military service or guns or protecting our freedoms. Women should be given the same opportunity of understanding—and appreciating—freedom too, not just men. Dumb Ass."

"Holy shit—are you finished?"

"Yeah," he retorted. "See, I told you this would help me think creatively. That's what the Government's worried about. Too much insightful thinking. That's why the Vietnamese wanted to kill all the intellectuals...and not just because they maybe smoked pot."

"They weren't all smoking pot," I said.

"You really amaze me, you know it, Charlie?" Buck said. "You managed to miss my whole point. Let me reiterate—"

"—No!" I shouted. "We're here to talk about our hassle back home, remember?"

"You need some reeducation, Charlie, like they gave to the ones they didn't kill. They wouldn't have killed you, Charlie. You know why? Because you wouldn't have posed a threat to them. Dumb Ass."

Jade laughed loudly.

"You girls have had too much to drink," Buck said smugly. "And Hotel Security will be up here pretty soon if you don't quiet down."

That was as good a cue as any to get down to business. I said, "I think I know of a surefire way to get Sullivan off our backs—and get Victor released too, both at the same time."

Jade gradually stopped laughing. Buck was already serious. I said, "How about we go ahead with the idea of kidnapping Kimberly Patch? It'd be a ransom for justice. All or nothing."

Chapter 12

We hid my Mercedes down a two-track Buck knew about from deer hunting before it became illegal to hunt in the area because of the exploding population growth. The unused and grassed-over old farm trail twisted and sloped down toward the Minnesota River, and in some places it was entirely hidden away by brush and low pine branches. Over time, it'd become a large deer-path. The trail ended at a small opening on the slope about halfway down to the river. The two-acre circle was heavily brushed-over with mostly small oaks and maples, also many clumps of wild black-raspberry bushes. At the north edge of the opening, facing back uphill, an expensive and apparently forgotten tree-house had years earlier crashed down, along with the dead tree it was built around. The octagonal structure had been made of good lumber, and it even had a trussed roof with real shingles. It'd been screened for mosquitoes at one time, but now most of the panels were damaged and hanging loose. The trunk of the huge cottonwood it'd been built around still pierced upward at an angle through the center, its gray roots exposed to the sky.

About three hundred yards away from the gazebo-like structure, straight back up the slope, was the Stamate's pretty bluff property with the watering trough and horses. Victor's plants had been growing nearby, in another smaller opening just over the ridge.

"See, I wasn't bullshitting!" Buck said.

The three of us were breathing hard and sweating profusely because we'd just high-stepped through the thick tangle of wild raspberry shoots and weeds in the hot July sun.

"See, it's exactly like I said," he said excitedly, "perfect to squirrel someone away for a while. Not to mention ourselves. It just needs a little fixing up. Shit, people pay good money to camp out in weather like this—it's a little warm right now, though, huh? See, using the buck-saw, we can cut the trunk off and pull her upright again, using the rope and winch I brought along just for that purpose. What'd I tell you? It's perfect...see, I wasn't bullshitting. Maybe you'll believe me sooner next time.

"Don't you girls think this kidnapping idea might be just a tad-bit extreme—I mean, now that you've gotten a better idea of what the living conditions will be like for the next few days?"

His last comment made me feel anxious and impatient. I was already wondering whether Jade would be able to cope with the ruggedness of our new surroundings. I watched her as she twisted down sideways to study the inside of the tree-house. An albino squirrel suddenly shot past her feet and she jumped back and screamed, getting a laugh from Buck. Somewhat embarrassed, she began picking at a mess of briars and brambles running down one entire side of her slacks. She occasionally stopped to study the tree-house's interior.

"Have you got a better idea, Buck?" I asked him. "Sure

it sounds extreme—but extreme times call for extreme actions, remember?"

"Well—how about an anthrax scare instead then? A five-pound bag of concentrated anthrax powder could wipe out the whole Twin Cities. They'd damn sure take *that* serious! Or, how about just a quarter of an ounce or so at the Mall of America...maybe float some up to the various levels from Camp Snoopy, you know?"

"You're sicker than I thought," I said, still catching my breath.

"Hey, Butt-hole, I'm just postulating," he said. "Do you think I'd actually do that? Of course not...I like kids. Just not as much as regular people."

"A lot of regular people don't like kids," I said.

"No, Charlie, I meant I don't like kids as much as I like regular people. Never mind, it's not worth it. Anyway, I'm talking about the great publicity a threat like that would generate—yes, partly because of the audacity."

"The bomb scare didn't work," Jade said absentmindedly. "The media brushed it aside—as a favor to someone, I suppose. An anthrax threat certainly couldn't be brushed aside so easily. It would likely—"

"—I figured you guys were behind that," Buck said. "You weren't fooling me. I was just biding my time, waiting to see whether or not you were ever going to tell me."

I quickly said, "We thought you'd be better off not knowing—for legal reasons.

"Bullshit."

"Sorry Charlie—and Buck," Jade said. She quickly changed the subject back to the anthrax idea. "You may be onto something, Buck...a threat of bio-warfare would surely be a lot easier to accomplish than a real kidnapping."

I laughed nervously. "What's the matter, Jade—are you chickening out?" I glanced at Buck. "I just thought it might be nice to involve the Senator directly—you know, go after one of the individuals directly responsible for Victor's troubles. And get this whole mess over with quickly. I'm sure the honorable Senator would be eager to help us if he had enough reason to." ·

I was relieved when Buck agreed without hesitation. "You're right—Charlie's right, Jade. We need to take fast, direct action. No more game-playing. They can't brush off a real kidnapping."

I quickly pushed ahead. "The media will have to be more responsible in their coverage if a Senator's daughter is kidnapped, that's for sure!"

Buck and I both watched Jade picking at her slacks.

"Might as well wait 'til you walk back through," he advised her. "Unless you want to wait here while I whack this shit down...I'll make you a walk-way. How's it look to you? The tree-house?"

"Fine," she answered. "A bit small, but better than I expected."

"Oh! I didn't have a chance to tell you yet," he said, "I'm going to build a lean-to for myself, right over there." He pointed back toward the two-track. "That way I'll be able to guard the trail, plus it'll give you pansy-asses more space and privacy. All I need is some of that mosquito dope we bought...which reminds me." He patted his front shirt pocket, then reached in and brought out a large doobie and lit it and declared to nobody in particular, "Man, this is really nice out here!"

"Speak for yourself," I said. "And we'll find out who the wimp is. Just fix the screens right away though, okay?"

"Sure. But would you mind helping me unpack the cars first? We really did a super job of getting supplies, didn't we? Especially considering all the shit we needed, not only to fix things up, but also having to buy all that food for four for a week, too."

"Fo-fo-what?"

"Food for four for a week, too. Here," he said, thrusting the joint at me. "We should all get on the same wavelength."

Jade pretended to wail with grief. "A week! I thought this would only take a couple of days."

"What did we just get food for four for a week for? " I asked her.

"Two hundred dollars worth," Buck added. "Gees Jade, we've been here less than five minutes and—"

Jade put up her hand. "I'm not complaining," she interrupted as I passed her the joint. She took a big hit on it and blew out most of the smoke. "I'm sure this'll be just fine," she said to assure us—but then quickly added, "I hope you won't mind if I stay right here by the gazebo tree-house most of the time."

"We won't mind," said Buck. "We'll need someone to keep things orderly and stay with the brat, anyway. You'll have to keep your mask on, though—whenever she's not blindfolded, I mean. And you can't be too nice to her, otherwise she might try to take advantage of you."

"We'll be here most of the time, too, Jade," I said. "Don't frighten her, Buck."

"That reminds me," he said. "Did you hear about all the damned cat sightings they've had around here lately? It's been in the news. A shit-house load of panther and cougar sightings—even one near the Mall of America, if you can believe that. One guy claimed he saw two black cats together. An occasional wolf or black bear has been known to cruise through these parts, too, but I've never seen one, personally. Just a bunch of deer and a few coyotes and wild turkeys. Maybe a few foxes and skunks...possums, that kind of thing. I haven't seen any big cats, but they're around somewhere, huh? Don't worry though, Jade, they've got plenty of squirrels and rabbits to eat—and especially a lot of stupid geese. Just remember though, if you see any baby cougars or bears, head in the opposite direction. You don't have to worry about them attacking you out of hunger—only out of protecting their young. They've got enough to eat without bothering with you." He laughed, then paused. "You've still got the Colt with you, don't you? Don't worry, I brought along my 10-guage too, just in case."

Jade shuddered and said, "I'm sure a rabbit would taste much better than me."

I caught a glimpse of mischief in Buck's eyes. He glanced at me and snickered, but he resisted carrying it any further. "Come on, we don't have time to be joking around," he said. "We've got a lot of work to do here before dark...we've got to get serious and make this place habitable."

"At least Kimberly shouldn't be too hard to nab," I said. "I made a phone call yesterday and found out that she's still planning to stay with her folks until school starts. I pretended to be an old high school friend looking her up. I'm sure she won't remember Beth Ann Smith."

Buck quickly became perturbed. "What the hell did you use her name for?"

"It was the first name that popped into my head. It doesn't matter anyway, because they don't know one another. By the way, isn't Beth Ann going to wonder where you're at for the next few days?"

"No more than usual," he answered. "Familiarity breeds contempt, absence makes the heart grow fonder—blah, blah, blah."

Jade asked, "Are you two thinking of breaking up?"

"No," he answered, "we just get along better if we don't see too much of each other, the same with a lot of other people. But—now that you mentioned it, she has been getting on my nerves more than usual lately...that's true. And she's been wearing all these wild, weird, revealing clothes in public lately too—which by extrapolation is a bad reflection on me."

"Yeah, I noticed that the last time I saw her," I said. "That short, emerald dress she had on fit tighter than my skin. At least I can sit down in my skin."

"Do you mind if we change the subject? Gees, I've already got enough weirdness on my mind right now. So the Patch girl rides horses?"

"Yes," Jade answered, "and most often all by herself. I've seen her several times."

"That's it then," Buck said. "We'll make it look like she got thrown off her horse and then maybe wandered off in a daze. They won't even consider the possibility of a kidnapping until they hear from us. That'll keep any heat off us—"

"—Until they hear from The Helpers," Jade corrected him.

"Yeah, The Helpers...whatever," he grumbled. He looked down and paused a few moments for effect, trying to look hopelessly despondent. "You guys could've told me right away, you know. I don't have a big mouth—unlike some people I'm glad I don't know!" He glanced up at me. "Like your dumb-ass brother, Edwin, for example. What do you think Victor's going to do about that little situation when he finds out? Have you talked to him about it yet?"

"Who, Edwin?"

"Yeah."

"I just brought up Victor's name, that's all. Right away he mentioned Victor beating him out on a cherry '69 Roadrunner at an auction up in St. Cloud. That was shortly before Victor was busted. Maybe it's just a coincidence. To be honest with you though, he still sounded pissed about it. It was a limited edition with a 440-six-pack. *Stored*, not re-stored. Three thousand miles. Trophies up to the ass."

"Hey—there's no excuse!" Buck hissed through tight lips, picking up steam. "And you shouldn't have mentioned Victor's plants to the asshole in the first place. To think the son-of-a-bitch actually sold the information to someone else...he should change his name to Judas. That's what I'm going to start calling him from now on whenever I refer to him."

"We're not even sure it's true yet," I said. "Anyway, let's not get side-tracked with it right now, okay?"

"Okay," he answered, "I don't blame you for wanting to change the subject. I'd kill the bastard myself if he were my brother. I believe one should forgive one's enemies, but not before they're hanged!" He glanced over at Jade. She was listening intently, having finally picked herself clean. He turned his head to the side and spit with rancor. "Snitching mo-fo!"

We grew quiet after sundown because homes were scattered thinly along the ridgeline not too far away. The closest one was less than a half-mile away, a castle-like abode with a huge pool taking up a good half-acre. A warm breeze blew in from the Northwest carrying the distant sounds of small children playing in the pool: *"Watch me Daddy! No, watch me! Mommy! Mommy! Watch me!"*

The night was pleasant and we sat around listening to The Grateful Dead while taking occasional hits of home-grown from a softly gurgling, cream-colored ceramic bong. I lit some sandalwood incense and, stoned, we watched hoards of blood-hungry mosquitoes trying desperately to penetrate the new screening. Drifting smoke sometimes made the bugs scatter. We quietly planned for the next day until we became tired and crashed.

The sun came up hot Sunday morning, chasing away most of the mosquitoes. Buck fixed us strong, fresh-ground coffee with lots of sugar and cream in it, along with mushroom and cheese omelets and thick-sliced bacon he'd retrieved from one of the two ice chests we'd brought along. Both were packed to the brim with meat and ice and dairy products. He was obviously pleased for the opportunity of playing the capable woodsman breakfast host—and instructor.

"Don't worry about the smell of the bacon," he said, "the wind's pushing it south. Tomorrow morning I'll show you how to make the best French toast you've ever had," he crowed, "along with maple syrup, peanut butter, honey and powered sugar."

"I just know I'm going to gain ten pounds here," said Jade. "And I'm probably going to get spoiled, too."

"Don't worry about that," Buck told her. "There'll be plenty of work to do around camp to burn off the extra calories. And I sure don't mind doing most of the cooking as long as I get out of cleaning up afterwards—including the dishes. That's the part I hate the most. That's why I'm glad you're staying around the camp here most of the time, Jade, instead of me."

I stopped eating long enough to use my cell-phone to call the stable near the Senator's estate. It was called *Tiffany's Thoroughbred's*. I pretended to be an acquaintance of Kimberly's calling to confirm already-scheduled riding time, and I got a lucky break. *Yes, she's penciled in for later this morning, at eleven o'clock.* "Thanks—just as I thought," I said.

She was skipping church, which somehow made it seem all the easier. "We have to speed things up," I told my fellow Helpers.

"Sounds good to me," said Buck. "I'm just about through eating, anyway. Okay, let's get this straight now: we're going to take your car to the airport, get a rental, and be in position to grab Kimberly—all between now and eleven, right?"

"Right," I answered, looking at my watch. "Plenty of time. It's only quarter to nine. As a matter of fact, it should work out great with only a reasonable degree of good luck."

"That's all we're asking for," said Jade, crossing her fingers and holding her hand up to the sky. "A reasonable degree of luck. Charlie, Buck—for the first time in quite a while, I have a good, strong feeling that Victor's going to be free soon! It feels wonderful to finally be getting some control!"

"We're going to have more than *some* control," I said, "pretty soon, we're going to have *complete* control."

Buck asked, "I wonder if we should we give them the opportunity of cleaning up their act before we involve the media? Which way's better? I think I know, but what do you girls think?"

I looked at Jade. She shrugged her shoulders. "I guess maybe I'd give them a little time to act first...."

I said, "But what's going to prevent the cops from re-arresting Victor—and maybe *us* too—as soon as Kimberly's released? I'm thinking the media should be informed up front, to prevent anyone from retaliating—you know, either before *or* after she's released."

"Some kind of guarantee would be nice," said Buck. "I can see where a threat of publicity hanging over their heads could help keep most of them in line...but I think it's important to get that son-of-a-bitch, Sullivan, off the street right away. We should front him off to the media and cook his ass, first thing. Which reminds me, Jade, keep that revolver right at your side while we're gone—the safety off. I'll try to find a holster for it later on."

"Maybe I should just go along with you guys this morning," she suggested.

He answered, "We already went over that, Jade...you can't go because if we get nailed switching cars or kidnapping Kimberly, it's better if one of us is still free."

"We won't be gone long," I told her. We'll only be a few hours. Just stay in the gazebo away from the bugs."

"I'll be fine," she said. "I'll clean up while you're gone."

"Don't worry about wearing your mask yet," said Buck. "We'll bring her in blindfolded. And don't play any more Grateful Dead music for awhile...it'll make you feel too damned peaceful and gentle. Play something like The Doors or The Animals, okay? Put the Leon Redbone CD away, too."

"Be careful with her, okay?"

He answered, "We'll be as gentle as we can, but most of that will be up to her. We'll let her know right away that she won't be hurt as long as she cooperates. In other words, we'll let her know up front that the kidnapping is kind of a bluff, not for money."

"She might be scarred psychologically," said Jade.

I said, "She's been sheltered her whole life...she's been on easy-street for a long time."

"Yeah, she's probably got it coming anyway for some

asshole thing she did and got away with," said Buck. "What goes around, comes around. You've already confirmed that she's a natural bitch, right? What more do you want?"

"Hey—let's stop justifying what we're doing!" I scolded. "The *bottom line*, Buck, is that her father is at least *partly* to blame for what's been happening. And also for what happened to Schruder too, in a roundabout way. Let's not forget that, either. We can't start feeling sorry for her now."

"Well," Buck disagreed, "it's okay for us to feel sorry for her, but we just can't let her see it very much—at least until we find out what kind of attitude she has."

"That's what I meant," I said.

"Sure you did, Charlie. Good ole tender-hearted Charlie. Wouldn't hurt a flea Charlie. You just don't want to blow the whole thing out of being too nice, right? That's why you're the one going with me instead of Jade. She's not rough and tough enough. It takes a mean bitch like you to help me with the tough stuff, huh Charlie?

"Look at Charlie's muscles, Jade. Flex them for us once, Charlie. See? She's a real scrapper in time of need."

"Lay off," I said menacingly. "Stop insulting me like I'm a dyke or something. And Jade just might not be the softy you think she is. She's helping us pull off a kidnapping, isn't she? Braving it out here in the wild...."

Jade frowned, then whispered as harshly as she could, "Will you guys knock it off! You're confusing me. Right now I don't know whether I'm a wimp, or a heroine, or a martyr, or what. Just hurry up and accomplish your mission, okay? Don't worry about me. I'll be strong."

Chapter 13

We arrived on time in a forest-green Mercury Villager with black trim. It was Buck's idea to get something that would blend in with the forest, underneath the camouflage netting he'd found at an Army Surplus store. It was my idea to get a larger vehicle. We didn't want anything too big though, so we settled on the minivan.

Buck had stopped for some *fortification* along the way, a bottle of blueberry schnapps. We found a good spot near the stable and quickly hatched a plan to get Kimberly down off her high horse. Part of the plan called for me to wear a blonde wig and large sunglasses. I also put on some bright-red lipstick of Jade's.

I'd pretend to have an injured foot, then ask Kimberly if I could pet her horse. Instead, I'd fasten onto the horse's bridal while Buck snatched the girl out of the saddle. Kimberly didn't weigh more than a hundred and ten or so. Buck was a solid two hundred pounds, at least. He assured me that I didn't have anything to worry about, because the schnapps was only *thirty-five* percent alcohol.

We settled in to wait.

"Help yourself, Charlie," he said, "it'll loosen you up a little bit." He handed me the antique flask he'd filled. "Also, it'll go good on top of that omelet you had earlier. Just don't drink too much...it's pretty sweet and might make you sick since you don't have much of a tolerance going. Unlike me."

"No more than one for my nerves," I said. "Because also unlike you, I seldom get drunk."

"I know, you're the type that only gets completely whacked out on weed, huh?"

"I limit that too, in case you haven't noticed."

"Yeah, I've noticed. Well, that's good, because they're saying now that women get lung cancer easier than men. It's not like I've had a bunch of car accidents or anything."

"Your ticket just hasn't been punched yet, Buck," I assured him.

"One thing I've noticed though, when I drink I start getting pissed-off about shit a lot easier."

"I know, and you start swearing a lot more too."

"I can't help it," he said. "It just comes with the territory of getting pissed, I guess...which reminds me." He reached into a hip pocket. "I wrote this last night, before I went to sleep. I told you I was going to do something about that hair-testing shit. Here, read this, tell me what you think. I'll keep my eye out for the girl."

"I thought you were totally bombed last night."

"I wasn't as tired as you two. That red hash Jade was holding out on us got me focusing on some deep shit, like about how businesses and politicians are supposed to take their cues from public opinion, you know, and they ignore us instead."

"Yeah?"

"Why do you always say that like a question?"

"What? What'd I say?"

"You always say 'yeah' like a question, instead of just agreeing with me about what I'm saying."

"I didn't notice. Maybe I'm subconsciously compelled to question everything you say...because you're so full of shit most of the time."

He disregarded the insult. "Well, read it...go ahead. I'll leave you alone while you read it."

"Okay." I started to read to myself.

"No—I mean out loud. I want to hear it again, too."

I rolled my eyes. "Okay, 'Dear Anheuser-Busch—'"

"—See, I feel especially strong about drug-testing because I used to be a truck driver and the bastards made it hard for me. Until I found out how to fool the system, that is—I'll tell you about that later. Basically, all you have to do is substitute someone else's fresh, warm piss with your own. Get it fresh and keep it under your arm, you know...go ahead and read. Sorry."

"Are you finished, because if you're not...."

He solemnly nodded his head and—as though to prove his sincerity, I guess—took another drink of the blueberry schnapps. "I was just pointing out how discriminating it is against certain groups of American workers. Go ahead now, sorry."

I stared at him and waited a full ten seconds before beginning again. "'This is to advise you that I will no longer be purchasing any of your rank beer. I spent time in the Marines, and it wasn't so alcohol producers could violate my civil liberties. How hypocritical. You want to test for drugs, including marijuana, while you peddle another drug that's legal but much more damaging to peoples' health,

and to society at large. You expect me to give you my business after finding out that you hair-test your employees?
Forget it.'"

"That's with an exclamation mark."

"Actually, there's two here, Buck," I said, glancing at
him and pausing again. "'Forget it!! I've noticed that the
first to be down-trodden are either kids, or prisoners, or
else soldiers. Those without many so-called rights.
Mandatory DNA samples for prisoners, mandatory shots
and drug testing for soldiers, mandatory drug testing for
kids in after-school programs. Testing kits for parents. Poor
people are welfare will probably be next. Maybe the
homeless. You freedom stealers always target the weakest
first, the ones with no voice—like your employees, then go
after the rest of us. I hope the Beermakers Union tears your
ass up. The same goes for General Motors and those hypocritical pricks that run the casinos. Here is what I'm doing,
personally, to resist your freedom-stealing bullshit.'"

"I just made up some lies here."

"'My poker club, my entire genealogy club and most of
my friends at the local American Legion and VFW halls
have decided to stop drinking your putrid products.
Additionally, I am starting a grass-roots effort at banning
anything connected with Anheuser-Busch. The effort is
already succeeding. You should feel shame over this hair
testing. Drug-testing companies are making tons of money
stealing our freedom. You are off base, un-American, and
most people think alike. I have so far dissuaded nineteen
hundred and eighty-four good citizens from drinking your
unwholesome, un-American products. Those who would

take away our precious liberties in the name of safety deserve neither, Ben Franklin. Your customers aren't taking this lying down, so prepare to lose a significant amount of business, Butt-holes!'"

"Well, what do you think of *that!*"

"It certainly can't hurt, I guess, unless they try to sue you."

"That's the only reason I changed 'Assholes' to 'Butt-holes.' Is that all?"

"What'd you want me to say? You made a few good points, but it won't do much good. Watch out for Kimberly—and don't get carried away with that schnapps, okay?"

"Sure. Why won't it do any good?"

"Lack of public sentiment...no one gives a shit. Most people figure if you don't have anything to hide, why should you care. Of course people *should* care, because it's all about personal freedoms. Sorry to say it Buck, but your views will probably just be thrown on the steaming dung heap of wasted personal opinions...just more hot air rising up. That was a good idea beefing up the numbers, though."

"Thanks," he said. "Say, how come politicians don't have to get tested? The bastards—they're the ones who should be tested first, setting an example, as long as they think all this freedom-stealing is such a good thing. Why aren't they tested? I might write someone a letter about that too. Who would I write, Charlie? How about George Bush? I mean the little one—the former coke-head who let that Christian women get whacked by the State of Texas. The one who got the gravy job during the war because of being born with a silver spoon up his ass. Oh well, at least he did serve...just barely...just enough to have a little fun."

I said, "I'd go right to the top on that one."

"Yeah? The President? That asshole? All he'd probably do is move the drug-testing companies to Little Rock and then buy stock in...sshhh, I hear a horse coming!"

As planned, I quickly slipped out of the bushes and sat down on a boulder beside the trail and took off one of my hiking shoes and a sock. I felt the schnapps glowing warmly in my stomach as the single horse's hoofs sounded louder and louder in a canter. I rubbed my exposed, moist foot nervously. The sun's direct rays felt good soaking into it, and the hot July breeze quickly dried it. A pair of unusual visitors suddenly flew out of a nearby bush and perched in a nearby oak. It was a pair of rose-breasted grosbeaks. I'd expected to see common sparrows or robins, or perhaps a couple of blue-jays or cardinals.

Kimberly suddenly came into view riding a large white and liver-spotted appaloosa. Her pretty blond hair was flapping loosely behind her in the wind. I pretended not to see her at first. A slight rustle of the bushes off to my right indicated to me that Buck had re-positioned himself one final time, and he was ready.

I pretended to carefully stand up on my *good* foot and hobble around a few steps, then I sat back down as though to study my injured foot. The handsome quarter horse slowed to a trot. I looked up and smiled and waved through my false pain. The pretty blue-eyed rider gave me a short wave back and expertly brought the excited stallion to a halt with one firm pull on the reins.

"Are you all right?" she asked.

"I think so," I answered, grimacing, feigning sharp pain. "It's probably just sprained. At least I hope that's all it is. But it sure hurts."

"Well, I'm in kind of a hurry, but do you need a lift?"

"A lift? Oh, no, that's okay, especially if you're in a hurry," I said. "I wouldn't want to put you out any...I can hobble back to my car on one foot. Thanks anyway." I stood up and pretended to test my injured foot with some weight and winced, then managed to cheer up some. "That sure is a beautiful horse. Do you mind if I pet him—just on the forehead? What's his name?"

"I don't mind," she answered, "but *he* does...Charlie's real skittish with strangers."

I felt like laughing. "Oh, is that his name?" I'd have to stall her and come up with another idea. "Is he yours?"

"Yes. Well, I hope you make it back to your—"

Buck suddenly clapped his hands loudly and shook the bushes. The handsome appaloosa bolted sideways off the trail and began bucking all around wildly in an area thick with young white pines. Kimberly held on gamely for about five seconds, then she flew high up into the air—as though in slow motion—and come back down, landing heavily and squarely on her ass. She was momentarily blinded by fluffy pine boughs.

Buck sprinted over to her with his Zoro mask on, as planned, and shooed the horse away. Then he quickly gagged and blindfolded and bound the girl before she could even begin to think about what was happening. The poor thing—it was just one disappointment after another. And here she'd been in such a hurry, too.

I cautiously obeyed all the rules of the road on the way back to our hideout...well, except for being a bit stoned, about enough to help me fit into the weird circumstances unfolding. Buck and I didn't communicate much on the twenty-minute ride back. That felt weird too.

He came up with the idea of using Chevy engines for our temporary names. Jade was Helper 283, I was Helper 396, and he was Helper 427—of course. When I suggested Helper 454 for my name instead of Helper 396, he routinely brushed the idea aside as being ridiculous. Then he reminded me to keep a sharp eye out while I turned off the main road onto the trail. "Helper 396, keep your eye out," he commanded.

I felt the schnapps kicking in and saluted him, saying, "Aye, aye, Sir!—I mean Helper 427!"

He pretended to think deeply, then said, "Oh, I see...I guess maybe I shouldn't have offered that to you back there."

"Too late now," I said. The flask had jammed up halfway out of his left hip pocket when he'd sat down. I reached over and snatched the container before he could stop me. After first glancing up into the rear-view mirror, I quickly went down the slope about fifty yards out of sight and stopped and took another swig of the schnapps.

"You're going to sleep like a baby tonight," Buck said, grinning.

"Yeah, but during your watch, Helper 427. Don't worry about me."

"Don't say I didn't warn you," he said. "Jade's never seen you drunk before, has she? This should be pretty funny."

"Just keep your hands to yourself *this* time," I warned him sternly, "and everything will be all right."

"You don't have to worry about that. The only way I'll ever get physical with you again will be to help keep your ass out of trouble. You'd probably get off on it too," he said sourly, his voice trailing off.

"Try it again and you'll find out," I said.

"What in the hell are you getting so frisky about? Get drunk enough and maybe I'll *have* to get physical with you," he half-joked. "Go ahead, have another drink."

Jade came out of the gazebo tree-house cautiously, as though possibly uncertain about whether or not she was supposed to have her mask on. She saw us being frivolous.

"What's wrong, didn't you find her?" she asked, concerned. Her voice came out a little too loud. She looked at us sheepishly.

Buck raised an index finger to his lips and said in a low voice, "The mission has been accomplished, Helper 283." He hastily began covering the Villager over with one of the camouflage nets, but stopped for a moment to look back at Jade again. He saw the look of unbelief on her face and jerked his thumb toward the rear of the minivan. "Come see for yourself," he said casually.

Jade carefully minced her way through the weeds to the rented minivan, following the narrow path Buck had smoothed down for her. She peered in, then put her hand to her mouth in astonishment. "I though you were just kidding," she said. "Wow, that was fast!"

Buck and I both laughed at the expression on her face.

"We don't fuck around," Buck said drunkenly.

I agreed. "No, we shlurtainly don't!"

Jade's eyebrows went up and she looked even more concerned. She sounded urgent. "Well, let's hurry up and make her comfortable. She's probably scared to death."

"Leave her blindfolded for now, though, okay Helper 283?" Buck said. "And tell her she'll be gagged again if she makes so much as a *peep*," he added harshly. "You guys go ahead and take over now. I'm going to take myself a little a nap. I was up real late last night writing that damned, probably worthless letter."

"What letter?" asked Jade, thinking she was missing out on something. "I thought we were going to—"

"—It wasn't anything important," I interrupted, gazing over at Buck. I grinned stupidly and stuck my tongue out at him.

"No, this is what's important to you," he said, pointing to his crotch. "Dick and nuts, Baby, dick and nuts!"

Jade looked at us—back and forth, very much astonished. Buck and I both laughed hysterically.

"What's going on with you two?"

"Helper 427," I said, "maybe you should offer Helper 283 some of that schnapps, too, before you go crash."

He agreed, saying, "Now Jade, you know that virtue is just insufficient temptation. Here, have one shot."

"Oh...*now* I see," she said, slowly moving her head back and forth. "No, thanks...under the circumstances, I don't think so."

"Now why doesn't that surprise me a bit!" Buck exclaimed. "This only goes to prove that virtue really *is* more respectable than money! You may be rich, Jade, but you're way past all the crap that goes with it, because you're virtually a...I mean, you're a virtual...uh, you're a *respectable* woman! Now Charlie, how does that make *you* feel?"

Chapter 14

After eating too much and taking an unexpected nap myself, I apologized to Jade and then asked her about Kimberly.

"Oh—she's okay, but how are you?"

I said, "Whew...I didn't think it'd hit me that hard."

"Sometimes we learn the hard way, huh? Well, Kimberly knows we aren't going to hurt her—that we're just forcing her father to help us with a good cause. Her blindfold is still on. She's taking the whole thing surprisingly well." She smiled gently and added, "I wish I could say the same about you."

"No shit," I answered. "I'm feeling kind of foolish...and not too great otherwise, either."

"There's some aspirin in the first aid kit."

"That's all right," I said. "I'm just thirsty. Real thirsty. Is Buck up yet?"

"Hardly," she said. "Actually, it's been nice and quiet. I finished the letter to the media...and I got a good start on the letter to Kimberly's Father. Short and to the point, just like you suggested."

"Good," I said. "I don't want this to drag on any longer than absolutely necessary. Let's still get them out today if we can."

"That was the plan," she reminded me.

"What time is it, anyway⸮"

"Just after two," she said, smiling strangely. "You must be hungry."

"Don't be a smart-ass, Jade," I said. "You saw how much I ate...that's partly what got me so tired...plus it's awfully warm out, too, isn't it. That's probably why Buck's still crashed."

Jade looked over in the direction of the lean-to. "We should let him sleep as long as possible," she advised me. Then, seeing the pained smirk spreading across my face, she added, "No, I mean so he can stay awake and keep watch tonight." She became more serious. "I hope he holds it together all right."

"Oh, he will," I assured her. "I'm an optimist, so—in the long run, anyway—I believe he'll end up doing more good than harm."

She rested a hand on my shoulder. "I'm not mad at you, Charlie...and I'm grateful for your help."

"Hey—we're all working together as a team and holding it together pretty well so far," I said. "Just not real well." I patted her hand. "It's going to work. All this hassle will be worth it in the end."

She suddenly brightened up. "Well, let's hurry up and get these letters out then, okay⸮ What're we waiting for⸮ Here, why don't you read the one to the *Star Tribune*. Don't worry, I printed it real sloppy with my left hand—same as before—and I changed the way I make some of my letters, just in case. And I made reference to the letter we sent them before—the one that didn't do any good. This one simply says that Senator Patch's daughter has been kidnapped and that she'll be held until justice is served—in other words, until Victor Stamate is released. Oh, and I mentioned that the Chief Prosecutor for Bunyan County was murdered by Luther Sullivan."

"I bet that'll perk their ears up," I said. The afternoon sun was intense and I squinted and fumbled through my purse looking for my sunglasses. "And what have The Helpers said to the rotten Senator so far?"

"Here," Jade said, reaching into her single blouse pocket. "Read it, tell me what you think."

"That's okay," I answered, "go ahead and give me the meat of it...damn, I might have to hit that first-aid kit after all."

"I basically just introduced The Helpers and told the Senator that his daughter had been kidnapped, then I accused him of helping to foster the climate that's making it so easy for innocent people to be locked up...mandatory Federal sentences and wrongful seizures, you know. I'm right at the point of telling him our demands. Do you think we should include one of the extra copies of the tape we had made? It'd require a special envelope."

"Yeah, we should probably go for the maximum effect," I said. "We should send a copy to the media, too. We can stop at Kinko's in Bloomington to get what we need. What did Buck do with them?"

"I don't know," she answered.

"Knowing him, he probably buried them somewhere...like an Indian, like he does with his dope. Let's get everything ready, then wake him up, okay?"

"Yes, good," she answered. "I just wish I could go with

you this afternoon, though, instead of staying here."

"Maybe Buck won't feel like going," I said. "He won't make good company for me—that's for sure. Not with a groggy hangover."

Jade fixed some extra-strong coffee, and I took a cup over to Buck.

"Hell no, I don't want no fucking coffee!" he yelled hoarsely.

"Sshhh," I said. "Don't forget where you're at."

"I know where I'm at," he groaned. "In Dr. Frankenstein's laboratory...and you're trying to turn me into a wide-awake, drunken monster...go away!"

"We have to go get the letters and tapes in the mail."

"Today's Sunday, Asshole."

"Knock it off. I know it's Sunday. Kinko's is open 'til six—I called. Come on, we've got to get the letters and tapes out—what'd you do with them?"

"They're in the bottom of my quiver...under a deckle. Get 'em and go."

"Under a what?"

"A deckle...it's a German...never mind. Go ahead and get 'em. You have my permission."

"Listen," I said, "do you want to just stay here and recover for awhile? Jade kind of wants to get away for awhile anyway. Watching Kimberly all by herself was quite a strain on her, I think."

"Good idea. Go."

"Just a minute—here, you should drink this coffee."

"Charlie, damn it, it's ninety fucking degrees out!"

"You have to stay awake to watch Kimberly while we're gone...I hope I can trust you with her."

"What the hell's that supposed to mean?" he asked, frowning menacingly. His eyes were fire-red from the alcohol. He tried to sit up and gave up after two tries. "What do you think, that I might go over and pop her while she's tied up—hey, *kinky*, not a bad idea! Ouch, my head."

"There's some pain relievers in the first-aid kit," I advised him. "No—I mean it, you can't fall back asleep. Would you rather ride along with me and let Jade stay, or do you want to stay?"

"Why can't we both stay and you go by yourself?"

"We already went over that last night, remember? It's too dangerous for just one person. Don't forget, there's a murderer out there, and he's probably looking for us...and the sick bastard has a gun named Dr. Jack."

"Okay," he said. He finally sat up, then drunkenly scooted himself back and rested against the rear of his flimsy lean-to. "I've got to get out of here...into the open air in the shade...in a few minutes, I mean. Couldn't you have made some cold coffee?"

"I didn't think of it."

"No, I guess not," he muttered. "Well, give it here. Thanks anyway. Don't leave yet—give me a chance to wake up first."

"You going to be all right?"

"Yeah. Between the coffee and a joint, I'll be okay...and something for the pain. Take the gun with you. I've got my bow, plus the shotgun if the action gets too heavy, which I doubt it will."

I said, "You can get some more sleep as soon as we get back. We won't be more than about an hour. This whole thing will be over...shortly."

"I've got a new line of jokes to work on, anyway, while you're gone," he mumbled weakly."

"Okay."

"About stupid warnings...on products, you know."

"Great. You'll have something to do, to think about."

"Oh, I've got plenty of shit to think about," he muttered, falling forward slightly and catching himself. He slowly sank back again. "Let me ask you a question, okay? I'm just wondering how you're going to answer it." He took a careful sip of the hot coffee and made a face at me. "Do you believe people have a right to overthrow the fucking government, you know, by force and violence if necessary?"

I said, "You really amaze me, Buck. How can you be thinking of something that profound in your condition? Why don't you give it a break for awhile. It's not going to help your headache any, I know that."

"That was my train of thought...what I was thinking about before you woke me up."

"Oh yeah? So now you're even dreaming about gun control, huh? I don't want to talk about it right now, okay. I'm telling you nicely, Buck."

"Can you just answer that one question?"

"No—because then you'll want to respond to what I say, no matter what it is. Forget it."

"Well, people have a right to abolish a government... if it isn't operating right."

"There, you said what you wanted to say. It's out of your system now."

"No, it's not out of my system," he said, scooting up a bit higher. "You should talk to some folks who lived under criminal governments and survived before you swallow the crap jammed down your throat by...by the attack dogs in the press. *Democrats.*"

"Holy shit, I'm getting out of here. Just stay awake, okay? And try to keep the girl comfortable—which includes not brow-beating her to death about gun control, or your conspiracy theory, either. None of it Buck, not about abortion, or the death penalty...nothing."

"You don't see it, do you Charlie?" he asked me, completely unfazed. "What we're doing here right now is overthrowing the government...or at least altering it. What I'm thinking is what I'm doing—see? And what I'm doing is what I'm thinking. That's why I'm here, today, doing this and thinking...the way I am."

"I've got to get going, Buck. One thing I'll admit though, is that you're even more noble than I thought you were. Keep up the good brainwork."

"Yeah, Charlie...I'm trying to make the world a better place for assholes like you to live in. See you later. And good luck."

"What's that supposed to mean?"

"Nothing. I just mean be careful, that's all. What did you girls end up saying in the letter to the media?"

"Not much. No preaching. We just made reference to the previous bomb scare, then just informed them of the kidnapping. Oh, and about Schruder's assisted suicide.

They're getting a copy of the tape, too."

"Good," he said weakly, "because those bastards are guilty, too—*shit!* Would you mind getting me those pills after all, Charlie? Thanks. Yeah, those bastards can have a lot of sway and impact on the average, stupid citizen. They're not objective, because of that liberal bias they usually have going—in the wrong direction. It boils down to a simple breach of trust, Charlie. I've been thinking about writing a letter to the Minnesota News Council about how the local media here is treating Victor's case...*mistreating* it, I should say. They avoid and misstate and suppress shit all the time. Maybe I should write to Rolling Stone and High Times, too. The media bastards—they're always on the wrong side, and they're right in bed with the politicians. *Democrats!* Oh, my head."

"I'm just glad Jade wrote those letters instead of you," I said. "See you later. We'll be right back. Think more good thoughts and try to stay cheerful, okay?"

He barely had enough energy to lift his hand, but he did manage to point to the general area of his crotch. "Dick and nuts, Baby," he said, grinning weakly, stupidly. His hand flopped back down heavily and he suddenly crashed through the back of his flimsy lean-to.

I pointed back at him and laughed as loudly as I dared to, then slapped my leg several times and laughed some more. "God's punishment!" I jeered. "Wow! Great! What a supreme asshole—can't even build an overnight shelter right!"

After leaving Kinko's, we headed straight for the West

Bloomington post office, where I deposited the letters into one of several drive-up mail drops. No time for pleasure cruising today. Everything went as planned—that is, right up until a large man driving a large, gold-colored car slammed on his brakes and started following us. That occurred on Old Shakopee Road, about halfway back to our hideaway.

I continued driving the Villager normally and told Jade that she might want to consider getting the old revolver out and taking the safety off, just in case. The gold car was still behind us when I passed by the trail turn-off. I impulsively tooted the horn once to alert Buck of a possible problem. He was suspicious by nature anyway, so I figured he'd think about the toot and take appropriate measures. Unless he crashed again.

I sped up to about seventy and the gold car stayed with me while keeping a nominal distance back. The road ahead suddenly dropped down into a deep ravine and began a series of sharp twists, then it dropped even farther on a short straightaway and rose back up to the ridge in a long, curving stretch. Then the land was flat again.

I glanced at Jade. The gun was trembling in her lap. "What are you going to do?" she asked.

"I don't know," I said. "But maybe you'd better put the safety back on for now."

"I didn't take it off yet," she said.

"Who do you think it is?"

"I don't know. He's hanging too far back to tell. But if he's a cop, he probably called in reinforcements by now."

"I've got an idea," I said. "And it might be the only way

for us to keep from getting nailed."

"Go for it," she said. "What do we have to lose? I won't have to shoot anybody though, will I?"

"That's not part of the plan," I assured her. I braked quickly and had just enough time to complete a three-point turn before the gold car came into view again. I punched the accelerator to the floor and sped up quickly. Just before we passed by the other car—a Caprice, the fat man inside plopped a flashing blue light down on the dash. I kept the pedal to the floor going back toward Buck.

"It's Tipton!" we both exclaimed together.

"I'm not surprised," I said. "They probably found my car at the airport and did some nosing around. That was kind of stupid of us—I mean me, huh?. They've probably been on the lookout for a forest-green Villager all after-noon. We should've used a taxi to get to the airport. Get ready to hold on," I cautioned Jade. "Put your seat belt on and don't be scared—I can drive good fast!"

We coursed back down through the ravine again, then shot up the other side. I kept the accelerator plastered to the floor until I hit eighty-five. Glancing up into the rearview mirror, I saw the gold Caprice coming on fast, about a quarter-mile back.

"Hold on now!" I yelled. I slammed on the brakes just as we dropped down out of Tipton's sight a short distance from the trail turnoff. Jade lurched forward violently and almost hit her head on the dash. The .44 Colt flew out of her lap and landed onto the floor with a heavy thud. I felt the wheels of the minivan lift as we almost flipped making the turn into the trail. I goosed the throttle on and off while keeping my other foot over the brake and we bucked and heaved and sideswiped quite a number of saplings while disappearing down into the lush vegetation. I drove another fifty yards or so and turned off the ignition.

"Come on!" I yelled to Jade. "Grab the gun and follow me. I don't know whether he saw me turn off or not—probably not, but we can't be sure. We'll be ready for him if he follows us in."

We hurried the rest of the way down the trail and found Buck in position where the trail ended at the circular clearing. He'd transformed himself into a camouflaged statue again, minus the face paint this time. He was casually leaning against the rough bark of a large white pine. A sharp broadtip hunting arrow was notched in the string of his bow, and he held two more arrows at the ready in his other hand.

"Trouble?" he asked.

"Maybe," I answered. "Tipton started following us—"

"We didn't know it was him at first," Jade said, very much out of breath. "Here!" She held the revolver out to him nervously. "The safety's still on...I think. It fell on the floor of the van."

"Charlie, you take it and go hide nearby and cover me if necessary," he ordered. "Jade, you go over and stay with Kimberly. She's still tied up. The shotgun's leaning against the tree-house—outside, in back of it—if you need it. The safety's on. Keep her quiet. Go ahead—move out *quickly*, soldier!

"Charlie, if he comes in, I'll get the drop on him with the bow here. All you've got to do is stay out of sight and cover me, okay? You got it? You just cover me if he goes for his gun, which he won't be able to do—I guarantee that! The fat bastard. What nerve! Okay—get into position out of sight now. *Move it, soldier!*"

"Knock it off," I said.

"Man, what a combination!" he said excitedly, "—alcohol, Tylenol, THC and, let me see, what else? Oh—caffeine! Not to mention a good dose of adrenaline to push it all along. What a rush! You can't slow me down now, Charlie! Tipton's ass is *mine*—that fat pig! I hope he does show up. Okay, hush now!" he whispered to me harshly.

I watched him fade back into the forest as a ghostly splotch of moving green and brown, then I moved off to the right about a dozen paces or so and squatted down behind an ancient oak tree to wait. I checked the old revolver's safety one more time. It was odd to think of the gun as old because it looked so new. The safety was definitely off, and I was ready.

Chapter 15

I was just beginning to feel smug about eluding Tipton when I heard a twig snap behind me.

"Don't even think about it, Little Lady," the fat lawman warned in low voice. He shot a hand over my shoulder and grabbed the gun while squeezing the back of my neck with his other thick hand.

I turned around slowly. He was dressed in civilian clothes, which included a loud Hawaiian shirt, this time mostly bright green and orange. Sweat was coursing down his fat face in tiny rivulets so profusely that the shirt's collar quickly darkened before my eyes. He'd apparently been unarmed until I was dumb enough let him have my gun.

"Where'd the other gal go—Mrs. Stamate?" he demanded to know. "And why'd you turn off into here?" His fat head swiveled back and forth on massive shoulders as he peered into the forest. "Huh?" He squeezed the back of my neck again, then roughly jerked me up to my feet. "You'd better start coughing up some answers, Girl," he said, squeezing my neck very hard this time.

"Ouch, you son-of-a-bitch!" I yelled. I tried to squirm away, but he tightened his grip.

"Who's going to help you out here? Huh Little Girl?" He paused for effect, then squeezed the back of my neck again with a vice-like grip. "Huh? Your pretty friend—that other trouble-maker? Where'd she go? You should've kept your nose out of things. Call her over—"

He suddenly let go of my neck and turned his head up to the sky and bellowed loudly up through the treetops. It was a long, bull-like wail that grew higher and higher in pitch and intensity until it finally came back down under the trees, ending with a series of short screams and little, wet, crying sputters. The first arrow had plowed deeply into one of Tubby Tipton's upper legs from behind, stopping immediately after hitting bone and making a sickeningly dull, almost rubbery, noise. In his excruciating pain, he accidentally squeezed off a shot with the revolver, blowing a large, dark, smoking circle into the tip of his left sneaker, exactly where his big toe had been just a moment earlier.

Another broadtip hunting arrow suddenly cut through the air, cleanly sailing through Tipton's forearm and causing his hand to let go of the antique revolver. As soon as the gun hit the ground, I snatched it up and quickly backed away. Tipton started turning around and around in little circles, faster and faster, trying to grab at the arrow stuck fast in his leg. But he was simply too fat to reach it.

I rubbed the back of my neck and backed up even farther away from the spectacle in front of me in disbelief. I paused long enough to look around for Buck.

Tipton's white sneaker was growing bright red at the top. Big droplets of blood were flying everywhere, including at me, so I backed up a little more before stopping again. He kept whirling around and around like a dog trying to catch its tail, except that he was trying to catch an arrow stuck in his leg instead. Finally he stood still, trembling, as he tried to take stock of his injuries.

Buck walked casually up to him and spit in his face. Just as casually, he watched the spittle while it mixed with sweat and ran down the injured man's chin and short neck, ending up on his already-drenched collar. The fat lawman's chest was heaving. He was breathing deeply through his mouth.

"Kind of hot out today, isn't it?" Buck asked him. "Certainly not the kind of weather a fat slob wants to be jumping all around the woods like a grasshopper with his balls caught in a lawnmower. What brings you out this way, Sheriff?"

"I...I...I...."

"Stop that damned shaking and *speak up, soldier!* Get a fucking grip! Now, suppose you start off by explaining to the *Little Lady* over there why you were hurting her neck, then maybe we can take a look at those little flesh wounds you got yourself there...you're awfully careless for a cop, you know that? It's just a good thing for you that I got a lot of first aid training in the Marines. You're going to need a tourniquet for that foot wound if it keeps bleeding like that. Your arm's all right. Your leg I can help some, but you're going to have to stop that damned moving around and shaking for a minute. Hold still now." He walked around behind the Sheriff and squatted down a moment, then quickly snapped the arrow off, causing Tipton to wail again once loudly. "The rest of the arrow, you'll have to wait on...they'll have to cut it out, unless you want me to...it's stuck in the bone pretty good. In the meantime, we'll pump you up with a ton of Tylonol and a couple of shots of schnapps—have you ever tried blueberry? It's not bad. You'll be just fine until we get you to a doctor. But unfortunately for you, that might not be for a few days. But don't worry, I'll help you keep the wounds nice and clean."

"Wh-what are you talking about! I've got to get to a doctor...and *fast!*"

"No, you don't have to worry about that," Buck said seriously. "We're going to take care of you for a day or two—or three, whatever it takes. The only thing is, you might not get as much to eat as you're used to. You should pretend like you're in a hospital—you know, like on a special diet or something. We don't have that much extra grub. Hand over the keys to the car now, Fat Boy."

"I left them in the car," Tipton whimpered.

"Did you call anyone else in?"

"No. Listen, Foster...my leg is killing me."

"Where's Sullivan right now?"

"I don't know...really, I don't. All I know is he's out looking for you guys too. You'd better hurry up and get me to a hospital, before this gets even more serious."

"*Even more serious?*" I interjected, rubbing my neck again. "What a joke. It's already serious enough—that's why you were crunching my neck a minute ago, remember Butt-head? Because the situation is so serious. Well guess what? You hit it right on the nose, because it's going to get even more serious."

"What do you mean? What are you going to do?"

I looked at Buck. He took the cue and continued the

speech. "We're going to keep you out of commission for as long as it takes for our friend Victor to hit the street again. That shouldn't take long though, because we just picked up Senator Patch's daughter earlier today. See, you're right on time here, because the party's just beginning. We're going to hold her, too, until Victor's released. See how serious it is? But at least you'll have one another for company—just not very good company. Now get moving...follow right along behind Ms. Pierce there, before I put another arrow into your fat ass. Now it's *your* turn to see what it's like to be fucked with.

"And is that a brand new Caprice I saw you drive up in? Nice. It should be bring a good price at a chop-shop. Probably bought with forfieture money—not tax money— anyway, right? I've heard that practically everything at the Sheriff's department was either bought with forfeiture money or else seized outright—refrigerators and big-screen television sets, even weight-lifting gear. Is that true? If it is, you should be ashamed of yourself. Hey, speaking of being ashamed, that reminds me. Did you hear on the news last week about that peeping cop shit? You guys can't do that. Cops aren't allowed to just go around peeking into peoples' windows, the same with going around hurting folks— right, Charlie?

"Stop fussing about those little flesh wounds now. I'll duck-tape the shit out of them to stop the bleeding when I tape the rest of you up—which will include your big mouth if you give us any shit. Yeah, this is some real serious shit, all right, isn't it? Get your fat ass moving a little faster—we don't have much daylight left. And in case you're wondering—no, I don't feel a bit sorry that you forced me to do this to you...any more questions now? No? Okay then, shut the hell up and keep moving, *soldier!* You stupid cops never learn, do you? Just like dumb grunts...move a little faster now, before I sink another one of these arrows into your fat ass. And in case you're wondering, no I'm not kidding. Am I Charlie?"

"I just hope my neck's okay," I said, wincing.

Jade had put her mask on when she'd heard the thunderous shot from the .44 Colt, then she'd taken Kimberly a short distance down a nearby deer trail to wait. It was good, clear, rational thinking. She came back into the clearing as soon as she spotted us. The girl was in tow, blindfolded. She led Kimberly back into the gazebo tree-house and sat her down, then came to the screen-door. "What in the *world*...."

"We done got ourselves another one!" Buck exclaimed proudly, prodding the sheriff to keep moving. "A *big* one this time—not a scrawny one!"

I was already beginning to feel sorry for Rudy Tipton.

Buck marched over to the first aid kit and shook out several large Tylonol tablets and handed them to the injured Sheriff. "Here," he said, "take these and...here, swallow them down with this." He took the flask out his back pocket and handed it to the shocked Sheriff.

"I need more help than *this*," Tipton whined. "I need a *doctor*." He was still trembling, though not as bad as before.

"Fuck all that shit," said Buck. He began removing small packages of pre-cut gauze squares from the first-aid kit.

"This is all you need...stand still now if you want me to help you." He opened the packages, one by one, then put several squares together to form a bandage and placed it over the wound on Tipton's forearm. "Hold it there a minute," he commanded the fat Sheriff.

He briskly walked over to the lean-to and returned with a new roll of shiny silver duct tape and began stripping off a long piece. He ripped the piece off by roughly tearing at it sideways, then he wrapped it around Tipton's fat arm twice, covering the patch. "There," he said, "next one now...turn around." He took a jackknife out of a front pocket of his pants and cut Tipton's bloody trouser leg off even with the bottom of his beefy buttock. "Lift your leg up," he commanded, then slid the severed pant leg down over the bloody sneaker.

"Keep on eye on him," he reminded me. "Keep him covered."

He said to Tipton, "Okay, hold this bandage in place now—same as the other one." He then wrapped the roll of duck tape around and around the poor Sheriff's thick leg and smoothly cut it off with the jackknife. "There. Now only one more. Take off your shoe," he commanded.

"I don't want to," Tipton whined. "It'll hurt...."

"I've got to stop the bleeding," Buck said. "Don't be such a pussy." He glanced up at me and snickered. "Not that I've got anything against pussy." He looked back to Tipton. "Get that damned shoe off now—I don't have much time. For one thing, I've still got to get rid of your car tonight. Charlie," he said, "we've got to talk as soon as I get this asshole tied up good."

"No shit," I answered. "I'd say things have changed significantly."

"Yeah, but maybe in our favor," Buck said optimistically. "It depends on how you look at it...for one thing, there's one less asshole out there hunting us down now."

Whimpering and still shaking a little bit, Tipton gingerly took off his blood-soaked sneaker. Blood poured out onto the wooden floor of the gazebo.

Buck shook his head back and forth. "What a damned mess. You might not want to look at it, Rudy," he advised. "And just for the record, I can't take credit for that one. Let me see it now—whoa, the sucker's *clean gone*, Rudy!"

"Oh no, oh no, oh no," whimpered the Sheriff. "No, no, no."

Buck asked, "You want me to go back and look for it?"

The Sheriff looked down at his foot for the first time and was instantly horrified. The fact that his big toe was actually missing seemed to take a long time to sink in. Finally, he looked back up at Buck with a glimmer of hope. "Do you think they'd be able to save it?"

"I don't know," said Buck, "but if it were me, I'd definitely give it a try. It'd help you to keep your balance better for one thing—not to mention not looking funny when you go to the beach. Stay here by Charlie and I'll go look for it—or maybe I should say, what's left of it. I'll put it on ice for you if I find it. That's the least I can do. You never know, they can work real miracles these days. You'd definitely be better off having that toe back—for balance, if nothing else." He chuckled good-naturedly. "Hey, that reminds me of that saying about beauty only being skin deep, you know, but ugly going all the way to the bone. Well, in your case here, there's no bone left for the ugly to go to."

Buck paused just long enough to glance up at me. "Will you remind me of that later on, Charlie? There's a good stand-up line there somewhere. Right now I've got to fix this Asshole's bleeding stump. He asked Tipton, "Is it starting to hurt yet?"

"That's a dumb question, Buck," I said. "Of course it hurts. Stop tormenting the man now...remember that cruel and unusual punishment stuff you're always talking about."

"I'm not tormenting him, I'm fixing him up," he answered. "Sometimes the pain doesn't come until much later, because of the shock to the nerves or whatever. Tear out some more of those guaze squares for me, okay? Thanks. A lot of them this time—twice as many."

I quickly put together about ten of the squares and handed them to him.

"Look away now," he told Tipton. He quickly placed the thick bandage over the bloody stump in one confident and smooth move.

"Oh, oh, oh!" Tipton yelped, giving Buck several reflexive kicks with the heel part of his foot.

"Hold still, damn it! Buck admonished him. "I'm trying to help you here!"

He grabbed the roll of duck tape again and cut off a short piece and smoothed it down over the already-red bandage on the stump, then wound more tape around and around the Sheriff's remaining toes several times. Finally, he ripped the tape off sideways and patted the loose end down roughly over the top of the injured foot, about the way a rodeo cowboy would finish a calf-roping event—with his arm outstretched to make sure the timer caught it.

"Ouch! Ouch! Tipton yelled.

"Sshhh. Keep it down," Buck warned him. "I'm not going to look for your stupid toe if you don't be more quiet. You must be getting some feeling back down there. Wow!—I was just thinking, it's a good thing you didn't shoot your dick and nuts off back there, huh Fat Boy? Ha! You'd have to look for that mess *yourself!*"

"Knock it off, Buck," I said. "That's totally unnecessary."

"Most *all* of this shit's been totally unnecessary," Buck shot back. "That's why we're all gathered together for this little party in the first place—because of all the *totally unnecessary* bullshit. "Wouldn't you agree with that now, Rudy? Huh? Speak up Fat Boy. Wouldn't it be simply wonderful if none of this had ever happened? Actually, we might be at the beginning of the end of what your sorry ass helped start in the first place: putting the lives of good, upstanding citizens in jeopardy just because of stinking greed...forcing us to behave so badly! I shouldn't even look for your stinking toe, Rudy," he said, slapping the Sheriff lightly on his bare knee. "But I will—just because I'm such a good, upstanding citizen."

Buck came back about five minutes later and told Tipton that he hadn't been able to find even a trace of the toe. Off to the side he told me there hadn't been enough of it left worth saving. "Only a little, quarter-moon-shaped piece—mostly just toenail," he said, suddenly looking worried. "Uh oh, I never thought of it until just now...I hope that fat pig doesn't have AIDS."

With great effort, Tipton was positioned inside the gazebo, but not too close to Kimberly. He'd been tied with rope and then wrapped with enough duct tape to make him look like a fat, silver mummy. At least he wouldn't bleed to death. Jade had taken her mask off, seeing that it no longer mattered to wear it.

Buck and I went outside and stood in some shade in conference. I asked him what he thought we should do about Tipton's shiny new car.

"I don't really have any chop-shop connections," he admitted. "I was just razzing him."

"I knew you didn't," I told him. "You may be a lot of things, but you're not a crook. Well, we can't leave it parked around here."

"I know," he quickly agreed, "I've already been thinking about that. And I've come up with an idea—a perfect solution. We can get rid of it in fifteen minutes—and not just by covering it up with brush, either."

"*Fifteen minutes?* Bullshit."

"Not by fire, either," he bragged. Want to bet?" By now he was smiling broadly. He jerked his thumb Southward. "The river's just over yonder, Charlie, remember? As soon as it gets dark—which won't be long now—we can send it rolling right into the Minnesota River. Yes, indeed. Right there by the Old Bloomington Ferry Road Bridge. It's closed off—almost certainly nobody around, either. I remember there's a place off to the right where the water's real deep close to the bank. I used to go fishing there, as a matter of fact. There's no guardrail in that spot, and it's a nice, easy slope to the water."

I raised my eyebrows in genuine surprise and slapped him on the back. "Sounds perfect! You know what, Buck? Sometimes, once in a great while, you simply *amaze* me. As a matter of fact, I'm thinking about changing your name to *Amazing Buck!*"

He looked very pleased and explained to me, "It seems like the more trouble I get into, the more resourceful I become. It probably has to do with my military training— you know, if you get caught, you're supposed to try to get away, that sort of thing. It's the same line of reasoning."

"Well, that explains it," I said. "Thanks for the overview."

"Smart ass. It looks like Jade can handle those two all right while we dump the car."

"She's doing pretty well," I agreed.

"Better than I thought she would," Buck admitted. "Why don't you keep her company for a bit while for I go through the car? My energy's peaking pretty good right now. Who knows, maybe there's something in it worth saving. The fat bastard owes us."

"Just remember, Buck, you're not a crook."

"Yeah, I know, like Nixon wasn't. Didn't you just hear me?" He grabbed up his bow. "The fat bastard owes me...and I'm not just talking about a couple of arrows. I wish I did know somebody with a chop-shop—just for this one time. Take a look at your own lifestyle right now, Charlie. For instance, I bet you could probably use a shower right about now, huh?" He chuckled. "See, that asshole cop over there is partly to blame even for you being funky right now."

Laughing, he squatted down on his haunches and pulled out his flat-bottomed briarwood pocket bowl. He pushed his finger into the top of it to pack its content down, then he lit it and inhaled deeply. He passed it to me and I took a big hit, too, causing it to glow red. It grew warm in my hand and then quickly became too hot to hold, except by the curved stem.

"That's why big thick ones are nice," Buck said, immediately realizing what he'd just said. He quickly added, "You know what I meant, Charlie—my house bowl is three-times the size of this little shit. It's flat-bottomed, also. What am I talking about? You've seen it. This one makes a good one-hitter, though." He reached for the little pipe and, through his nose, inhaled the light trail of smoke still rising up from it. He jammed the bowl back into a front pocket of his camouflaged fatigue pants. "Whoa—that little sucker's hot in there," he said.

"I know what you meant by that too," I said, laughing.

"Huh?"

"Never mind."

"You know what, Charlie? I've noticed that you've been thinking dirty a lot lately, always misconstruing what I say. Anyway, you should know I wouldn't talk about myself that way."

"Yeah, I know," I answered. "*Little sucker* doesn't sound like—"

"—Don't even go there," he cautioned me, "you don't

even want to be there." He burped loudly. "Damn, I just made room for another tiny nip of what's been biting my ass all day." He stood up and removed the antique flask from his back pocket and shook it. "Damn! That fat pig drank almost all of my remaining stock!" He frowned and unscrewed the top and wiped it off before downing the last few drops. He burped again and added, "I'll be right back."

Choosing not to take the trail, he cut through the woods and disappeared in the general direction of the Sheriff's car.

I felt like being by myself for a few minutes, so I ambled across the clearing toward the deer trail Jade had been on a little earlier. She saw me and smiled and waved, probably thinking that I was going to relieve myself. I waved back.

Buck's homegrown pot was kicking in pretty well. I drifted along the deer path, down into the dark, cool shade of large oaks. Soon I was floating effortlessly along the aged, hoof-worn path, occasionally drifting from side to side whenever I needed to avoid fresh deer pellets. My eyes zeroed in for just a moment on a tiny fawn print, then I floated to the other side of the path again to avoid another spilling of dark brown pellets.

We seemed right on the verge of accomplishing a noble cause. Victor would probably be released very soon. We were almost there. But Buck was right about my life being greatly affected by ignoble assholes like Tipton. Even so, I felt sorry for the fat cop.

I briefly wondered where Sullivan could be, what he could be up to. I didn't want to think about the evil man, about the threat he still represented to us. I banished the image of his face from my mind. I suddenly wished there were more Helpers in our group.

All hell would break loose tomorrow, when the letters were received and Tipton and his car were missed. I smiled to myself. *Maybe no one will even miss him...that'd be funny.* But I figured Kimberly's kidnapping would make immediate national news.

My mind stumbled into thinking about the camouflaged nets Buck had insisted on buying. I felt myself smiling again, for the first time fully understanding their importance. I knew Buck was having fun, but it was serious and dangerous fun.

I briefly wondered whether we'd end up having to do any time. In my mind, I could see Buck appealing to the Governor. Ventura would let us off with a joke and a grin. Buck would probably offer him a hit on his bowl—his house bowl, not the little one.

Now very high, I imagined all of us celebrating Victor's release in the Governor's mansion, high-fiving and grinning and choking on dense smoke from huge New Yorkers and Cuban cigars. I imagined poor Jade floating over to open a window, then I heard her begin to scream—short, terror-stricken bursts of screaming.

It took me a second to realize that Jade's screaming was coming from the real world—from the direction of the gazebo tree-house, not from the Governor's mansion!

I sprinted back up the deer path as fast as my legs could carry me, all the while instinctively looking around for something to pick up.

Chapter 16

I saw a figure crouched down low, running along the edge of the forest toward the tree-house gazebo. That turned out to be Buck. He was carrying his bow and something in a plastic bag bouncing against his leg...like maybe a box of some kind.

Then I saw Jade jumping up and down inside the gazebo. By now she was making pathetic little screams. I couldn't see much else because of the way the setting sun was hitting the new mosquito screening. I could see that Kimberly was still seated.

"He's dead! He's dead! He *died!*" Jade kept saying between little screams.

Buck reached the gazebo before I did. After arriving at the door, he leaned over sideways and gently tossed his bow and the box he was carrying to the ground, then very forcefully ripped the screen-door off it's hinges and flew inside. I heard him command Jade, "Shut the hell up, will you? Hey! No matter what else, get a grip and be quiet! Hey—shut up, damn it!"

Kimberly was still seated on a little rustic stool Buck had made. She was still tied up, but not blindfolded, and she was watching with amazement as the drama unfolded right in front of her.

I raced through the doorway to stop Buck from possibly slapping or shaking Jade. I figured that might happen next, considering his weird way of thinking. A damn good slap would shock her back into reality...back into shutting the hell up. Sure enough, his hand started to come up. I reached him just in time, grabbing his wrist, but he easily pulled his arm free with one jerk.

"You dumb ass, Charlie!" he yelled. "Am I going to have trouble with you, too? I wasn't going to hit her—I was only going to put my hand over her mouth to shut her the hell up!"

"Oh...sorry," I said, not at all convinced he was telling the truth.

I took hold of Jade's shoulders and gently shook her until she connected with my face. Finally, she quieted down. "Look what happened," she said, pointing at the heap of dead bulk on the floor.

The Sheriff of Bunyan County was lying on his back, still roped and taped into a sitting position. His eyes were popped-out and glassed-over, very much unfocused. He appeared to be perpetually surprised, not unhappy.

"Look at him," Jade said to me hoarsely. "He's dead. He just died."

"He doesn't look sad about it, does he?" I said. I couldn't help laughing.

"Hey, I've got two going nutzo now," said Buck, chuckling. He glanced over at the mound of body on the floor and zeroed in on the face, then started laughing along with me. "Yeah, he does look like he's shocked to be here, doesn't he? Our asses are in a real bind now, Charlie. That's not so funny."

I stopped laughing. "Hey, we didn't kill him—it was probably his fat heart that did it."

We paused together to look down at the Sheriff's surprised face again, then broke into laughter again.

"It was too much stress for him," Jade said quietly.

"I'd say so," Buck said through his laughter. "Any ideas on what we should do with him now?"

Sounding cloudy-minded, even dazed, Jade answered, "What do you mean? We need to...we have to call...."

"What?" Buck interjected sarcastically. "Who? Call an ambulance? Take him to a hospital or a morgue? I've got a better idea...how about if we just load his fat ass up and drop him off at the nearest police station? Forget it, Jade. For one thing, they'll wonder what a broken-off arrow is doing in the back of his leg...or won't that be any big deal?"

"Schruder died too," Jade said. "That's two now."

"Yeah, but that lard-ass wasn't murdered like Schruder was," said Buck, sounding irritable. "It was his heart, pure and simple. Sure, he was under a lot of pressure, but he was about ready to get tossed on the manure pile anyway. He'd sure make a lot of fertilizer all ground up, wouldn't he?"

"In a way, he was kind of cute," Jade said slowly, still sounding spacy and strange.

"You must really be whacked-out, Jade," Buck said. "Yeah, he was cute, like my pet pig. I hope she's all right—her and the little pups."

"Well, what are we going to do now?" I asked of no one in particular.

Kimberly spoke up in a small voice. "I certainly wouldn't

give up at this point."

Now what's this? I thought to myself. *A Patty Hearst-like trick?*

No one said anything, so she went on as though answering my question. "Why think about turning back now?" she said. "I certainly wouldn't. All you've got to do is hide the body a day or two. He wasn't murdered...I can attest to that."

Buck was typically sarcastic. "Oh, I see," he said, "it must be bonkers time. Somehow, I'm the only one who got left out."

"I'm not being irrational at all," Kimberly said. Her blue eyes sparkled with enthusiasm. She looked at Jade. "I understand what you guys are trying to accomplish—I really do. I know a little bit about your husband's case, Mrs. Stamate. In fact, I've even talked to my—"

"—Why should we believe anything you have to say?" Buck interrupted.

She eagerly answered his question. "Look, I can understand you're not wanting to trust me—under the circumstances, but I'm telling you the truth. I talked with my father about the Stamate case...I was the one to bring it up, because I knew Mr. Stamate wasn't getting a fair shake. It was obvious to me, slanted news accounts aside."

"Yeah, and just what did your Old Man have to say on the subject?" asked Buck.

"Well, to be honest with you, he was vague about it and he wanted to change the subject. He did tell me that it involved complicated political issues about illegal drugs and sentencing laws—basically, he wanted me to butt out, which only confirmed in my own mind that something was afoul, that my father was probably involved, you know, from a political angle. And now I've pretty much put the rest of the story together listening to you guys talk. And I know all about *him too*," she said, frowning and stabbing a finger at Tipton's body. My Daddy despised him...so did I, I guess. He was really crooked. So is Luther Sullivan. He visited my father last week, but I don't know why...I mean, for certain. Did he really force Mr. Schruder to kill himself?"

"It's all on tape, Sweetie," said Buck.

"Please don't call me Sweetie," she said.

"You *must* be a real sweetie to have such a sweet attitude about this whole thing," Buck said. "I meant it in a good way, see? Most people are kind of pissed when they get kidnapped."

"Well, you guys aren't doing it for the money," she said, apologizing for her own abduction, "that's different."

"Yeah, but we've still broken the law big-time," Buck said. "That's not different. We can't trust anything you say until this is all over and our friend is free."

"I don't blame you," she said. "I'm just letting you know that you don't have to worry about me...trying to get away or anything like that."

Jade spoke softly. "That's good to know, Kimberly. I'm glad you told us."

I said, "Come on you guys, we need to talk. By ourselves."

Jade and I both quickly exited the gazebo and walked far enough away so that Kimberly couldn't hear what we were saying. Buck lingered behind to check the girl's ties and to pick up his bow and the plastic bag with the box in it lying near the screen door. I noticed that a tag was attached to the plastic bag. Buck studied the tag and muttered to himself while ambling through the weeds toward us. "Whoa, an evidence tag," he said. "I wonder what the hell's in here?" He shook the box lightly. Speaking louder, he said, "Okay, you know we can't trust her, right?"

I immediately agreed. "Right—we can be nice to her, but we can't trust her. She at least has to stay tied up."

"She's no longer a threat to us," Jade said. "And she's the daughter of my parents' neighbors...and she's a lot nicer than I thought she was."

Buck said with exasperation, "That's exactly why we can't trust her—she might be putting on an act of nicety."

"This'll all be over tomorrow or the next day, Jade," I said. "We're almost there."

She asked, "What are we going to do about the Sheriff? His body, I mean?"

Buck and I exchanged glances. He beat me by saying, "We'll take care of him...don't you worry about that. Charlie and I'll take care of that little bit of unpleasant business. But you can't start trusting the girl all at once, Jade, okay? Otherwise, I'm out of here...."

"But what will you do with him?"

Buck became even more exasperated with her. "Damn it, Jade! What does it matter? He's dead! Let us worry about it, will you?"

I told her, "We'll take him away from here for the time being, okay? Then you won't have to think about it."

"But where will you take him¿"

"Just away from here," I answered. "It doesn't matter. We'll hide him until this is over—it's almost over now."

"Out of sight, out of mind," Buck said. "We'll cover him over with some brush and shit, and...."

I elbowed him in the side and gave him a cold stare, but it was too late.

Jade's head jerked up. "The bugs and animals!"

"No—forget that idea," I said. "We'll put him in the car...in a comfortable position in the back seat...then hide the car."

She batted her pretty eyes several times in rapid succession. "Okay," she said, apparently satisfied. "I'd better go see how Kimberly's doing now."

"She's doing fine," Buck said evenly, carefully, holding my stare. "You just left her a minute ago and she was as happy as a *mother-fucking lark!* Don't you remember¿"

I said, "Okay then, good, break it up...nothing's changed. We'll hide the body and we're right back on course, just as though he'd never followed us in here in the first place, right¿"

"Right," said Buck.

Jade looked over her shoulder in the direction of the gazebo and frowned. "Right," she repeated, showing little enthusiasm. "I'd better get back to Kimberly now."

We watched her as she minced her way back to our little hideaway. She paused at the doorway, apparently confused over the screen door lying on the ground. It was partly propped up by weeds, the screening itself undamaged.

"Speaking of trust," Buck said, "we'd better keep a

sharp eye on her, too, right along with the Patch kid. "She's acting really weird, Charlie. Why don't you help me load that piece of shit into the car now, before she gets another weird idea, like giving him a funeral out here or something. You'd better stay here with them. I'll hike back in from the bridge—the exercise will do me good."

"So you still want to run the car into the river, but now with Tipton in it?"

"Hey—why not?" he answered. "We don't want them to discover his body any more than his car, right? What better place for him to be anyway, short of a morgue? It'll be nice and cool for him. Even Jade would appreciate that."

"I don't think so," I said.

"Fuck it then, if she asks, we'll just tell her I drove the car into a brush pile or something...what do you suppose is in the box here? Kind of a strange box, isn't it?"

"Maybe you should leave it alone. It might be important evidence."

"Leave it alone? Ha! Are you kidding?"

He slit the top of the plastic bag with his pocketknife and grabbed hold of the metal box inside and let the heavy bag drop down to the ground. "Nice box," he commented, turning it over and over. He shook it lightly a few times up near his ear. It was made of brushed aluminum, a soft blue color. He pushed a shiny metal button and the top flipped open with precision, revealing a dark blue, velvet-lined interior loaded with a dozen golden Thai-sticks and many chunks of hash. The chunks of hash were of various sizes and colors ranging from blond to light green to shades of dark brown. A couple of the pieces were almost black.

Buck licked his lips, then, like a chocoholic eyeballing a freshly opened box of assorted chocolates, he picked out the darkest piece. He scratched at it with his fingernail and sniffed it, then started dancing in place. "This one's laced with *opium!*" he whispered excitedly. His eyebrows shot up as far as they could go and the corners of his mouth moved close to his ears in a wide grin. "Man, oh man, are the gods smiling down on us today Charlie, or what? First I get to shoot a cop with my bow, then *this!*"

"Yeah, good score," I said, full of wonder. I moved closer and poised my own hand over the beautiful box, then stabbed for a huge block of reddish-brown hash.

"Ha! Good choice!" Buck whispered hoarsely. He quickly surveyed the area all around us suspiciously. "Man, we should bury most of this shit right away...just in case...you never know. That's probably choking red you've got there. The more you cough the higher you get—good shit, but you don't want to do too much of it in a stretch. The Marines taught me some pretty good knowledge, huh?"

"I'd say so," I agreed. "Okay Partner, let's do a few hits and then hurry up and get rid of the body of the beast. I don't feel comfortable with bodies lying around."

"Yeah, that carcass will start stinking up the whole continent pretty soon otherwise. He needs to be cooled off right away, a fat bastard like that. Imagine all that bulk going rancid in this heat? Whoa, mama!"

"Can you get his car all the way in here? He's too heavy to drag or carry very far."

"It shouldn't be any problem. I might have to whack out a little bit of brush and a few tree limbs, but that's what I do for a living, remember?"

"Oh yeah," I said, "a professional tree-jumper, I almost forgot."

"Knock it off, will you? This isn't a good time to get on each other's nerves. Here, let me see that chunk of hash a minute."

He took his bowl and a lighter with a camouflage cover out of his pocket and warmed a corner of the rock of red hash, then rubbed at it gently with his forefinger. He held the pipe with his other hand while forming a funnel-like circle at the top so the crumbs of hash could fall through. "That should be enough," he said, gently tapping his forefinger into the bowl. He took his lighter out again and lit the pipe, then offered it to me.

"Go ahead, you first," I said.

He shrugged his shoulders. "Okay." He took an enormous drag on the curve-stemmed little bowl and held it for about five seconds, then grabbed at his throat. He couldn't hold the chest-full of ever-expanding smoke and ended up blasting our whole side of the peaceful little clearing with white smoke. Then he lunged at the smoke like a drunken fool, sucking in air loudly as if trying to catch some of it. "Come back here!" he whispered hoarsely. "Come back here!" Then he whirled around to look at me, bleary-eyed, still clutching his throat. "Man that hurt—and I sure hate to see all that smoke going to waste like that too. Be real careful Charlie—it expands while you're holding it in. I forgot about that."

I took a small toke and held it in a long time, until almost nothing came out when I exhaled. The hash tasted exquisite on the roof of my mouth. It brought instant flash-memories of the few times I'd smoked it in the past. A collage of colorful, fuzzy, happy snapshots mixed with a powerful taste of hash suddenly permeated throughout my brain, and I took another hit. A few seconds later, I brightly remembered our task at hand. "Okay, I'm suitably fortified for the mission now," I told Buck.

"What mission? Oh, yeah—let's go get that piece of shit," he said, "and get it away from here before it starts stinking up the whole damned neighborhood. Jade would sure change her tune if she had to be around that body up close in this heat for a while. There's nothing worse-smelling than a dead human body left out in the heat."

"I'm pretty fucked up," I said. "We'd better hold off on any more partying until we get rid of the corpse. What a yucky word, *corpse*."

"Yeah, it reminds me of funeral homes and coffins and red, velvety material and shit like that. Flowers. I mean *funeral* flowers—you know. All that funeral crap that costs an arm and a leg. I'd just as soon go back to the earth, like in the old days...except I don't like the idea of being buried in the ground...worms crawling through your eye sockets, shit like that. I'd rather go back to nature up on one of those platforms like the Indians used to do. Or find a cave somewhere and die. Even cremation would be all right. They sure waste a lot of good space burying people, don't they? Pretty soon it'll be against the law. Then they'll start digging everybody up and cremating *them*. What do you think? Look at how expensive the land is in Tokyo...what were we talking about, anyway, Charlie? Not Japan, I know that."

"Getting rid of the body," I reminded him.

"Oh, yeah...the *corpse*. That reminds me of when I used to work for that chiropractic college. As a security guard. Did I ever tell you what happened one Halloween night?"

"No."

"You sure?"

"Tell your story, Buck," I said, "but let's keep moving, too, okay? It's dusk out already."

"Okay, anyway, so they—the students—have to study these real corpses, that are rotated by the college, see, and—"

"—What do you mean *rotated?*"

"Hey, they can't keep them forever...you know? They have to rotate them, get new ones once in a while. Funny you'd ask that, though."

"Ask what?"

"About rotating."

"You're the one that brought it up."

"No, see, they used to rotate them physically, too. What are you looking at me like that for? I'm as serious as a heart attack. They used to dip 'em down into some kind of solution—formaldehyde, I think. Anyway, it would shrivel them up like overdone barbecue chicken—only without much sauce. It was really creepy. I had to inventory them every night. The place was under lock and key. Hey—slow down, will you?

"So on Halloween night some guys broke into the special dipping room and took one of the corpses, a shrunken little guy—looked like one of those little Peruvians or Bolivians. Had hair still on him and everything. First they put a bunch of peanut butter up his nose—don't ask me why. They were probably drinking. Then they propped him up on a bench in one of those little bus shelters by the entrance of the college. Slow down a little, will you? I can't talk good when I'm jarring around like this....

"And here I was, the security guard for the joint...and I didn't even know what happened. That is, until the cops started swarming the place outside. They rescued the little feller, and if I'm not mistaken, they had to dip him again right away—probably to kill any germs he'd picked up. I only *kind of* remember that last part...I think. Anyway, those corpses gave me the creeps. You're right, Charlie, even the *word* corpse sounds yucky, doesn't it?" He fake-shuddered. "*Corpse*...yuck!"

Chapter 17

We were ready to give up trying to move Tipton's blubbery bulk the short distance to the back of his Caprice when Buck suddenly remembered the winch he'd brought along to re-erect the fallen tree-house. So he and I hooked the dead Sheriff up to a thin steel cable and slid him across the weeds and up into the back seat of his large car using the winch and a couple of planks placed side by side. He was a tight fit, and he ended up costing us nearly an hour of hard work. It took both of us pushing hard to make the back door click shut. When Buck finally reached around through the front and slammed down the lock stem, it not only lessened the possibility of the door popping back open, it also signaled the end of a hellava struggle.

Buck left to deliver the car to the Minnesota River, leaving me standing outside in the dark, sweating and breathing hard. There was a full moon out and the sky was fairly clear, so I knew he'd be able to find his way back all right. And he wasn't the least bit afraid of the dark...unlike me.

I stayed by Jade and Kimberly and tried hard not to think about Luther Sullivan. I knew it was possible—however remote—that he was lurking around outside in the darkness. Buck had taken his bow with him. I had the revolver in my hands—in my lap—waiting for some kind of monster to show up out of the darkness. I was worried that Buck would purposely try to frighten me when he came back. I hoped he wouldn't be foolish enough to try sneaking up on me, or that he wouldn't try to scare me by making some horrible noise.

I ran my fingers over the valuable, antique gun and slipped the safety off and then back on again. It made a dull, metallic *click*. I did it again just to get the feel for it. There was one less bullet in the gun now. One of the chambers was still empty since Tipton's big toe had been blasted off. That bullet hadn't been replaced, which left five shots now. Just in case Sullivan showed up. Wanting to feel more secure, I used my heels to push myself back even tighter against the wall of the tree-house. Pretty soon I felt very tired and stopped feeling the gun. Finally, I put it down on the floor away from me, but still within reach. I practiced reaching out in the darkness for the handle several times to fix in my mind's-eye exactly where it was located.

A warm, gentle breeze kicked up over the clearing, swaying the upper branches of a tall cottonwood standing nearby. We'd been listening to some Jethro Tull turned down low, but I decided to replace it with something lighter and less chaotic. Using a pocket flashlight, I searched through the collection of CDs we'd brought along. Definitely not *Dark Side of the Moon*. I settled on *The Best of the Platters*, one of Buck's contributions.

Kimberly spoke softly in the darkness. "My father loves me very much. He'll be worried sick about me."

I thought Jade was probably sleeping. I didn't really feel

like talking, but I said, "That's the general idea of a kidnapping, isn't it?"

In the darkness, I saw Jade move up closer to Kimberly. "Did you know that your father is the Chairman of a very powerful committee?" she asked the girl, her voice sounding kind and gentle.

"Yes," Kimberly Patch answered. "Some kind of judiciary committee...law enforcement, I guess. I'm not loyal to all of Daddy's views though—some of them, I am. I know he has some good ideas, too."

"Well—he's crossed the line with one of his *bad* ideas," I said roughly.

"Unfortunately," Jade told Kimberly apologetically, "your father is a staunch promoter of mandatory minimum sentencing. What Charlie means is, my husband is imprisoned right now because some politicians have crossed the line between the political and judicial aspects of government. Politicians have tied judges hands, leaving them with no discretion in some cases."

As if on cue—and making us all jerk, Buck suddenly appeared only inches away from the re-attached screen door. He told our captive with vehemence, "That's what your father stands for, girl, power-hungry politicians! Mandatory sentences, with no discretion! Even in soft drug cases, the pigs and prosecutors have all the discretion. Why? Because politicians like your father are always pushing, pushing, pushing the drug war craze to get re-elected. You know what I'm talking about too, girl. Fight big crime...big *drug* crime. Yeah! Big shot, tough guy. Down with crime and criminals! Yahoo! The only thing is, good people like my friend Victor are getting caught up in the feeding frenzy. And assholes like Tipton and Sullivan are getting filthy rich. I don't know about your daddy."

"I don't agree with mandatory sentences, either," Kimberly said.

Buck shut up and waited for her continue, but she didn't add anything. Finally, he asked, "You don't?"

"No," she said. "That's one of the things I disagree with my father about. And I don't believe in zero tolerance, either. It's about the same thing, isn't it? Like being expelled from elementary school because your mother accidentally puts a plastic knife in your lunchbox."

Buck looked over at me in the darkness. I had to imagine the skepticism I knew was showing on his face. He quickly turned his head back to the girl. He couldn't resist the line of conversation. "I don't even like 'just say no'," he said. "That one should be reserved for prescription drug abusers, anyway, like Nancy Reagan and—"

"—But that's not the same thing," Kimberly said, cutting him off.

"Huh? *Kind of*," he said. He took a few seconds to recover his train of thought, then said, "They're both bottom-line, bullshit expressions that don't work—except by trampling all over peoples' rights. Does 'just say no' work? No. Does zero tolerance or mandatory minimum sentencing work? No. Well—they kind of do. People try to make them work, and that's exactly where the problems and the unfairness comes in. They're both bullshit terms...ideas. Now do you see what I mean?"

"'Just say no' doesn't really hurt anybody," Kimberly

said, growing argumentative, "zero tolerance and mandatory sentences do."

Buck scoffed, "Bullshit...'just say no' would certainly be
hurting somebody if the experts put resources into thinking it'll work, because then they'd be wasting their precious time and money...looking in the wrong direction.
Maybe I'm missing something, Sweetheart. How does 'just
say no' work?"

"Don't be mean to her, Buck," Jade said. "She didn't say
it worked, she just said it wasn't hurting—oh, never mind.
Why don't we change the subject? Maybe we should be
more quiet, anyway."

"I didn't mean to start anything," Kimberly said, sounding timid.

"You didn't start anything," Buck said. "Nice try,
though. Divide and conquer, right?"

She ignored the insinuation. "I don't think my father
would intentionally hurt anyone. Unless he were a criminal who deserved it, I mean."

"Or *she*," Buck huffed. "Unless *she* were a criminal too.
Your father's definitely guilty alright, but he's also in a
damned good position to right some wrongs...that's the
important thing. To *us* I mean, not to you."

"It's important for *all* of us!" Kimberly exclaimed hotly,
for the first time revealing her feelings of hostility toward
Buck. "And I'm not afraid of you, *Bucko Whacko*—or whatever you call yourself!"

Again, I could only imagine the shock and embarrassment written all over his face. He paused for just for just a
moment, then quickly strolled away from the screen door

and came back a few minutes later with the roll of duck tape. He ripped off a short piece and quickly strode in behind Kimberly and smoothed the tape down over her mouth. Then he started another piece and noisily began wrapping it around and around her head—mouth, hair and all. Finally, he angrily ripped the tape free from the roll and threw the roll off to the side. "Watch her closely," he commanded me. Then he strolled back over to the screen-door. "I've had a very long day and I'm tired," he explained. "And I'm going to bed!"

In the quiet darkness, I watched Jade go over and begin to remove the tape from Kimberly Patch's head. She took a long time doing it and spoke to her soothingly, all the while glancing over at me. And she kept looking outside at the moon-lit clearing on the other side of the screen-door. Back and forth, back and forth. I grew very tired and found it easy to remain expressionless and neutral as I drifted off to sleep. The .44 Colt was within easy reach.

Noisy crows and a variety of smaller birds chasing a big great-horned owl woke us up early. The owl occasionally moved from tree to tree, hoping to elude its tormenters, but the racket went on and on until Buck finally grew angry and came out of his lean-to in his underwear and began throwing sticks and rocks in their direction. The noise from the crows only intensified.

I sat up and pressed my face to one of the gazebo's screened panels for a better look. My effort was rewarded. I got to see Buck lose his balance after winding up and hurling a large rock like a discus thrower. He landed on his ass and skidded a few feet across the weeds, then jumped up right away and began plucking burrs off the back of his sagging briefs. He was actively reaching underneath from the front when he heard my stifled laughter.

"*Fucking birds!*" he muttered, tiptoeing his way back to his lean-to. He flopped back down heavily onto his air mattress on the floor and its plug shot out, making a fluttering, staccato-like whistling noise. He quickly flipped over and shoved the plug back in. Then he sat upright very still and began moving his head back and forth very slowly, like a radar dish. The birds had stopped their personal assault against him. Speaking in a low voice, he muttered, "I bet you thought that was a coincidence, huh? Dumb Ass. See, I knew what I was doing."

He pulled the plug out again, making the same flapping, whistling noise, and the bird racket resumed. He tried different air noises again and again, in-between pauses, but the birds kept up their racket until they gradually made their way up over the top of the ridge to the Northeast, far enough away to stop being a nuisance.

"Dumb Ass yourself!" I whispered, teasing him back through the mosquito screening. "I guess you're not so special with birds after all, are you?"

Kimberly and Jade were now sitting up, trying to wake up. They both squinted and scowled against the already-bright, early morning sun slanting in on them.

"Morning ladies," I said cheerfully. "Just about coffee time, huh?"

"Yeah, D-day," Buck said, coming into the gazebo. "Are you girls all decent? I hope not."

"Can't you at least give us some privacy¿" Kimberly groaned. "Go away, why don't you."

"Hey, who de-mummified your mouth¿" Buck asked. "I just came in to ask you girls how you want your eggs this morning."

"Why couldn't you have asked us from outside¿"

"Hey—what's biting your ass so early¿" he asked the girl. "Here the day's just starting—and a good one too, it looks like—and you're already bitching. Well, little miss fancy, I'm not going to let you ruin my day—not *D-day.* This is the day the shit hits the fan—and I can hardly wait! And little girl, you can watch everything unfold with us on our portable TV if you can manage to control your mouth. Otherwise," he said, "it's back to the tape again, eyes and all this time. I'm not bullshitting either. You're not going to ruin my day, that's for sure."

He took out his briarwood pocket bowl and paused to take a hit, allowing the words to sink in. He held his breath and scowled at her again. "Now then," he continued, speaking matter-of-factly and pausing to let some smoke out and take in a gulp of fresh air, "how do you want your *mother-fucking eggs¿*"

"He swears when he gets mad," I quickly explained to Kimberly.

Her blue eyes sparked. "Say, Bucko, in some states it's against the law to talk that way around women and children¿"

"Fuck 'em if they can't take a joke," Buck answered. "The judge, too. By the way, which do you consider yourself—a woman or a kid¿ You've got a smart mouth like a kid."

Kimberly's lips compressed and turned white. She turned her head away from him and looked outside, scowling hard and squinting against the sun.

"What a prude!" exclaimed Buck with apparent delight. "I'll be so damned glad when this is all over, because then I won't have to help baby-sit a little kid—a spoiled, rich kid, born with a silver spoon up her—"

"—Buck, don't you dare be mean to her!" Jade warned. "She hasn't done anything to you."

"Yes she has," he disagreed. "She's got a big mouth— had everything handed to her on a silver platter all her life. Out riding around on fancy horses while Victor sits rotting in jail, in part because of her old man."

"That's not fair, Buck," Jade said. "Nobody can help what circumstances they're born into...." She glanced at Kimberly. "I didn't mean that in a negative way...there's certainly nothing wrong with having wealth."

"No, there's not!" said Buck angrily. "Unless it happens to turn you into a snotty bitch!"

"Buck, let's go make those eggs now," I suggested, rising to my feet. I pretended to forget that I was only wearing panties and a tank top. I purposely stumbled around a few seconds before picking up a pair of white shorts to put on. The trick worked. His eyes opened wide and fastened onto the lower half of my body while I put them on. I'd successfully diverted his attention.

He looked back and forth between Kimberly and my bare legs, open-mouthed and momentarily confused. "Hey, fuck it—why not? We need to talk, anyway."

"What about?" I asked him. I moved toward the door.

"You'd better put something else on," he said, glancing at my legs again, "you'll get all scratched and bitten up."

"You're right, thanks, " I said. "Go ahead—I'll be right with you."

"This is *D-day*," he reminded us all. He shifted a cold stare toward Kimberly, and then the expression turned sour. He purposely grazed Jade with the look when he turned to leave. "I need to talk with you about setting up an observation point, Charlie," he said, "up on the ridge. But there's something else we've got to talk about too, just as important."

"I don't trust either one of them," he told me for the third time.

After eating an uneasy breakfast, Buck and I walked straight North through the forest to the ridge above, coming out close to the corral with the watering trough by the single large oak tree. The horses were lying down in a patch of shade near the road, twitching their tails at deer flys. The trail turnoff was just down the road to the East a few hundred yards.

"To be honest with you, Buck, I didn't sleep very well last night," I said.

"Me neither," he said. "We know we can't trust the kid—that's a forgone conclusion. The question now is, can we still trust Jade?"

We stayed within the fringes of the forest and surveyed the area. By now it was mid-morning and the July sun was cranking the heat up fast. The mosquitoes were still a problem in the shade, but we were protected by dope—the bug repellent kind, that is. I nevertheless inhaled one while walking and quickly coughed it back out, feeling the need to spit afterward. "Yuck!"

"Sshhh!" Buck cautioned. "The reason we're even up here right now in the first place is because someone might decide to snoop around. Well, I mean as soon as the shit hits the fan...as soon as the letters are delivered."

"That won't be until this afternoon, probably."

"I know, but we can't take any chances. This whole thing could still backfire and be covered up, even at this late stage. Who knows what kind of connections Sullivan might have—or Senator Patch, too. That's why we can't take any chances on someone hearing us down below. This is a good spot right about here to keep an eye on the road. We can switch off if you don't mind...I get tired of being in one spot too long. It'll probably just be for one day anyway."

I told him, "I think seeing Tipton keel over did something to Jade's head."

"Well, the poor woman's been under a lot of constant pressure," Buck said. "And for quite a long time now, too. We need to face-up to the reality of the situation, Charlie. I know she's your friend—she's my friend too, but we can't let her fuck things up right now when the gig's almost over. All I'm saying is, at this point she might have to be protected against herself."

"What do you mean?" I asked. "We can't tie *her* up, too."

Buck laughed. "Why not? No—I'm just kidding. But

one of us should stay with them most of the time from now on. I think Jade's been beguiled by that snippy little rich bitch down there. I don't feel comfortable being up here even a few minutes, but I wanted to show you the layout of the land up here...and talk privately."

"I've been here before," I reminded him.

"Oh yeah, that's right—right before Victor was busted, huh?"

"What's that supposed to mean?"

"I just meant time-wise," he answered. "I didn't mean anything by it. I know it's not your fault Victor was busted...even though you probably *unwittingly* helped facilitate it. Loose lips sink ships and all that. But I know you didn't snitch him off."

"Thanks a lot," I said.

"What? I'm just telling it like it is. The same goes for not being able to trust Jade anymore. I mean, as long as she's playing the role of the great protector for the Patch kid. I know she's your friend, but Victor's your friend, too, and *mine*. The way I see it, the most important thing we have to do right now is to hold the plan together and give it some time to work. And that includes watching—get down, quick! Somebody just drove by real slow...."

I'd already crouched down behind a bushy white pine. "I know—I saw it too. It had some kind of lettering or a decal or something on its front door."

"He didn't see us," said Buck, "I watched his head."

"Maybe he's looking for the trail."

"No, I don't think so," Buck answered. He took his pocket bowl out and took a hit off it and then passed it to me. "Hash," he said, "not choking red, either. Nobody knows the trail's there. The only reason Tipton found out—sshhh, stay down! The car's backing up!"

Buck hastily withdrew a pair of small binoculars from one of the pouches fixed onto his web belt. "Now you see why I've been carrying these with me all along, huh? I'm no dumb-ass, no siree, I'm gonna live to be a hundred and three—at least. Sshhh," he whispered. "Stay down low...here, you want another hit? He's too far away to see a tiny bit of smoke."

"That's okay," I answered. "What's the lettering say?"

The dark blue vehicle stopped. It was possibly a Bronco, or a Blazer. Buck adjusted the focus on the binoculars. "Holy shit," he whispered, "it's the fucking *media* already!"

"Huh?" I dropped down a little lower. "What's he doing?"

"Quick—lay flat!" Buck whispered harshly.

We both stretched out low to the ground.

"He's got binoculars too!" said Buck. "But don't worry, he didn't see us. He can't see us low to the ground like this...just lay real still, okay? It's a good thing you didn't wear anything real bright...it's a good thing you changed out of your shorts too, huh?" He grinned at me. "Sshhh, he's getting out of the car...just keep down, we're all right."

Buck dropped his head flat to the ground next to mine, then slowly came up again with the binoculars to his face. He quickly ducked back down again. "He's looking here, but he's still looking all over too...he started walking this way, but then stopped."

Buck lifted his head again slowly, this time without the binoculars. He peered out over the grass and taller weeds for a minute or so and then said, "He's walking back toward the car now. Come on, Charlie, he's got his back to us. We should move back a little farther into the woods in case he decides to take a walk around. Wow! The media got here already!"

I leaned forward at the waist and ran loping back south toward the ridge, dodging trees and brush. "Maybe it doesn't have anything to do with the letters and tapes," I whispered, my words seeming to bounce around in front of me. "I mean, it's awfully early, isn't it?"

Buck stopped and turned around and brought the binoculars back up to his face. He answered, "We're getting some kind of action though, aren't we? That's probably not bad. Let's hide behind these big oak trees here, okay? I can still see him a little bit from—holy shit, Charlie! He's coming right this way! Get down again and keep still, okay?" Buck paused. "I've got an idea. When I say *go*, drop back a little farther and then circle around a little bit and run out to the road and pretend like you're just out for a walk, okay? In other words, lure him back the other way. I can't, because I look too suspicious. Maybe you can pump him for some information then, too."

I followed Buck's instructions and soon found myself out on the road, hiking past the dark blue 4X4 Blazer. It was a plain model without much trim. One line of lettering on the door simply read, *The Minneapolis Star Tribune*, and underneath that in larger letters was the single word, *REPORTER*.

I slowed my pace and purposely scuffed my tennis shoe against the pavement and watched out the corner of my eye. The reporter—a very young man—saw me and waved and started walking back toward me and his Blazer. I kept walking, pretending not to see him. Out of the corner of my eye, I saw him picking up his pace. "Excuse me," he shouted, waving an arm over his head.

I stopped and turned around. In the forest beyond the well-dressed young man, I saw Buck waving too, just like the newsman. Though I couldn't see his face, I knew he was grinning from ear to ear. I waved back to both of them, thinking to myself, *how very bizarre—and here the day's just starting!*

Chapter 18

"Hi—I'm Tucker Westmoreland." The newspaperman with the red hair and blue eyes and freckles plastered across the bridge of his nose jumped the small ditch gracefully, athletically, greeting me with an outstretched hand and what I supposed was a genuine smile. He shook my hand politely. "Do you live around here?" he asked.

"Hi. No, I'm just visiting a friend," I answered, "but she couldn't join me in my walk today—hurt her ankle."

"Oh, I'm sorry to hear that," the young man said pleasantly. He frowned politely. "That's too bad. Sorry to bother you, but I was hoping you could tell me something—anything, really—about this piece of land."

"Beautiful, isn't it?" I said. "The whole stretch along here is so pretty. That's why I decided to go this way today. Why are you interested? Did something happen here?"

"Hey—you should be a reporter," Tucker Westmoreland joked.

He was in his early to mid-twenties and handsome, in a Beach-boyish way. He came across as clean and fresh and quite intelligent.

"I thought about becoming a photo-journalist back when I was in high school," I said, turning to look at the landscape. "That'd be a nice shot over there, wouldn't it?"

I pointed in the direction of the horses now standing under the single large oak. "Are you interested in buying land around here or something?"

Tucker Westmoreland laughed good-naturedly. "Sure, maybe in twenty years. I'd say it's a little pricey for me this early in my career though. Besides that, I don't think the present owners want to sell...in a roundabout way, that's kind of why I'm here."

I managed to look puzzled. "How is that?"

He chuckled. "It's a long story. Are you sure you have time to hear it?"

"Yes. I have a little time. How about the short version?"

"Okay. Why not? I'm here because a man named Luther Sullivan is interested in putting a—um—night spot here. Actually, sort of a...dancing place."

"Oh—you mean a strip-club, a nudie-joint," I said.

The reporter was slightly embarrassed, but amused. I saw a touch of color creeping up out of his collar. "How'd you know?" he asked me.

"I watch television," I answered, smiling. "And sometimes I read the paper—your *Tribune*. Only Sunday's edition, though. That's all I have time for."

"Yes, well, that's good...I suppose," he said. "Anyway, one of the present owners of this land is in jail right now, awaiting sentencing for—if you can believe it—growing a crop of marijuana. Right over *there* somewhere," he added, pointing loosely over his shoulder and chuckling nervously.

I turned around to look with him and caught a glimpse of movement.

"Hey—did you see that?" Tucker Westmoreland asked.

"What?"

The young man's alert and now curious eyes roamed the edge of the forest along the ridge. "It kind of looked like...no, it's not even hunting season yet. Nothing."

"You were saying...."

"My boss at the newspaper seems to think there's a clash of some kind going on over this property here. Apparently, this Luther Sullivan guy wants it for another club, but the owners don't want to sell. But there's a few other intricacies involved too."

"Like what?"

The fresh young man laughed again. "You really should consider becoming a reporter," he said. "I mean that—seriously."

"What else complicates the situation?" I asked, smiling.

"Well, just rumored stuff. I probably shouldn't even talk about it. See, I'm an *investigative* reporter. I have to be careful about my sources. You understand, I'm sure."

"Oh! Goodness, I'm sorry," I said. "I was just curious, that's all. No harm done, right?"

"No—of course not," he answered. "Well, let's see...there's talk about the possibility of homegrown terrorists being involved in all this. Then there's some fishiness about a recently deceased prosecutor. And if that's not enough, the Sheriff of Bunyan County can't be located—along with the other owner of this land—Jade Stamate—and some of her friends. And to top all of *that* off, now a Senator's daughter is missing too! Supposedly a horseback riding accident. They're almost certainly not all related, but you never know. It sounds ridiculous as well as complicated, doesn't it? I told you it was a long story."

He swept his arm back toward Buck. "This beautiful property here may very well be the key to the whole thing. That's why I came here to see it up close—an investigative reporter's curiosity, you might say. What do you suppose is just over the ridge there? I'm thinking about taking a closer look."

"The mosquitoes are real bad in the shade," I said.

"I brought along some repellent just in case," he said. "I thought I saw a footpath or a trail or something that may lead in back there—down the road there a piece," he said, pointing east. "Mrs. Stamate's husband, Victor—the one in prison—had a couple of hundred big plants growing down in there somewhere."

"I heard it was just over the ridge there," I said. "Near the top."

"Oh—so you've already heard about *that* too?"

"Yeah, well, my friend heard about it and told me.

"Do you mind if I ask you what your name is?"

"No, not at all," I lied. I quickly came up with the first name that popped into my head. "Rosie. Rosie McDonald. It was nice talking with you."

"Well, you certainly learned more than I did here, today," Tucker Westmoreland said. He smiled warmly and shook my hand again, then went to his vehicle and drove off, heading east.

I started walking the other way until I figured he was well down the road, out of sight. But when I turned to look, I saw the Blazer's brake-lights come on just as it dipped down out of sight, almost even with the trail.

I leaped over the small ditch and ran across the clearing toward Buck, yelling all the way. "Buck! Head back to the camp! Hurry up! I tried to steer him away, but I think he's going down the trail—and I mean right *now!* Run!"

"We live in a structured society," Tucker Westmoreland said. "You can't just take the law into your own hands."

The race back to our hideaway had gotten Buck's adrenaline pumping. "Well pal, we're in the process of undoing some of that elaborate structuring," he told the cub investigative reporter. "Now get your ass moving, before I restructure it with one of these razor-sharp hunting arrows."

"By the looks of it, you're already into some pretty deep shit," Tucker Westmoreland told him. "Why make it any worse?"

"Why make it any worse? Good question," Buck answered. "Well, we've already bet the whole plug, so what difference does...*detaining*...you for awhile make? You're not being kidnapped—like I already told you. You're just being detained. Now get your ass moving...that's right, over to the little building there. It's not much, but it's been a good headquarters for us. Don't give me any more shit now, because I won't mind zinging one of these arrows your way. I've had a lot of practice lately, but I could always use some more...I'm not bullshitting, either."

"Do you mind if I ask what's going on here?"

"Never mind that for now...I'll explain it as we go along. Hey—just what we needed!" he yelled happily ahead of himself. "A representative of the media!"

He took out his pocket bowl and took a big hit and automatically held it out to the young newspaperman.

"No thanks."

Buck goaded him. "Too good for you, huh? Well, this shit's been sanitized by the law...you'll never guess where I got this hash from. Good ole Sheriff Tipton himself."

"You're kidding, of course."

"Nope. Had it in the back of his car...so-called evidence."

"Buck," I cautioned.

"It doesn't matter now, Charlie. It's minor compared to everything else."

Tucker Westmoreland looked at me. He appeared to be both surprised and disappointed. "I thought you said your name was Rosie?"

"Sorry," I answered, "only in emergencies."

"Hey—that was a good one, Charlie," Buck said. "I figured you secretly liked Rosie O. She's a mighty fine pig, really...I hope her puppies are all right, shit. Yeah, newspaperman, Tipton won't even miss this good stuff, the crooked bastard. He's dead. He had a heart attack—too much stress, I think."

"Dead?" The cub investigative reporter asked in disbelief. He looked around. "Where is he?"

"That doesn't matter for now," Buck said. "He's not here. He's dead, like I just told you. It doesn't matter where he is now. But that's all right, I'll forgive your curiosity— you're a newspaperman and you're supposed to be curious. Well, we're not hiding anything here. Whatever you want to know, I'll tell you, but you've still got to be tied up—same as our other *bitchy* hostage friend here."

"Hostage? So I'm being held hostage? For what?"

"Not exactly," Buck said. "Relax, will you? Just consider yourself a *detainee* until we get a little justice going. It won't be long now. You can watch everything unfold on TV with us—if you behave yourself, that is. Otherwise, you get to pretend like you're a mummy for awhile."

Buck stayed back with his bow outstretched while Tucker Westmoreland and I entered the gazebo tree-house. He called ahead again, "Hey—wake up in there! We've got another keeper! Wow, this place is like *fly-paper!*"

Jade rushed over to meet us. "What's happening?" Her pretty brown eyes worriedly searched my face for some answers. Kimberly was still tied up, but I saw that the ties had been loosened.

"Just some more company, Jade," Buck said from behind. "Nothing to worry about. I was getting kind of bored anyway."

"You're Victor Stamate's wife," Tucker Westmoreland said.

"Yes, I am," Jade answered.

Buck said, "Well, meet a real live newspaper man, Jade. Where's that roll of duct tape?"

I handed it to him and he quickly turned the reporter around and taped his wrists together behind his back. Then he sat him down on the floor, away from Kimberly. Finally, he taped his ankles together.

"There, that should about do it now," Buck said. "I hope you didn't drink a lot of coffee this morning, because taking a piss is definitely going to be a problem for a while. Did you have breakfast yet? I never had a chance to talk with a news-hound before...you must have a pretty good nose, huh?"

"Thanks, but I'm not hungry," Tucker Westmoreland. "And yes, I manage to follow a good scent...that's why my new Blazer's already got over a hundred thousand miles on it."

Buck asked, "Is it yours, or the *Trib's*?"

"Well, it belongs to the newspaper, but I'm the sole driver."

"You're pretty lucky then," Buck said, "because you're probably going to end up getting a brand new vehicle out of this whole ordeal."

"I am?"

"Yeah," Buck answered. "Is there anything in the Blazer you want to save?"

"Yes! My camera equipment's in it—and my writing materials!"

"I'll save it all for you, don't worry," Buck said. "But the vehicle has to go—and I mean right away. Charlie," he said, "this won't take long. Can you hold things together here for about an hour or so while I'm gone? I can make a lot better time in daylight than I did last night."

Jade asked, "Buck, what'd you do with Tipton's car and body?"

"Never mind that for now," he answered. "It's in a good spot and well-protected. That's all you need to know."

She asked, "But why is this man going to get a new car? I don't understand."

Buck shuffled his feet around and looked at me, his eyes asking for help.

"What'd you do with the Sheriff's car?" asked Jade, suddenly becoming alarmed. She raised her voice. "And his body! That poor man!"

"Shush up, will you?" Buck snapped. He scowled at her and said, "His stupid, fat ass is all right and the car doesn't have a scratch on it. Neither will this guy's. Now quiet down, will you? Gees! Give me a break, will you?"

"Everything's okay," I said to Jade. I patted her on the back. "He just doesn't want to talk about it in front of Tucker here."

"That's it, in a nut shell," Buck said, relieved. "Good bottom-lining, Charlie. There's certain things we can't say just yet, Jade...just in case. If there's one thing I've learned in all this so far, it's that you can't trust the media."

"Oh, I wouldn't say that," Tucker Westmoreland said defensively.

"I don't have time to discuss it right now," Buck said, holding his hand up. "But you can bet I will as soon as I get back. All these damned shootings—who's fault do you think those are? The media's. Giving people with warped minds bad ideas. But we can talk about that later. I don't mind talking about it. What's your name? Tuck? Tucker? Now Tucker, you're probably overlooking the enormous sway and impact the media can have on the average stupid citizen, and when newspapers take sides, they naturally attract negative responses. They become targets to vent anger and frustration upon. That's where I come in, so if I don't seem to have much patience with you as a media man, that's why. Oh—I almost forgot, and sometimes the newspapers don't cover shit at all. That's about as bad, see? But we can discuss that a little later."

"I don't call those kinds of shots," Tucker said.

"No, you just play along, covering the insignificant crap they tell you to cover, right? You're just doing your job. But you're right about one thing, free speech is eroding at a higher level than *you're* at—just like how the government is covertly, subliminally paying the big TV networks to carry their propaganda on popular shows. And Charlie here thinks I'm just being paranoid. That's definitely calling shots at a higher level, isn't it? And you and me are paying for it, my friend. Imagine that? We, the taxpayers, are paying for government-scripted anti-drug messages added into—"

"—Sorry to interrupt you," Tucker said, "but I just thought of something. Maybe I can help you guys out here."

"Thanks, but there's no need for your help now—it's too late for that," said Buck. "The media's going to be involved big-time anyway, and hopefully very soon. The same goes for this brat's father—Senator Patch. He's going to be involved big-time, too, helping us out. He's one of the assholes that caused this whole fiasco in the first place. By stirring up a bad atmosphere."

I could tell Buck's frustrations were coming to a head. "Hurry back, okay?" I prodded, trying to keep him on track.

"Sure. We can talk about all this when I get back. Because there's some things this young whippersnapper probably needs to be taught, like about how—among the ten guarantees listed in the Bill of Rights—the Second Amendment is the one that makes any of the other ones possible in the first place, including his big one, freedom of speech. The right to bear arms is the one freedom that protects all the other ones, see? I try to look at the big picture. A little crime is a small price to pay for freedom—but shit, I'll be right back. Just hold that thought. What's your name again?"

"Tucker."

"Okay, Tucker—that's kind of a weird name. Just hold that thought, Tucker, because you wouldn't even be able to be an investigative reporter if it weren't for the citizens being able to have guns—I'll explain it all to you later."

"No need to," Tucker responded. "I already know what you're going to say—that newspapers are protected by the Second Amendment."

"You damned right they are!" shouted Buck. "So why in the hell are they trying to dismantle the very thing that's protecting them?"

"We're not trying to dismantle freedom of speech...what are you saying?"

"You asshole! You guys are cutting your own throats!" Buck yelled, totally exasperated now. "Do you think the Government's going to let you say anything you want to after the guns are all gone? Maybe for awhile. Ha! Then they'll start putting all kinds of restrictions on you guys too—like in the interest of national security. Or to control protests. They'll call it imminent lawlessness, or whatever. See, now we hit on it. That's one of the problems these days—where in the fuck are the protesters. Where's the dissension? Huh? Nobody gives a fuck anymore! One little battle in Seattle. Whoopie! That's why we had to take matters into our own hands, see? You guys aren't help—"

"—Buck, don't lose it, okay?" I warned him. "You're making me kind of nervous. Maybe you should reload your bowl with some of that black hash and go chill for awhile."

"Fuck the *hash!*" he yelled, now almost out of control. "I'm going to have myself a *mother-fucking drink!*"

I couldn't help feeling sorry for Tucker Westmoreland. He was pressed down tight against the gazebo wall like he was expecting to be clobbered when Buck left. I apologized for my friend's misbehavior. "He's got some pretty strong opinions," I explained. "Also, he can be quite profane when he's angry. But in his favor, he's very loyal to his friends. This has been extremely hard on everyone."

"Wow—what does he do for a living?" Tucker asked me, amazed.

"He's a tree-jumper," I answered. "Actually, a tree-*doctor*. Plus he makes and sells rustic furniture."

"He'd of made a good strike-breaker back in the thirties."

"He means well," I said casually. "At least he cares about things."

"He may be caring about his *prison conditions* before long," Tucker said. "You too. Aren't you worried about having to do some time over this?"

"Not really," I said. "I figure the authorities will bend

over backwards to clear all this stinking mess up right away. The newspaper you work for and Senator Patch are both going to receive some peculiar mail today, including a copy of a tape proving that Luther Sullivan killed Joe Schruder. I imagine the Senator will have our friend freed very quickly when he finds out that his missing daughter has been kidnapped by a ruthless group of terrorists. That's us, by the way, in case you can't tell. We're prepared to face the fallout. There wasn't much else we could do."

"They were going to put my husband in prison for the rest of his life," Jade said quietly. "And he's not a criminal. All he did was grow some pot for his own use...not to sell. He smokes marijuana to relax because he has Post-traumatic Stress from serving his country. He also has Tourette Syndrome and Obsessive Compulsive Disorder, and it helps him with those, too. He's a good man, not a criminal."

"I believe you," the young newspaperman said. "He'd have to be a good man to garner such loyal support."

"I'm not going to press charges," said Kimberly quietly. "I can't stand that Bucko Whacko nut, but I don't want Jade or Charlie here to suffer any more than they already have. I just wish my father weren't mixed up in this mess."

Tucker asked, "Where do you suppose Luther Sullivan might be right about now?"

"Probably looking for us," I answered. "The same as Tipton was."

"What exactly happened to him?"

"Like Buck said, he had a heart attack. But not before he had to be stopped from almost breaking my neck."

"Why, what happened?"

"He...sneaked up on me, and Buck had no choice but to shoot him. In the leg and arm, with his bow and arrow. And just so you'll know when they find his body, he shot his own big toe off, by accident."

Wide-eyed, the young red-haired reporter exclaimed, "Wow! This is going to be a big story! Big-time *national* for sure...probably be my once-in-a-lifetime, lucky break! I wonder, would you mind taking some pictures of us here...like this...I mean, right now? If you don't mind. Buck put my camera right over there."

"Maybe a little later," I said. "I'd better check with him first." I laughed, then added, "Come to think of it, he'll probably want some pictures too."

"I don't like him!" Kimberly suddenly exclaimed. "He's *so* uncouth."

Jade said, "He's really not such a bad guy, Kimberly—admittedly a little rough around the edges. But he means well. I don't know what we would've done without him."

Kimberly repeated, "I just don't like him. A guy like that, he should've stayed in the Service. He's an animal."

"He's not usually this bad," I said. "He's just stressed out and on a mission. It's kind of what he was trained for in the Service, you know? Just try not to provoke him, okay?"

"I sure won't make that mistake again," Tucker said.

Curiously, Jade produced a joint and lit it. The timing and setting seemed odd. She took a small drag on it and passed it to Kimberly. *What's this?* I thought.

"Nobody has to know, right?" Kimberly said, looking

first at Tucker Westmoreland, then at me. She took a large drag on the joint, causing it to run, then casually passed it over to me.

I was surprised, but didn't show it. I fixed the run with the tip of my tongue, then took a hit on it myself and passed it to Tucker to see what he would do.

He took it from me, and it suddenly dawned on me just how quickly things were changing when he took a long drag on it too, inhaling deeply.

"Right—" he agreed with Kimberly, nodding his head and holding the smoke in. He slowly let some smoke back out and chuckled nervously, then finished the sentence. "— Nobody has to know. Wow, I haven't been high for quite some time now, myself. For one thing, I had to stop long enough to pass the drug test they gave me before I was hired by the newspaper. This'll be my first buzz since...I can't remember when."

"Almost for me too," said Kimberly. "I simply have no...I mean...."

"Connections?" I asked. "Well, now you do."

She giggled nervously.

I said, "Well, at least we all have something in common here, huh?" I looked at my watch. It was almost eleven o'clock. I leaned down and picked up the portable TV and turned it on. "Might as well catch the eleven o'clock news," I said.

Apparently, the letters hadn't been received yet.

Chapter 19

By the time Buck returned, we were all very high. Jade was polishing her nails while I tried to explain to her not only how a construction crane worked, but also how a sky-scraper was erected. Kimberly was engaged in an active dialogue with Tucker, something about astro-biology. Both were still loosely bound, making for a weird, confusing picture. She was trying to convince the young reporter that there's more weight of life below the surface of Earth than above it. Their lively chatter was occasionally punctuated with short bursts of hysterical laughing and wrist-bound finger-pointing. The portable color TV was flickering unnoticed on the floor.

"Hey, anybody care to hear the special news bulletin that's on right now?" Buck asked loudly, sarcastically. He purposely let the screen-door slam shut. "What the hell's the matter with everybody? Look what's on the damned TV. Hey assholes! Here the hour's at hand and—. What's happening here? Nobody's paying attention. Charlie!"

"Relax, Buck," I said, "we're all buzzed. I've been doing my job...almost too well, as you can see. Everyone's calm except you. Why don't you sit down by me here and watch TV for awhile."

He'd obviously started drinking. I could smell the sweetness of the schnapps on his mouth as soon as he sat down by me. Then I detected the underlying sour smell that comes with heavy drinking and day-old sweat. He reached into his back pocket, producing the antique flask. "Don't mind if I do," he said. "Hey! People! We're on TV—don't you want to watch yourselves?"

Everyone quickly hushed and looked down.

"Wow! Look at me!" Jade exclaimed. On the TV was a picture of her in a leopard-patterned bikini on a tropical beach. "I wonder how they got that? It's from my earliest modeling days."

Buck exclaimed, "Wow! I must be seeing things. You never told me—"

Two more pictures flashed on the screen, quickly shutting him up. One was of him—a recent mug shot showing an unremorseful, unshaven, grinning prisoner with a broken-off tooth. The other picture was of me, from my college yearbook.

Buck looked at Tucker . "Now you see why I don't like the media, huh? See how they're doing me?" He abruptly broke out laughing and slapped his knee once.

Not knowing how else to respond, Tucker easily joined in with Buck's laughing, quickly forgetting the TV on the floor. "Yeah—that's what you get for all that social tinkering!" he hollered.

"We're all Tinkerbells!" exclaimed Jade, joining in fully now too.

Letting go of all his troubles, Buck yelled hoarsely, "Drinks on the house!" He tipped the flask to his lips and drank thirstily, then passed it to Tucker, who did likewise. Tucker quickly passed it to Kimberly. She wiped it off and took a delicate sip and passed it on to me.

"What the hell," I said. "Why not?" Glancing down, I saw the face of Luther Sullivan.

"Hey guys—listen!" I shouted, "sshhh—look, there's the enemy!"

Everyone immediately hushed again. We all fixed our eyes on the sinister-looking face now taking up the little TV's whole screen.

"*Reliable sources have named this man, Luther Sullivan, as a possible suspect—we repeat, suspect—in the death of Joe Schruder, the former Chief Prosecutor for Bunyan County. Additionally, he is being sought for questioning to determine what his role might be in the federal government's re-opening of a marijuana-cultivation case against Victor Stamate, whom—if you recall—is a much-decorated Vietnam Veteran who was previously sentenced under County law.*"

"Hey, there I am!" Kimberly suddenly exclaimed. "Look at my hair!"

"*In an unrelated story, the young woman shown here— Kimberly Ann Patch, the only child of Senator Warren Patch—is still missing after a presumed horse-back riding accident yesterday. Helicopters, volunteer searchers and tracking dogs are still on the scene. Stay-tuned to this channel for updates.*"

"I don't understand," Jade said. "Did they get the letters yet or not?"

"It's hard to say," said Buck.

Kimberly looked perplexed as well. "Perhaps my father was able... to persuade...."

"The media," Buck finished for her. Turning to Tucker Westmoreland, he said, "Nothing against you personally, newspaperman, but that wouldn't surprise me at all. Patch is a stinking democrat. So is your boss, I bet. You can tell him I said so too."

"Well, I'm a Democrat too," Tucker said, chuckling. "There might even be another one or two of us here."

"I hope not," said Buck. He stopped laughing. "Anyway, the cat's out of the bag—we just saw that. The good news is that now Sullivan will probably be too busy watching his own ass to be much of a threat to us anymore—I hope. If he sees or hears the news, that is. And it might not be so bad for us if the kidnapping *is* being covered up. Do you see why? Because the whole thing would then be less complicated to straighten out. Without the stupid public being involved. The stupid public. Bottom line: it looks like Victor will be released *any time now!* I just hope we'll have some say in what were and were not war crimes, if you know what I mean."

Jade somehow managed to smile and frown at the same time. "But how are we going to know when Victor *is* actually freed? Oh—I miss him so much!"

Buck answered, "We'll just have to watch the TV here, I guess."

"I've got a better idea," said Tucker, causing all heads to swing his way. "I mean, if you want to hear it."

"What?" asked Buck. "Go ahead...we're all open-minded here. Most of us anyway," he added, glancing at Kimberly.

She stuck her tongue out at him and made an ugly face, then flashed him a middle finger from her lap.

He laughed loudly, seeing that he'd hit the mark.

Compressing his lips together, he made a lousy attempt at masking his next words. "One in each end, baby—then rotate."

"What'd you say?" Kimberly asked in disbelief.

He answered, "I said, 'one way for this to end...maybe...is to locate—"

"You did not. I heard what you—"

"—Hey, uh, guys," Tucker pleaded.

Buck beamed with pleasure. He said, "Okay, what's your idea, newspaperman? Quickly, please."

"I think I know of a way we can end this real fast."

"Will it guarantee Victor's immediate release?" Buck asked. "Otherwise, I don't even want to hear it."

"What would happen," Tucker said, "if Kimberly simply went back home, saying that she had in fact fallen off her horse and then wandered around—you know, like in a daze, but also, *I* went directly back to the paper just as though nothing had happened to me here?"

"What about the Blazer I just got rid of?" asked Buck.

"That's a minor detail."

"It's not if I have to pay for it," Buck said. "And exactly what is it about this plan that guarantees Victor his freedom? Wait—let me guess: your trustworthiness, right? And the trustworthiness of our other dear friend here. Well newfound friend, it's nice to be smoking dope and drinking with you and all, but if that's your whole idea, it's a joke. Tell me your not joking. Where's the guarantee?"

"I guess there's not one."

"No—I guess there's not, is there? Otherwise one of *us*," Buck said, pointing at his own chest, then to Jade and

I, "would've already thought of it."

He suddenly cocked his head sideways, becoming quiet for a moment. He grinned widely again and nodded his head several times while shaking his finger slyly at Kimberly. "I just got some special insight," he said. "Maybe *you* thought of that." He looked back at Tucker. "It sounds like something maybe *she'd* come up with, not you Tucker...you fucker.

"I'll tell you what," he said, laying down the law now with drunken authority, "if either one of you two go any-where, it'll be with one of *us*. Trusting you enough to party with is one thing, but trusting you with our freedom is an entirely different matter. You dig? Now Tucker, try not to take it too personal...it's just that we've got a lot invested here."

Jade asked, "Well, can we at least go someplace else now?"

"What do you mean?" asked Buck, "to talk?"

"No," she said, "I mean, away from here. Like maybe back home...or at least to a hotel."

"There's nothing wrong with staying right here," Buck answered, frowning. "Besides, we shouldn't be talking strategy in front of our *new friends* here." He looked at me. "Right, Charlie?"

I glanced at our two captives. They both had hope in their eyes, waiting to see which way I'd go. Without answering Buck directly, I said to Jade, "I guess it wouldn't hurt to have a little pow-wow, would it?"

"No," she said, quickly springing up to leave. "Because I don't like it out here...I never did. It's hot and the mosquitoes are real bad and there's weeds everywhere, and—"

"—Holy mackerel!" Buck cut in. "Give me a *fucking break*, will you, Jade?" He paused just a moment for the shock value of his angry words to sink in. "Can't you at least wait on all that damned complaining until we can get our heads together...in *private?* Gees!"

Buck carried his bow with an arrow notched at the ready and glanced back toward the gazebo tree-house every few seconds. "This is getting complicated fast," he said, walking a short distance away and then stopping. "What do you think, Charlie?"

"About what?" I asked, very buzzed.

"Shit," he said. "Don't you remember?"

"No."

"Shit," he repeated. "Jade, what was the main question? Just the main one, please."

Seizing the moment, she eagerly answered, "We were talking about leaving, don't you remember? We don't need to stay here any longer. Kimberly and Tucker aren't threats to us any more. We can just let them go now."

"Oh, I see," Buck said. "Their word is suddenly and mysteriously as good as gold, is it? Did it ever occur to you that they might be trying to fool us?"

Jade's eyes pleaded with me for support. "Charlie...."

Buck turned around and gazed into gazebo tree-house closely. "Yeah, how do you see this, Charlie?"

"I'd just as soon not have to be in conflict with either one of you," I said.

I can understand that, but what does it *boil down* to for

you?" he prodded. "Bottom-line it, if you don't mind."

Jade cut in, "I'd like to leave here as soon as possible. This is an awful place to me now...I don't like it anymore. I'm going to check into selling it. I don't think Victor or my father will mind, under the circumstances...the bad memories....."

"Hold on a second Jade," Buck said. He reached into a front pants pocket and produced something shiny. He held it out for her in his fist. "Here, it's a gift from me to you...to give you courage. I've carried it around in my pocket during this whole episode. Here."

Jade held her hand out timidly, as though expecting a prank. "What is it?"

"My lucky silver bullet," he answered, letting it plop down heavily into her upturned hand. "It's to give you courage, because you sound like you're starting to fall apart, right at the end here. Jade, listen to me. You've got to hang in tough these last few hours."

"Where'd you get it?"

"Never mind...it's special," he answered. "You probably can't read it, but it's autographed by Charleston Heston. Remember him? A good, manly actor—same as Reagan was. Not like all the fags in Hollywood today. Except that Reagan allowed politicians to grab power over judges on his shift—you know, the breakdown between the judicial and political, the powers not being separated. What was that all about? I guess his mind was going. What in the hell were we talking about anyway? Gees, *my* mind must be going. I know it wasn't Clinton—that asshole."

"About where you got it."

"Got what? The clap? What'd I get?"

"*This,*" Jade said impatiently, holding the special silver bullet delicately between her fingers.

"Where I got it doesn't matter, Jade...it has nothing to do with why I'm giving it to you. It's just to remind you to be brave."

"I know, but where'd you get?"

"From the fucking *silver bullet* fairy!" Buck exploded. "Why do you keep asking me that? Can't you just accept a gift gracefully? Man! Shit!"

"Settle down, Buck," I said. "Don't be mean."

"I'm not being mean," he retorted, "can't you see I'm trying to be patient and nice here? Now Jade, damn it, do you want the *fucking bullet*, or not? Because it's special to me. You can have it...you're welcome to it, but I don't feel like giving you the whole history of it, what it's made out of, the manufacturing process, the shipping details, et cetera, because otherwise I'd just as soon keep it myself."

"I only wondered," she said softly.

"Okay—no problem." Buck pressed his lips together and ground his teeth, struggling to be patient. He glanced at me, then looked at Jade again. "It's special," he repeated. I'd like you to have it. It's a gift—you know, to help you with your courage."

"That's okay, thanks, but I don't need it," she said quietly, holding it up close to her eyes and frowning. "Anyway, with me, it wouldn't be the kind of courage you're looking for. It'd be more like being afraid of being thought a coward. Anyway, I don't have a pocket suitable for carrying something like this around. Plus, it's special to you."

"What the hell's all that supposed to mean, Jade? Believe me, it's even *more* special to me now!" he yelled at her, snatching it out of her fingers. "I can't believe I'm hearing all these damned excuses for not accepting a *fucking gift!*"

"Buck, that was uncalled for!" I scolded him, jabbing a finger into his chest.

"She's acting really weird, Charlie," he responded. "Maybe I should just bomb out on her. Believe me, if it weren't for—"

"—What do you mean, 'bomb out'?" I interrupted.

"Just pulling up my stakes and leaving—and I mean right now."

"That's what I want to do, too," Jade said, looking spacey. She suddenly leaned forward and kissed Buck's unshaven cheek. Then she deftly snatched the special bullet back out of his hand.

The gesture gave Buck an instantaneous and complete makeover. I'd never before seen him turn so red. He looked at me sheepishly before quickly dropping his gaze to see what sort of weeds might be growing up around his camouflage boots. Even our two prisoners temporarily escaped his attention.

As though to finish him off, she added excitedly, "Victor will be so *proud* of you."

Triumphantly, she turned to me and whispered loudly in my ear, "Come on, let's start packing!"

"Hey, not so fast," Buck said. "I heard that. Just because you want to leave this wooded paradise so soon doesn't mean we can trust those two all at once. Jade, hold up a second there. We still need to talk about a few things."

I gently pulled on her arm to stop her.

"What?" she asked, looking puzzled, "I thought it was it all settled? I'm going to go see Victor now. I think. Either that, or he's coming here."

"Oh shit," Buck mumbled near my ear, "this is getting too damned nutty." He reached into his back pocket for his flask and held it up and shook it and then winced sharply. "And now, to top it off, I've got to go refill *you*, don't I? Well, you're just going to have to wait a little while...." He reached into his shirt pocket and took out his pipe and the camouflaged lighter and took a big hit. As though muttering to himself, he said, "I wonder where Victor is right now? I miss him too."

"I was wondering about Sullivan a minute ago, myself," I said.

"Actually, Charlie," Buck whispered into my ear, brushing by me slowly, "I'm just trying to stir her brain a little bit, to better see where she's coming from. Listen now: *Jade*," he asked in a normal voice, *"where's Victor?"*

"He'll be here any minute," she answered sweetly. "And he's going to help me pack, too."

Buck clapped his hands once sharply. "Hey—I thought you just said you wanted to leave? Just what I thought! Coo-coo time!"

"Buck," I warned.

He said, "Okay, Jade, why don't you go cheer the other two up over there while me and Charlie talk about...this other thing. Plus, I've got to refill my flask so I can celebrate when Victor gets here. But don't untie our guests yet, okay? Promise? I kind of wanted to do that myself...symbolism, friendship, that sort of thing. We're just going to the Villager for a minute...we'll be right back, okay Jade? How do you feel?"

"Like I just went straight to the top on *Who Wants to be a Millionaire!*" she answered, jumping up and down. "It worked! It worked!"

"Well, I wouldn't be surprised if Regis shows up with Victor, too," Buck grumbled, showing uncharacteristic despair. "He sure wears nice ties, doesn't he? Real shiny ones. Probably gets them by the dozen."

"He's got nice hands, too," said Jade seriously. "I doubt whether he'd bother to hike in here though, because it's so yucky. I'd like to get high with him, wouldn't you, Buck? He seems so nice...almost like a teddy bear. We'll go see him if he can't come with Victor today. Later on, I mean. Does he still live in Las Vegas? I'm so *happy* this is over!"

"Yeah, me too. We all are," Buck said sadly after she was out of earshot. Then to me he added, "I wish I was whacked-out like her and it was over for me too. What do you suppose happened? It's weird how your mind can snap like that, huh?"

"Yeah—it's weird alright," I said, very concerned for her. "Must be the stress. Well, what should we do now?"

"Obviously, she'll have to be watched right along with the other two while we're still in the hiding-out mode," he answered. "Would you mind keeping on eye on them until I get back from the van? This is definitely going to take a refill. Don't let anything change until I get back, okay? I'll just be a few minutes...."

Chapter 20

I met Buck at the screen-door when he returned. I didn't feel like telling him that Jade had already untied Kimberly.

"Buck, you'll need to be real flexible and extra-sensitive right now," I cautioned him.

"That's what I got this for," he said, holding the flask up. "This'll definitely help me be more flexible...I don't know about that other, though. Something I should know about?"

I lowered my voice. "Try not to make a big deal of it, but Jade did some untying in the few minutes we left her alone...Kimberly."

Buck thought for a moment. "Do you think it'd help to get her drunk?"

"Who?"

"Who in the fuck are we talking about, Charlie!" he whispered harshly. "Jade! Maybe you should cut yourself off for awhile—lay off that dope some."

"Relax," I said, "I knew who you were talking about. I was just making sure. Getting Jade plastered could go either way...I wouldn't recommend it, though."

"It might mellow her out for awhile, change her brain chemistry around in a positive way, you know? Maybe even make her crash. Right now I'm going to re-tie that

Patch kid."

"Do you have to?"

"Yeah, I'd say so. You never know what Jade's going to do, but at least we can be sure about the brat."

"She might try to stop you."

"In that case, then, you'd have to help me" he said drunkenly. "If it comes down to it, you'll have to keep her away from me while I tie her up."

"Not Jade!" I whispered.

He groaned and slowly slid both his hands down his face. "Am I going to have trouble from you, too?" He tried to keep his voice low. "No, not *Jade*—try to follow me, will you?"

"I'm following you right now," I said. "But you need to relax some."

"You're making it hard!" he said, raising his voice even louder.

Jade snickered. "What're you guys doing over there?

Buck turned around and gave her an impatient look, then turned back to me. "Don't get any ideas from that dingbat...I'm not talking about my *dick*."

I said, "Hmmm, I could go many different ways on that one...care to take it back?"

"Take what back?" he answered. "Forget it—right now we don't have time to talk about it."

"I doubt if it's worth talking about, anyway," I teased.

"Another two or three shots of this schnapps could always change that!" he warned me, elevating his voice again.

Jade snickered again and a faint touch of red began to

creep up Buck's neck toward his ears. "Watch my damned back for me while I re-tie her now, will you, Charlie? Pay attention! What in the hell are you laughing about? Pay attention now, Charlie...this is serious business."

He pretended to stumble around the gazebo, rearranging things, then he swiftly swooped in behind the girl before she could mount a resistance. She was subdued without injury and quickly re-tied. Jade and Tucker were both astonished, but not me.

"You pig! You pig! You pig!" Kimberly kept on screaming, right up until he deftly smoothed a fresh piece of duct tape down over her open, screaming mouth. Beaming with pride at a job well done, he suddenly squatted down and gave the tape covering her open mouth a little kiss. "There—finished!" he declared.

Kimberly jerked back with big eyes. She desperately tried to squirm out of her bonds.

Next, Buck drunkenly whirled around to address Tucker. "Don't even *think* about it, *buster!*" he told him, red-eyed.

He glanced at Jade. "And the same goes for you now, *girlfriend.*"

Jade lowered her focus down from Buck's face and suddenly flung her arm out, pointing at his crotch. "First I thought you were crazy," she exclaimed, "but now I see your nuts!" She broke out laughing hysterically and continued to point, making little jabbing motions toward his crotch. "The horsies are going to get out! The horsies are going to get out!"

"Huh?" Buck looked down and quickly zipped his

trousers. "You're getting nuttier and nuttier," he said, looking at her sheepishly, "completely out of your usual character. Man, is Victor in for a surprise."

I gave him a hostile look for saying Victor's name.

"I know—too late," he said.

But Jade only said, "That's from a joke I heard a long time ago."

I looked at Tucker. He was having trouble suppressing his mirth.

"It must've been from a *real* long time ago, Jade," I said, smiling myself.

She looked around at everybody slowly, individually, then raised her eyebrows and opened her mouth and slowly put her hand over it.

Buck looked confused. "I think she might want a drink now."

Jade looked astonished. "What'd I just say?"

He handed her the flask. "Never mind—here," he said, sounding unsure of his own words. "Welcome back...at least for now. Maybe it was just a case of temporary insanity."

He looked over at me. We both shrugged our shoulders.

Tucker said, "I take it you're not letting us go for a while then, huh?"

"That's all relative to whether we can trust you or not," Buck answered. "But she's already blown it too many times," he added, nodded his head drunkenly toward the girl.

Kimberly struggled against the ties again. Her blue eyes were wild with anger, but all she could do was jerk occasionally and make muffled noises.

"Speaking of relative," Buck said to her, "you've become about as useless as a relative now—and about as trustworthy, too, I might add."

She jerked and squirmed even harder and made guttural noises.

"Keep that up," Buck said, "and you're *definitely* not going to Disneyland with me next time I go...not that I really plan on going anyway. That damned German World was a bunch of crap...walk around in the heat, then they won't even let you sit in the shade with a beer unless you buy the whole damned meal. What a rip-off. First you have to pay through the nose to park and get in there, then the prices are sky-high at the shops! And that damned China World is about fifty times the size of some of the other worlds. What's that all about? I wouldn't be surprised if Clinton had something to do with that...some kind of kick-back...what a asshole."

Kimberly squirmed again and made more ineffectual noises.

"Now, you I like, Tucker," Buck said with bright, red eyes. "You've got a weird name though...kind of reminds me of that Friar Tuck guy. You know who I mean, don't you? That fat guy from Sherwood Forest, over there in England—the real old England. You ever been there, Tucker?"

"No, but I like Eric Clapton a lot," Tucker replied. "I saw him the last time he was here, at the River Center."

"You did? So did I!" said Buck excitedly. "I went to see

ZZ Top at the Target Center, too, just lately, but the bastards there make it hard to toke up. You have to take in joints. You can't take in a big bowl or anything like that. They give you a pat-down before you go in and then they kill your eyes lighting the place up all the time. They try to make it look like part of the light show, you know, timed with the music, but it's actually for security... so they can keep on eye on things better. It's probably because of the rappers. It's the slippery slope, see? Then they go after the rest of us, too. Just like with profiling people—stopping them for no reason. They started with blacks, now they're even doing it with weird-looking students. Instead of a war on drugs, now we've got a war on violence. See how it goes? They always start on the ones with no voice. Same with mass murderers. They make it hard for everyone. You're always going to have a certain amount of crime with guns, Tucker—that comes with the territory...that's part of the high cost of freedom. I always try to look at the big picture—the grand scale of things, Tucker. The way society is headed. It's like that Orwell guy said: *if you want a picture of the future, imagine a boot stomping on a human face—forever.*"

Jade was quiet. She'd been listening to Buck's monologue ever since taking a drink of schnapps and having a few hits. We were doing our best to keep her mind off Victor. I'd discreetly turned the TV off earlier. We simply needed to give our plan some time to work.

She suddenly jumped to her feet. Stretching her arm forth like a great orator, she shouted, "'*Balls!*' *said the Queen! 'If I had two, I'd be King!'*"

Buck looked at me with astonishment and hurriedly took another sip of schnapps. He chuckled nervously, then grew quiet. Finally, he mumbled, "Shit, here we go again."

Choosing to ignore her latest outburst, he turned back to Tucker. "When I was a kid, I wanted to live all by myself in the woods to get away from all the bullshit. I'd like to do the same thing right about now, except to grow pot, too. There's a real showdown coming over marijuana, Tucker, and just think—you get to be in on it."

Tucker glanced at me nervously and wet his lips, then gave his attention back to Buck. "What do you mean?" he asked.

"All the political hypocracy over marijuana is finally coming home to roost. Did you see that John Stossle segment on *20/20* a while ago? Sure, now everyone knows the truth. The politicians have been treating it like a big joke from their pasts—especially Clinton, but they still slam the shit out of pot smokers by keeping the same tired, bullshit laws. Down with crime, all that shit. Americans are getting tired of it. And now we're going to keep having the medical marijuana and commercial hemp issues popping up all around us, the federal government against the states...what's the matter? You look kind of uneasy. Did that black hash get you too high? Probably just temporary paranoia."

"I'm all right," Tucker replied, looking uneasy.

"All I meant was, you get to cover it...if your boss let's you, that is. It'll be interesting to see how Ventura handles it this time around. It should be a blast! He's either going to be chased around by a dozen manure-spreaders flicking shit or end up disappointing his earliest constituency—the young voters. Oh, there's definitely going to be a showdown. Say, don't reporters have some kind of protection, like for their notes and film outtakes—stuff like that?"

"Yes, why?"

"I was just thinking, maybe I'll let you cover my crop next year. You can get some good color pictures through the whole growing season...and you can interview me explaining exactly how the experts grow good dope outdoors. I like to start with plastic cups inside first. Don't worry about *me* though, Tucker, because I've got an old Bugs Bunny mask I can put on."

"I don't know if my boss would allow it."

Buck frowned. "Oh—I forgot, freedom of the press is kind of limited to those who own one, huh?"

Jade said, "They don't have to run porno ads, either. But they do, for the money."

Buck responded casually, "Jade, I can't help but notice how filthy your mind's been getting lately."

"Porno ads," she repeated. "They don't have to run porno ads, but they pretend like they have to—for people like Luther Sullivan."

"Yeah, him too." Buck looked into her face closely. "What was I saying now? Oh yeah, about the showdown. No, about putting together a story on my crop next year. Except that now maybe you can't because of your asshole boss, right? Okay, we're back on track now.

"See, Tucker, times are changing...everything's different now," Buck said. "Pretty soon the politicians will have to cave in and allow for some pot. Medical, industrial, whatever. And Minnesota farmers will be able to make *kazil-lions*—about five times what they do in wheat. Not to mention *save the Earth* and all that shit, too."

"Sorry to disappoint you, but they're not going for it," said Tucker. "They've already declared that medical marijuana as a necessity isn't a defense, even if you have a prescription from a doctor."

"How right you are about that, Friar Tuck," said Buck, pleased that the young newspaperman was conversant in one of his favorite subjects. "But there's a showdown coming, like I said. Everyone's confused over it for now...what to do...complicated appeals and all that crap. How can the people vote for it, then the Feds come in and fuck with them? The cops have been catching hell for years over having to enforce stupid pot laws, but I guess they deserve it, don't they? But it's the politicians—the hypocritical power freaks—who are to blame. The political cultural tinkerers. You don't mind me calling you Friar Tuck, do you? It's got a nice ring to it."

"No, I don't mind."

Buck continued with his train of thought. "Good. Now, here in Minnesota, we're still waiting for some kind of Federal approval—like for them to re-schedule pot as a soft drug with potential medical uses. Isn't that a hoot? That's why everything's all gummed up in this state right now...because we're waiting for the fucking Feds to reclassify pot for us. Meanwhile, it's the Fed's who're going after pot patients even as we speak!"

"But the Czar said we're going to start turning to treatment," said Jade.

"The who-what?"

She groggily clarified her statement. "We can't win the war against drugs until people stop wanting drugs. As long as people have money, they're going to buy drugs. I heard our governor say that."

"Oh," said Buck. "I see...where was I now?"

But she cut him off and continued on talking as though in a trance.

"The Czar said that once America gives in to a drug culture and all the social decay that comes with it, it would be very difficult to restore a decent civic culture without a prohibitively high cost to civil liberties."

It took Buck a full minute to analyze what she'd just told him. Finally, he was able to sum it up and bottom-line it. "Social tinkering," he said. "Sounds like a premeditated excuse for future goon squads, if you ask me."

Jade answered, "The Government is ill-equipped to handle the needs of the people."

"No shit!" Buck agreed. "Slow down now Jade, will you?"

"If people don't have hope, they'll fall into apathy," she said.

"Jade, wait a damned minute, will you? Slow down now—you're covering too much all at once. For another thing, what you're saying should agree with your common sense a little better than it is."

"All we want is a kinder, gentler nation."

"Holy mackerel!"

"Buck," I cautioned.

"Okay...okay."

Jade said, "What I'm saying is my reasoning and my common sense. Drug treatment works and cuts crime, but 'just say no' doesn't work. Here Buck, I'm giving you my cell-phone. I'll keep your special silver bullet with me, just in case."

She turned to me in a daze and began taking off her rings. "Charlie—here, you can have my rings...I mean, just in case anything happens to me."

Buck was fast losing what little patience he had left. "How do I turn this woman—"

"—*Buck!*"

"Carl Sagan smoked marijuana," she said, her eyes suddenly brightening up. "It inspired his essays and gave him wonderful scientific insight. He was highly motivated by it...not at all lazy. He certainly wasn't the scum of the Earth."

"Anything else new and up-to-date¿"

"Yes, Buck. If you want to know, Florida is developing a marijuana-killing fungus, but it's not nice to fool with mother-nature that way. You have to do something like putting a daffodil gene into rice."

Buck ran both his open hands down his face in exasperation. "That's good to hear," he said quietly. He looked at me. "Shit, you might as well go on, Jade, you've got the floor. Go ahead."

"Well, Gary Johnson is cool."

"Who¿"

Tucker Westmoreland spoke up. "He's the Governor of New Mexico. He supports legalizing all drugs."

"Oh, I see," said Buck. "We're back on the treatment

thing."

Frowning, she asked no one in particular, "Why is Michigan drug testing its welfare recipients⸮"

"I don't know," Buck quipped, "but it's refreshing to have a question from you for a change. I'll be glad to take the floor and try to answer that for you. To begin with, everything's changing so—"

"—Nothing's changing," she automatically cut in to correct him. "They executed a Christian woman in Texas. Where's the Pope when you need him, anyway⸮"

Chapter 21

I noticed that the clouds had thickened and turned much darker. They were now moving across the sky very fast, heading Southeast. I looked the opposite way and saw what was chasing them. Spots of dark gray and black were growing and mixing with the remaining white clouds and coming straight at us.

Soon the Minnesota River Valley became dark, as dark as it ever gets in mid-afternoon, and enormous, single drops of rain began falling, slow at first, then at a normal rate, soon in torrents driven by mighty gusts of wind. The big cottonwood and oak leaves—all working together—gave off threatening hissing noises that came in sheets, the sounds synchronizing with the driving, monsoon-like rain.

Jade and Buck had finally talked themselves out, and they were napping peacefully. Tucker had nodded-off too. Kimberly and I were awake watching the little TV. I'd removed the tape from her mouth right after Buck crashed.

The noise from the storm stirred them all awake again.

Buck's eyes were redder than ever now. "What in the hell's going on?" he asked, rubbing at his eyes, trying to see better. "A fucking *hurricane?* Hey—what's the TV been saying?"

"They still haven't reported the kidnapping," I answered. "Kind of odd, isn't it?"

"My father probably covered it up," Kimberly said.

Tucker said, "My boss—Mr. Schumer—knows the Senator quite well, but I don't think he'd cover up a major story for him."

I suggested, "Maybe law enforcement in high places wants it covered up...the DEA or FBI."

"That wouldn't surprise me at all," said Buck. "Look at all the shit you don't hear about until later—like that Ellsburg crap I heard about several months ago."

"What about Ellsburg? Tucker asked. "Are you talking about Daniel Ellsburg?"

"None other," Buck confirmed, "a real *snitch* if I ever heard of one. We're just now finding out he's the one who blew the end of the Vietnam War for us. Yeah, he worked for the government on top secret shit and then snitched about it to the media—fronted Nixon off about his big plan for ending the war. Ha! The same plan we ended up using in Kosovo!"

"That sounds pretty weird," said Tucker. "I'm not following you. Are you sure about that? I haven't heard anything—"

Buck interrupted by putting his hand up. "Now don't get me wrong Friar Tuck—I'm not saying you have your head especially far up your ass or anything, because hardly *any* of our fellow Americans caught the connection. The democratic media probably helped squash it, for one thing. Now, what kind of war did we fight in Kosovo, Friar Tuck? Mostly a political war. Same as in Vietnam. But see, Ellsburg fronted Nixon off about his plan to bomb the shit out of Vietnam, while not having any of our ground troops there any longer. Do you get it now? It's almost hilarious when you think about it! We used the same strategy in Kosovo that Nixon was going to use to end the War in Vietnam, but Nixon got burned while it worked for Clinton. Why? All because of a fucking snitch, *Ellsburg*. And now they'll probably make a national hero out of the son-of-a-bitch—with the media's help, of course. Yeah, it's funny what you find out later, huh? That fucking rat should've gotten a hundred and ten years for treason."

Jade said, "I heard that Tim Allen's a snitch, too. He's not funny to me anymore. I don't like snitches, either."

This time Buck looked at her with fondness. "Oh—now I see, Jade, you've just been saying stuff you know I like to hear. I'll take that as a compliment, I guess."

She looked confused and smiled at us.

Tucker said, "But Nixon wasn't being honest with the people."

In an instant, Buck became outraged. He spun around to face the cub investigative reporter. "So look at Clinton! When have *any* politicians or presidents ever been honest with the people? Wake up, Friar Tuck! Look at Clinton!"

"You don't mind that Nixon—"

"Fuck Nixon! I only mind that he couldn't end the war better—with better results, with *honor*, and with all of our POW's freed. You can thank wise-in-his-own-eyes Kissenger for that blunder. People like me get tired of hearing all that *greatest generation* crap all the time too, from assholes like Brokaw. Almost all soldiers are just stupid asses who don't know much about why they're fighting. They just want to serve and survive, the same in any war. You have your heros and cowards in every war. What a bunch of crap. Greatest generation for ripping off the boomers! Fucking old people everywhere, taking up all the space in restaurants, eating up tax dollars and shitting out dry, crusty old tax-dollar turds!" He laughed loudly and slapped his knee. "I was just kidding on that last one."

"You've got a good sense of humor," Tucker told him. "You remind me of Judge Judy. You know— *justice with an attitude!* But better than that, with humor mixed in too. Do you mind if I have another hit or two?"

"Speaking of better than that," Buck replied while looking at me strangely, "I'm also going to untie you."

Nothing was making much sense, but it no longer seemed to matter. I looked at Buck blankly.

Thunder boomed not too far off and rain continued to pour down, but the wind had subsided.

"I won't take off," said Tucker. "Unless you want me to—later on, I mean."

"Consider yourself a free man," Buck said with the air of a drunken aristocrat. He waved his arm once to signal his royal pardon. "From now on," he said, "you're a free investigative reporter just covering a damned good story. And feel free to take all the pictures you want to, okay?" He stumbled up to his feet and wobbled over and unbound the pleasantly surprised young man.

"Sounds good to me," Tucker said. "But what about her?" He jerked his head toward Kimberly.

"She doesn't have anything coming," Buck said flatly, looking over at her. I knew he was testing her attitude.

"She's blown it with me too many times now. I can't trust her—plus she's got a big mouth. Most rich, bratty kids do, you know."

Kimberly didn't move. She had a slight glimmer of hope in her blue eyes

Jade, sensing the suspense, said, "You should untie her, too, Buck."

But he was firm. "Didn't you just hear me, Jade?" He gave her a long, puzzled look. "We can't trust her," he said, summing up the situation.

"Ask her," said Jade.

"Ask her? Ask her what? What good would that do?" Buck asked in disbelief. "We can't believe a thing she says anyway, the little snip."

"I believe her," Jade said firmly.

"Well, I don't."

"You're not in charge," said Jade.

Buck immediately swung around to me with angry red eyes, pleading for support.

I struggled to give him some. "Nobody's in charge, Jade," I said. "It's true that Buck's been making a lot of the decisions, but he's just been...kind of...taking the lead...a lot."

"I want to take the lead once," Jade said resolutely. She immediately got up and began untying Kimberly.

Buck's neck and face turned very red and he laughed and reached for the flask in his back pocket. He tipped it up a long time for show and then licked at the last few drops. "See if I give a fuck," he said. He laughed again, letting it trail off into a light-hearted but fake-sounding chuckle. "I was getting tired of all the responsibility anyway. Just remember though, Jade, if the brat goes haywire on us, snitching and shit, it was your idea, not mine."

"Okay," Jade said, unfazed by the comments. She tugged at the knots in the ropes until they finally came loose, then she began to run her fingers through Kimberly's hair to straighten it out. She pulled a loose strand of duct tape off the girl's chin and started massaged the front of her shoulders.

Kimberly backed up a step. "That's okay...thanks...I'm fine." She began rubbing her hands up and down her arms as though to regain the circulation in them.

"I'm sorry—we're sorry," Jade said.

Thunder cracked close by and Kimberly leaped up to her feet with fright. She glanced down at the portable TV and soon began yelling, "Oh—look! Turn it up! Turn it up!"

The storm was causing terrible interference with the reception. Broken lines and flickering images raced crazily across the tiny screen, making it difficult to see anything. Buck tried to adjust the flimsy pull-out antenna and ended up snapping it off at the base. Then he had to touch the antenna back to the metal base and hold it there while the picture and sound came back clear enough to understand what the newswoman was reporting:

"I repeat, Victor Stamate has just been released from custody. He is shown here arriving at his home—I'm sorry, actually, this is the home of his in-laws, who are away vacationing in Europe."

"Victor! Victor!" Jade screamed at the TV.

"Sshhh!" Buck admonished her with a scowl and a wave of his hand over his shoulder. "I'd like to hear the rest of it, even if you don't."

"*You may recall that Mr. Stamate, a Vietnam veteran suffering from PTS, was fined heavily and sentenced to probation two years ago for growing marijuana on a tract of land he and his wife own overlooking the Minnesota River in Eden Prarie. He was re-arrested about two weeks ago when Federal authorities stepped in to re-open the case—which is technically possible in some drug cases.*

"*In a strange twist, a reliable source has called this station just about a half-hour ago to suggest a possible link between Victor Stamate and Luther Sullivan. Sullivan is a former Minnesota State Police bodyguard, and he now owns and operats as many as seven strip joints along the Winconsin side of the LaCroix River. The caller—a confidential source—suggested that Sullivan may have been interested in the Stamates' choice bluff property as a new site for another strip joint, although current zoning laws there would have prohibited such a business from starting up. The FBI is now looking for Sullivan, shown here, for questioning in last week's death of Joe Schruder, who until recently was the Chief Prosecutor for Bunyan County. We reported only last week that Joe Schruder had died of an apparent suicide. It is interesting to note that any future prosecution of Victor Stamate would have been coordinated through Schruder's office, which is one of the reasons the Minnesota State Police and the FBI are now looking into the matter more closely.*

"*In an unrelated story, Kimberly Patch, daughter of Senator Warren Patch, surprised everyone earlier today after wandering home—dazed but apparently unharmed—after falling from her horse and suffering a possible concussion. Many police agencies and volunteers had been out looking for her. She is reported to be* in good spirits and recovering at home, where she's being attended to by a private physician."

Chapter 22

"It could be trick," said Buck, "but I doubt it—they wouldn't have the nerve to fake Victor's release. But then again, if they lied about this stupid kid wandering home on her own," he added sourly, turning to look at her, "then I'd say—shit, she's gone!"

We all jumped up and peered through the wet, dripping mosquito screening. Through the pounding rain, I caught a glimpse of Kimberly's blond hair disappearing into the forest, bouncing like a deer's tail, heading south in the general direction of her home.

My immediate reaction was, *now this is odd*. What was her intention? Was she trying to escape, or was she trying to fulfill what the news had just reported about her? Maybe both.

"I wouldn't want to be in her shoes right now," Buck said, laughing. "Between the rain and the mosquitoes and the rising swamp, I doubt if she'll even make it to the river. She'll probably turn back as soon as the swamp down there rises up to her ass. Believe me...I know from hunting these parts years ago. It gets nastier and nastier the closer you get to the river. But if she *does* make it to the river, she'd better slow down unless she can swim real good, because it's awfully deep close to the banks along that whole stretch down there."

"Maybe she'll circle back around to the road," I said, now even more worried than ever about her.

"You should go after her, Buck," Jade said.

"I'll go," said Tucker.

"Buck knows the layout of the land better," I advised the newspaperman. "You might get lost in this rain."

"Shit!" Buck complained. "I don't want to go out there and get all muddy and fucked up trying to find that ignorant fool! What the hell did she take off for, anyway? She was already untied—practically free."

Jade said coolly, "Maybe she was afraid you were going to tie her back up again, Buck. You should go after her. If you don't, I will. We can't stay here in comfort and let her...possibly drown."

"Oh, I wouldn't say *that*," Buck said. "I could let her drown, easily." He laughed and took a large drag off his little pocket bowl and handed it to me. He strolled over to the screen-door and opened it. "But I won't," he said, letting out a little smoke. "I was just letting her get a head-start to make it more fun."

I wasn't worried about leaving Jade and Tucker alone, so I took a quick hit myself and handed the sizzling pipe to Jade, then braced myself for the harsh environment outside. I leaped into the pouring rain and ran after Buck, yelling out to him, "Hold on, I'm coming too!"

Of course he didn't wait.

Luckily, I was able to follow the trail of broken-down vegetation left by the two as they coursed generally southward for about three hundred yards, then turned westerly on an easy-to-follow deer-path for another hundred yards or so, then finally turned north on another smaller deer-path.

I caught up with them almost to the road, but just out of sight of it. Kimberly was lying on her back, breathing heavily. She was shielding her eyes from the rain, which was now falling even heavier. Buck was sitting almost casually nearby on a decayed log, hanging his head down low, catching his breath. When he saw my legs come into view, he looked up and grinned. Then he quickly shut his mouth and breathed through his flaring nostrils to prove to me what good shape he was in, despite all his partying.

Turning to Kimberly, he scornfully said, "You dumb bitch. You thought I was really trying to catch you, huh?" Ha!" he scoffed. "I just let you run yourself out!"

No one talked for a long time.

Feeling the hit of hash now after the mad dash, I turned my head back and forth very slowly, surveying my bright green surroundings. Fascinated, I watched the rain pelting everything around me while I waited for my breathing to slow down. I tipped my face up and let the rain wash the sweat off me. It felt good to be clean and in good shape. I'd had a pretty good workout, and now, suddenly, everything was clear and wet and very clean. My world had become lush and green and surreal, strangely wonderful in spite of being drenched. In a moment of clarity, I suddenly realized just how much my friends meant to me. Yes, Buck Foster included.

After Kimberly caught her own breath, she got up and started hiking the hundred yards or so toward the road.

She occasionally looked back, as though half-expecting Buck to give chase again. When she reached the ditch, she turned around and—bending over at the waist—screamed back at Buck, "You're a dangerous lunatic! I hope to see you hang!"

Buck stood up, wobbling. He almost fell over when he whipped around to face the girl. He laughed loudly and stumbled, then roared in the rain like a lion, almost falling again. But he quickly re-gained his balance. Pointing at his crotch, he bellowed out, "Dick and nuts, Baby! Dick and nuts!" He put his hands up to his mouth and shouted through them, "And the same goes for *yo daddy*, too!"

The two of us headed back for the gazebo tree-house pretty much as the crow flies, but when we got there both Jade and Tucker were gone. There was a note from Jade taped to the TV. It simply said: "*Got tired of waiting for Victor. Went to find him. Took the van. Be back soon. Jade.*"

"That's how this whole damned thing started for me," said Buck wearily. "Going to find Victor, remember, Charlie?"

"Yeah, I remember," I answered, "you almost blew your engine up trying to catch up with me."

"Well, it looks like it was worth it," Buck said. "Victor's free now. I'll be damned glad to see him, too."

"They probably won't be long," I said. "We might just as well wait here with all of our stuff until they get back. I don't know about you, but I'm exhausted." I rested my arm over one of his stocky shoulders and smiled up at him. The rain had washed us both clean.

He leaned forward and grazed my cheek with a kiss,

then backed up and reached into his drenched pants pockets for his pipe, looking a little embarrassed.

"Jade left it over there," I said, pointing to a throw-together table in one of the corners.

He took his time meticulously carving the buildup out of the little bowl with his pocketknife. Then he took a yellow pipe cleaner out of his pocket and began to slide it back and forth through the stem of the pipe, reaching all the way through to the bottom of the bowl. In a conversational tone, he said, "Sometimes I don't even bother with a screen anymore...I usually just start with some real course shit down in the bottom, then work it up finer to the top. It works pretty well. "Do you have any weed, Charlie?" he asked. "Yeah? Good, thanks. I'll fill it up with a mixture of weed and Lebanese Blond this time, okay?" He chuckled, then started laughing. "That Tipton wasn't such a bad guy after all, was he? I wonder what he was going to do with the box of goodies?"

We took our time loading the pipe together. I took a hit first, then Buck took a huge hit and held it so long that I thought he'd possibly pass out.

"Whew!" he finally said, forcing out only a small bit of leftover smoke, "I'm so glad everyone's gone, especially that pain in the ass, Kimberly!" He slapped his knee weakly, being now very drunk and high. "Friar Tuck was all right, but Jade was getting to be a real pain in the ass too, wasn't she? As a matter of fact, Charlie, I can honestly say that I'm glad she's not here right now. Isn't that awful? I hope she's going to be okay, though. She might need some psychiatric help...or some counseling or something. Maybe

Victor will give her a big kick in the ass, who knows." He was thoughtful for a long time, then said, "She's not quite okay and I'm not quite okay, but that's okay. How are you doing¿ Are you okay¿"

"I feel fine," I answered. "Why—what's wrong with you¿"

"Oh, I don't know," he answered, looking drunk and exhausted and haggard. His head was dropping down to his chin. "I just feel like getting off by myself and resting for a long time. The cops are probably going to squeeze the shit out of me for awhile over this. Maybe I'll take off up North for awhile...there's a veterans-only place up near the Boundary-water area that's real nice and quiet. I can rent a boat...maybe a pontoon. Then I won't have to worry about tipping over...just falling off.

"But the first thing I need to do is check up on Rosie and her pups. *A fucking bald eagle!* Who'd believe it¿ I sure hope Victor and Jade get back right away. I don't feel so great, to be honest with you, Charlie. I feel really burned-out. I'm not getting that old yet, either."

I suddenly remembered some good news for him. "Oh—by the way," I said, "I got Kimberly on tape when she said she didn't consider herself as a kidnap victim. Remember when she said that¿ I don't know if she was lying or not when she said it, but it can't hurt anything...just in case."

Buck picked up some. "Wow! Really¿ That's a relief, but I doubt that she'd press charges. Her old man probably wouldn't let her, even though she'd like to see me hang. Remember she said that¿ The little bitch. No, they'll probably want to cover this whole thing over and forget about it quickly...just like cats burying their shit."

"I know I shouldn't be worrying about Sullivan at a time like this," I said, "but what do you suppose he's doing right now?"

"I don't really care as long he leaves us alone," Buck answered. "Maybe they'll profile the son-of-a-bitch on America's Most Wanted—in Canada too. Actually, Charlie, I *do* care. I hope the prick rots in prison for the rest of his life. What have you got planned for the next few days?"

"Oh, I don't know—just a lot of resting up, I guess. Why?"

"Well," he said, "I was just thinking...how would you like to go up North with me for awhile? I mean, just to rest up, you know. Nothing else. Really. I mean, as long as we both just want to rest up for awhile anyway. It's just an idea. You won't hurt my feelings if you don't want to go. In fact, I wouldn't blame you if you don't even want to go at all."

He grew more and more embarrassed. Pretty soon I saw redness creeping up his neck, so I decided to play with him some. I turned and looked behind myself, then said, "Huh? Are you talking to me?"

"Well, yeah," he said weakly. "What are you looking at me like that for? I wasn't asking you for your hand in marriage or anything like that. Gees! Don't get any ideas. Well, just forget the whole idea, then! And stop looking at me like that, will you? First Kimberly, then Jade, now you. Give me a fucking break, will you? Do you want to come or not? What're you stretching it out for? I know what you're up to...trying to embarrass me, aren't you? Well, forget it—I just changed my mind. I need time to *myself*, anyway...."

"Sure," I said casually, "I'll go with you. But I think we need to take a little break from one another first."

"Really? Great. I mean, *great!* Like Tony the *Tiger* great! Listen, I'm going to be practicing some new lines for the next few days, then I'm going to try to get another gig set up. Let's plan on leaving right after that—maybe in a week or so, how would that be?"

I gave him a provocative smile, causing even more color to creep up his neck. Soon his entire head was crimson.

"Sounds good to me," I said, raising my eyebrows up and down, teasing him some more. I took his hand. "But what would you like to do right now, until they get back, I mean?"

Buck's ears turned darker and darker red, until they became purplish-red and seemed about ready to pop. He carefully avoided looking at me.

"Hey, I was just *kidding*, Asshole!" I yelled, slapping him on the back.

He looked terribly confused. "You mean about going up North, or ...what?"

"Come here, I'll show you," I said.

He hesitated, then stepped up to me just close enough for me to grab his crotch with both hands. *"Dick and nuts, Baby!"* I said, squeezing.

Chapter 23

"Ladies and Gentlemen, tonight I have the privilege—the honor, really—of welcoming back one of our all-time favorite guest comedy performers, a good and honorable man who believes in sticking by his friends at all costs, Mr. Buck Foster! Buck Foster! Let's hear it for him, Ladies and Gentleman!

"Now, the last time Mr. Foster was here, we had...a bit of a problem from an audience member who took offence at something Buck said. So I want to warn the audience tonight—behave yourselves! Anybody particularly sensitive to fat people jokes may want to consider leaving at this time. Your cover charge will be woefully refunded.

"Once again then, let's hear it for Buck...Fossster!

Buck had managed to pick up three or four bookings as a result of his marginal success in LaCross the month before. The gig tonight was at *Cat-calls Galore* in St. Cloud. Sullivan was apparently on the run, no longer a threat to us, so tonight Buck and the Stamates and I were determined to have a good time celebrating Victor's new freedom.

He was eating good again and working out hard for his upcoming fight with some whacko going by the name of *The Jolly Green Giant*. The fighter's costume was a Jolly Green Giant getup, like in the TV add. Victor told us he'd consider a one-time name-change for the fight, and he also said he'd wear a one-time *Jack the Giant Killer* outfit for the occasion. But he was buzzed when he said it.

Yesterday, Jade's parents arrived home early. Victor had called them, advising them of her poor mental state. It's a good thing, too, because we were all getting tired of hearing her going on and on about Tipton's death. She kept saying, "I saw the light go out of his eyes," and, "I was the last person he saw on Earth." Buck had gotten really pissed at her one time, telling her, "Okay, okay, we get the message...it's no big deal. Why, I've seen the same thing happen in a deer's eyes a hundred times. We're all just animals anyway...just forget about it." Jade had answered, "Well, Rudy Tipton wasn't a deer." "I know!" Buck had shouted back in frustration, "he was a P-I-G, *pig!*"

But that's all past us now. For one thing, Jade's on mild tranquilizers. Thank goodness she and Buck didn't have any trouble letting bygones be bygones.

As we settled in to hear Buck's new routine, I smiled to myself, thinking, *Well, at least he has Victor to help him tonight in case anyone attacks him.*

His opening remarks contained several successful audience-warming—if not slanderous—remarks about President Clinton, then he gave a special dedication to Victor.

"Now here's a guy who's been to hell and back—and more than once, too," Buck told the small crowd. "Nothing to do with his marriage. A true war hero, he's more decorated than he'd ever admit to. He's been awarded everything except a purple star. Just released from Federal custody. Think I'm kidding? No, I'm not. They were going to railroad him—double-jeopardy-style—just for growing a little bit of weed. Hey, what good is freedom of choice if you don't have anything left to choose from, you dig? And as our own greatly respected Governor recently said, '*We call our country home of the brave and land of the free, but it's not. We give a false portrayal of freedom. We're not free—if we were, we'd allow people their freedom. Prohibiting something doesn't make it go away.*'

"My friend sits among us tonight, audience. Victor, please stand up and be recognized! My best friend, Victor Stamate, ladies and gentlemen! Hey—Victor's a good fighter too, I might add, in pretty good shape for his age! Ha! Ha! Just kidding, Victor...take it easy. So if someone out there doesn't care for one of my jokes, don't get any ideas of revenge. Think I'm kidding? I'm not."

Victor stood up quickly and sat back down to a smattering of clapping, the most vigorous of course coming from our own table. A dozen or so patrons must've either had some regard for veterans or else just felt like clapping. Or—who knows, maybe a few of them had been following the story on the news and were happy to hear that Victor had slipped the Federal noose.

"You know," Buck told the audience, "the world is getting crazier and crazier. Too much foreign influence is one of the reasons. They're inundating us with all these stupid labels and warnings that either make no sense at all—or worse yet, are confusing. Like the one that came with the kitchen knife I just bought the other day, which happened to be made in China. It read, '*Warning: keep out of children.*'

Okay, nothing wrong with that, is there? It even makes good sense. Well, what about the one my little kid got in trouble over last week while he was shopping with me in the grocery store? On a bag of Fritos, made right here in America: '*You could be a winner! No purchase necessary. Details inside.*' Thank goodness the manager of the store had a good sense of humor—and a few kids of his own, because mine had just pillaged about twenty bags of chips...he was caught pushing the bags to the back of the shelf. Think I'm kidding? I'm not."

Buck received some light laughter and applause, so he went on with greater confidence. "Last year I bought a string of Mexican-made Christmas lights, which seemed odd, because I thought they're all being made in China now. Anyway, the label on the string of lights said, '*For indoor or outdoor use only.*' Hey, again, no harm done, right?

"Talk about overkill, let's look at a few of the safety warnings I found recently. Oh—and by the way, that's part of what's fucking society up these days: too much concern over safety. It's effecting our basic freedoms. So anyway, I bought some of that Nytol sleep-aid shit the other day and they had this intelligent labeling on the bottle, '*Warning: may cause drowsiness.*' And I got some of that Boot's children's cough medicine for my kid. It had a warning too: '*Do not drive car or operate machinery.*' What the hell? Might as well cover all the bases, right?

He had the audience rolling pretty well now. "My wife bought a new iron the other day. '*Do not iron clothes on body,*' the warning read. Let me guess why—'*Iron will be hot after heating,*' right? Or how about this warning on some bread pudding I picked up at the store the other day: '*Product will be hot after heating.*' Sure enough, that did happen. Let's see, what else about heat? Evidently, anything that gets hot is a big problem for the label people. Oh—one of my personal favorite warnings, which I found on my wife's old Sears hairdryer: '*Do not use while sleeping.*' All I can say is it's a good thing that doesn't apply to computers.

"How about the helpful instructions on this hotel-furnished shower cap, ladies and gentlemen? Yeah, I brought it along with me just in case you didn't believe me. Look for yourself." He held up a cheap plastic shower cap and pointed at the label. "Here, read it for yourselves, '*Fits one head.*' Now, that could be confusing if you were high, right?

Quickly changing course, he asked, "Now, would anyone here be excessively put off or offended if I told a few of what I call my *fat-gal* jokes? If so, please raise your hand, and I'll go in a different direction. I've discovered that some people have little or no sense of humor at all when it comes to my *fat-gal* jokes, which are—incidentally—some of my favorites."

I looked at Jade and Victor and grinned. "Some people never learn, do they?" I said. They smiled at me, their eyes twinkling with a strange, glazed-over shininess in the dim light.

I focused for a moment on Victor. He was enjoying Buck's performance, and he was smiling, full of confidence. I glanced back at Buck. He, too, was happy and full of confidence. I looked over at Jade. Her brown eyes twinkled warmly for me and I smiled back.

Fuck Sullivan, I thought to myself. *The bullshit's over now. I'm going to have a good time with my friends tonight, just being happy.*

Maybe it was because of the crummy strip-joint atmosphere and the dim light, I don't know, but I couldn't help giving in to the impulse to glance over my shoulder into the darkness behind me. Maybe Luther Sullivan was back there in the shadows, staring at us.

Just being paranoid, I guess.

"The right of citizens to bear arms is just one more guarantee against arbitrary government, one more safeguard against the tyranny which now appears remote in America, but which historically has proved to be always possible."
—Hubert H. Humphrey

"The most foolish mistake we could possibly make would be to allow the subjected people to carry arms."
—Adolf Hitler

"Among the many misdeeds of the British rule in India, history will look upon the Act of depriving a whole nation of arms as the blackest."
—Mahatma Gandhi

"The great ideals of liberty and equality are preserved against the assaults of opportunism, the expediency of the passing hour, the erosion of small encroachments, the scorn and derision of those who have no patience with general principles, by enshrining them in constitutions, and consecrating to the task of their protection a body of defenders."
—Justice Benjamin Cardozo
The Nature of the Judicial Process
(New Haven, 1921)

Resources

(FAMM) Families Against Mandatory Minimums

(NORML) National Organization for the Reform
of Marijuana Laws

(ACLU) American Civil Liberties Union

(NRA) National Rifle Association

(MAP) Media Awareness Project